Neal — you
for your guidance and
friendship over these
many years.

Jim L

Sub Rosa and Other Stories

JAMES LAMBERT

BALBOA.PRESS

A DIVISION OF HAY HOUSE

Balboa Press books may be ordered through booksellers or by contacting:

Balboa Press
A Division of Hay House
1663 Liberty Drive
Bloomington, IN 47403
www.balboapress.com
844-682-1282

Because of the dynamic nature of the Internet, any web addresses or
links contained in this book may have changed since publication and
may no longer be valid. The views expressed in this work are solely those
of the author and do not necessarily reflect the views of the publisher,
and the publisher hereby disclaims any responsibility for them.

The author of this book does not dispense medical advice or prescribe the use
of any technique as a form of treatment for physical, emotional, or medical
problems without the advice of a physician, either directly or indirectly. The
intent of the author is only to offer information of a general nature to help
you in your quest for emotional and spiritual well-being. In the event you use
any of the information in this book for yourself, which is your constitutional
right, the author and the publisher assume no responsibility for your actions.

Any people depicted in stock imagery provided by Getty Images are
models, and such images are being used for illustrative purposes only.
Certain stock imagery © Getty Images.

Print information available on the last page.

ISBN: 978-1-9822-6188-7 (sc)
ISBN: 978-1-9822-6190-0 (hc)
ISBN: 978-1-9822-6189-4 (e)

Library of Congress Control Number: 2021900873

Balboa Press rev. date: 01/19/2021

We don't have to live great lives. We just have to understand and survive the ones we've got.

—Andre Dubus

Everything you love will be lost, but in the end, love will return in another way.

—Franz Kafka

Table of Contents

Blood in My Hair

I always wanted to go home. I just didn't know where home was. I didn't know how much blood would be spilled getting there. All that flowing blood was, for me, a kind of highway home.

The first time I felt warm blood in my hair, I watched my grandfather pistol-whip a man to death. I was eight or nine. It was summertime. My brother, Jimmy, and I were visiting Grandpa at his house on the grounds of Angola Penitentiary, where he worked as a major in the security force. Grandpa lived in a little village inside Angola they call B-Line where guards and their families still lived.

My given name is Dwayne, but around here, they call me Cowboy. Here is a dormitory at the Main Prison complex at Angola, where I'm serving life without parole. My home is Ash 1, and I share it with sixty men of all ages, races, and backgrounds. Pretty near everyone has a nickname. I got mine from riding bulls. I rode bulls all around the country for twenty years before I caught a charge and got sent up. The journey from B-Line to Ash 1 has been a little like a bull ride—rough, fast, and bloody.

Grandpa Floyd worked at Angola for forty years and raised my daddy and his brothers up here in B-Line village. All my people were originally from Avoyelles Parish over on the west bank of the Mississippi. A lot of folks from Avoyelles work at Angola. Those jobs seem to pass down through the generations from father to son,

1

and now even from mother to daughter. Daddy couldn't wait to get away, and as soon as he could, he got a job in the oil patch. He married my momma, and they settled down in Port Arthur. Daddy pulled twenty-eight-day hitches offshore, and Momma pulled all kinds of crap I'd rather forget. When summers came around, it was easy for her to ship Jimmy and me off to Grandpa's for the summer. We loved being at Angola. Grandma and Grandpa loved having us. Jimmy and I spent most days around a fishing pond near Camp J. Nearby were all the hills and woods a boy could want. There were plenty enough children to choose up baseball teams. It's true that everyone on B-Line was constantly surrounded by killers and robbers serving life sentences, but according to Grandma, we were some of the safest kids around.

Grandpa Floyd was a big cheese in the prison security. He and Grandma had a full-time servant assigned to help cook and clean around their house—Clifton Thibodeaux, from down on Bayou Lafourche. Clifton had worked as a cook on an offshore supply vessel for years before he got sent up for killing his wife and her boyfriend. He didn't get the chair on account the jury found he hacked them up due to hot blood. Far as I knew, he was a gentle man and one hell of a cook. He handled the laundry and cleaning, too. Since he worked for Grandpa, Clifton didn't wear the usual prison stripes but wore blue denim shirts and blue jeans. I sometimes forgot he spent his nights in a cell block.

With Clifton doing the heavy work, Grandma spent her summers running after us boys, tending her considerable vegetable garden and flower beds, and getting spruced up each afternoon for the return of her white knight. Us boys would be cleaned up, Grandma wearing a fresh cotton dress, two martinis mixed and fresh flowers on the dinner table. Grandpa would roll out of his huge Department of Corrections truck, plop himself down in his

La-Z-Boy, and down the martini. Grandma planted a big kiss. The smell of fried chicken or crawfish etouffee wafted into the dining room. We all sat down at the table. After that, the conversation could begin, which usually consisted of Jimmy and I recounting every adventure we had that day. Grandpa never talked about his work. All he cared about were his wife and grandsons. As far as I knew on those summer days, I was a thousand miles from a prison, much less the bloodiest prison in America.

Jimmy and I spent that afternoon catching catfish from a pond on the other side of the levee. We ran them home for Clifton to clean and cook. Grandma fried her special hush puppies and fresh okra out of her garden. It was hotter than blazes that night. The attic fan was pulling the air through the front screen doors, down the central hallway, and out the back doors. Clifton was bent over the stove, frying our fish. I stood on a chair behind him, admiring the huge breaded fish bodies and curled up tails sizzling in the black iron skillet. Clifton slipped me hush puppies right out of the hot grease. Grandma was upstairs putting on the last of her lipstick. The martinis were cooling in the icebox. Jimmy was taking a bath. For some reason, I gazed down the hall to the front yard, just enjoying the breeze from the attic fan on my face; in my nose, the smell of fried fish, and in my ears, the crackling sounds of okra frying.

The screen door flung open. A man wearing prison stripes walked into the kitchen. Clifton wheeled around and turned white as a sheet.

"Henry Jones, what the hell you doin' here?"

Jones muttered something and walked right past me, out the front door onto our lawn. He wasn't tense. He moved slowly and deliberately; I felt no fear whatever when he passed. Clifton stayed by the stove, frozen. I knew something was out of place but

3

didn't understand what. I walked out on the front porch and heard Grandpa's truck wheel around the corner. It came to a sudden stop outside the front gate. He and one of his men jumped out of the truck with guns drawn. They ran through the gate toward Henry Jones, who stood there in Grandpa's front yard, calm as a lamb before his shearer.

Grandpa drew his pistol and pointed it at Jones' head. Just then, Clifton burst out the front door and yelled from the porch, "Please, Major Floyd, don't kill him, not here, not in front of Dwayne! Please, Major." Clifton ran onto the front lawn, continuing to plead with Floyd, pointing toward me on the front porch.

Grandma yelled from her upstairs window, "Floyd, what's going on down there, honey? Is there trouble?"

"You stay up there, Elsie!" Grandpa shouted. "Keep Jimmy with you."

Grandpa charged Jones and smacked him with his service revolver. Each time he whacked him, he'd curse him, "God damned you, Henry Jones, God damned you! Comin' over here by my family!" With every blow, Jones slumped a little more. Blood ran down his face.

"I'll teach you a lesson you'll never forget. Comin' over here by my wife, you son of a bitch—I'll teach you! You stay the hell out of B-Line!" The pistol rose and fell. Each blow, the sound of steel splitting flesh and bones. The other guard grabbed Grandpa's arm. I stood transfixed, gazing at the scene. Jimmy and I had just come back from paradise with a mess of big fish, and now this.

Grandpa holstered his pistol and walked calmly up the steps onto the front porch. Jimmy and Grandma were standing at the front door to greet him. He passed me by and patted my head. Grandma gave him his martini and guided him to his recliner. I felt something warm and wet in my hair. I felt my hair and looked at my fingers. Warm blood. They were covered with Jones' blood. It scared me, this first anointing. I ran right up the stairs and scrubbed my head under the faucet.

We found out the next day that Jones was dead. Not a word was said about the business with Jones the rest of the summer. I never told Momma or Daddy. I never let them send me back to B-Line for the summer. I don't know why I couldn't go back there. I still loved Grandpa Floyd. I cried like a baby when he died. I guess his house didn't feel like home anymore. It wasn't long after that I started fighting and playing with guns.

———◆◆———

Daddy finally threw Momma out when I was thirteen. I thought things would get better. Jimmy and I could do a better job of running the house without her drinking and strange men, but it just didn't work. Daddy stayed offshore, pulling twenty-eight-day shifts. Things went to shit. One of Mama's brothers stepped up and brought us out to live on his farm. Uncle Bobby taught me to ride his mules and ponies. I felt my power the moment my legs wrapped around a four-legged. He got me involved in youth rodeos. God bless Uncle Bobby. Rodeo was my ticket out of Port Arthur.

Years later, I was riding the pro circuit and traveling with a buddy named Simmons Sanchez from Roswell, New Mexico. He joked that he'd never seen a little green man around Roswell until the day a bull kicked him upside his head. We drove between rodeos up and down the high plains in his old crew cab pickup. Slept in it most nights, unless we picked up some road whores and sprang for a cheap hotel room. There was a whole lot of fire water at night, and some bar fighting sprinkled in for good measure.

Sim used to say, "Bull riders live life eight seconds at a time." That was me. The rest of my time between rides was just a slog:

liquor bottles, cocaine, hazy mornings in strange beds, ERs, stitches, a broken bone here and there. The times in between were something to be endured until I could climb on another mad bull, wrap the reins around my right hand, and feel the rush of the next eight seconds. The adrenaline surge couldn't be equaled. Believe me, I tried.

Amarillo was where the adrenaline surge ended, and the pain began in earnest. My second bull was named "Out for Revenge," and he was a doozy. As I lowered myself onto his back, I looked at the hand who would open the gate. Something funny was in his eyes, like he was looking at a dead man. I might have lasted two seconds. All I remember was the blast of air in my face as the gate flew open, my hand catching in a bind. When I came to, I was lying in the back of an ambulance headed to the ER with Sim next to me.

"Hey, little buddy, you with us?" he asked me.

"Sure nuf, son. What happened?"

"That was a real kicker you got there, Dwayne. He threw you around like a rag doll. You got in a bind. Your hand never released. How's your shoulder?"

"Tell you the truth; it hurts like hell. Can't lift my arm," I said. "Did I get knocked out?"

"You were out cold all the way here. I think he got you upside your head."

I raised my left hand up and felt warm blood in my hair all over the right side of my head. It took thirty stitches over my right ear that night to stop the bleeding.

Sim sat by my stretcher in the ER, waiting for someone to come sew me up. He talked about our years on the road. He wanted to make sure I stayed awake. "Dwayne, you know most folks looking at the two of us would think we're crazy to be out here doing what we're doing. Livin' in a truck, getting the shit kicked out of us, and not two dimes to rub together. I know my people back home sure think so. But what they don't realize is that you and I—we've really got it made when you think about it. We're fucking free, man." He started laughing silly and slapped me on my knee. I wholeheartedly agreed with him at that juncture of my life, lying there with warm blood in my hair.

Jimmy Swaggart and I got something in common. We both got busted at a dump on Airline Highway known as the Travel Inn. Jimmy got done in by a private eye working for another preacher. Caught him slipping around with a prostitute who he fell in love with. Me, I got cuffed and beaten out in the parking lot by a pair of Jefferson Parish deputies. After the beating, they told me I was a cop killer. News to me.

I had busted out of the rodeo circuit due to my bum shoulder and a bad habit of getting drunk and fighting younger, stronger riders after hours at the bars. Sim had long ago washed his hands of me. He claimed I hadn't been myself since that spill in Amarillo. Tell me about it. Hell, I had a hard time sometimes remembering what day it was.

Another rider, Sammy LeBlanc, drove me down to New Orleans. His uncle got us on as fitters at Avondale Shipyard. We spent our days slinging hot iron and doing prep work for the welders. Our nights were a blur of honkytonks and whores. One of those ladies got us fixed up at the Travel Inn. Dirt cheap, and the clerk floated us the first week until we got our paychecks.

Convicts have their own language. Up here in Ash 1, a lot of fellows talk about catching a charge like they were catching a cold, some unseen virus you just happened to run into. I had heard the expression before I got sent up, and I always thought it was bullshit. That's what I thought—until the night of September 23, 1998—the night when I caught my charge. Best as I can tell, my charge caught me.

Sammy and I went down to Belle Chase after work one night to watch some amateur barrel racing. After the competition, we stopped at a bar on Barataria Bayou. We had a few Dixies and were playing pool. Three bikers rolled in with a really bad attitude and a desperate urge to play pool on the only table in the joint. I guess we weren't moving along fast enough for them. One of them said something about stinking goat ropers (must've been the boots), and it was on big time.

The three of them jumped us, so I used the cue to even things up. There were broken beer bottles involved. Blood was flying. I chased a couple of them around the table. Women screamed. Two Jefferson Parish sheriff's deputies burst in the front door, guns drawn and started yelling. One of them wrestled Sammy to the ground and cuffed him. They both drew a bead on me. I was the one holding the bloody pool cue.

Maybe it was the two guns pointed at me. Maybe I heard the faint echoes of the noises Henry Jones let out as my grandpa crushed his skull. I burst out the back door and ran into the pitch-black night. Three steps and I fell into the bayou. I'll never really know what made me keep going at that point. I'm no swimmer to speak of, and the charge I was facing at that point was probably drunk and disorderly, simple battery at worst. It was a bar fight, not an armed robbery. I had been in plenty of bar fights. But for some reason, that night, I swam like I was an Olympic champion.

I reached the other side of the dark water. I was laughing. Having been sobered up by the adrenaline and the cold water, I decided to make my way back to the hotel. I thumbed a ride back to the East Bank. I was walking along the Travel Inn driveway and saw a set of flashing lights a block away on Airline Highway. They put a spot on me and pulled up to a screeching stop. I raised my hands before the car doors opened. Two deputies rolled out with guns drawn and ordered me to the ground. After they cuffed me, out came the clubs. By the time I got to the car, my head and face were streaming warm blood. My ribs were cracked, and my bum shoulder had been yanked out of its socket for the umpteenth time.

As I landed hard on the back seat behind the cage, I yelled, "What the fuck are you guys doing? It was only a bar fight! Nobody got hurt! Those guys jumped us. You ask the folks in that bar!"

One of them shot back, "Hey, asshole, shut the fuck up. We're bringing you and your sidekick up for the murder of a law officer. You remember the officer who swam after you? He drowned, you son of a bitch! He drowned chasing you, you miserable bastard!"

"What are you talking about? I didn't see no police in the bayou! I just swam like hell to the other side."

"His name was Calvin Theriot, and he was twenty-six. He's got a wife and two kids, and he died chasing you from a crime scene. So just shut the fuck up until we get you to the courthouse, and then you can talk all you want to the nice detective."

You can search the law books on Louisiana criminal law high and low, and you'll never find a case like mine. Believe me, I've looked. I was tried for capital murder since I "killed" a police officer in the line of duty. They claimed I tried to drown him. The jury came back with the lesser verdict of second-degree murder, which came with mandatory life without parole. When a police officer dies, heads are going to roll. I got life. Sammy pled guilty as an accessory. He served five in the parish jail. I couldn't blame him, although it hurt like hell to see him on the stand against me.

From the moment the blood started flowing that night, I knew in my gut that something had shifted. I was sitting in the back of that patrol car with my shoulder out of joint, and my head covered with warm blood, I felt myself moving from one world into another. The moment I heard the word "drowned," the blood in my hair seemed to turn cold. I had passed through a portal into the world I now inhabit, Ash1 Bed 27.

———◆◆◆———

Convict poker, to a rodeo hand, was the bottom of the barrel. No skill, no courage, really. Just blind luck and the ability not to give a shit if you live or die. Yes, the money was good. $250 to the winner, the last man standing, or sitting to be more accurate. Four guys sit at a card table in folding chairs. A trussed up bull is released and coaxed by the clown into charging the table. The last convict in his chair gets the prize, while the other three are tossed into the air, maybe gored. Ten seconds of sanctioned violence and arbitrary fortune. The crowds screamed bloody murder. They always wanted more.

Uncle Floyd took me to the Angola Rodeo as a boy. I loved it. When they told me I was going to Angola, rodeo was the furthest thing from my mind. I thought I was going to hell on earth. What I knew of the place was from the time of Grandpa Floyd. I knew of the inmate guards with shotguns, the Redhats cell block that was nothing more than a sweatbox, the stabbings at night while you slept. I heard of rape and being turned out to serve another inmate. Angola was always on the front pages. The papers called it "the bloodiest prison in America." I was a cop killer, and that didn't sit well with anyone.

The ride up in the DOC van did nothing to change my mind. I was chained hand and foot. A freeman had a shotgun pointed at me most of the time going up. Once, he put the barrel against my lips.

"Go ahead, boy, start sucking. Might as well get some practice in ahead of time. Just a couple of more hours and someone's gonna have his cock in your mouth." I closed my eyes and said nothing. Both freemen in the van started cackling.

I'll never figure out freemen.

Since I was a cop killer, for my protection, the folks in classification put me in a cell block where I spent twenty-three hours a day alone. Each day through my bars, I could see the horse pen where riders and grooms work the rodeo horses. Men rode high and proud in the open air, a freedom I once knew. I wanted it so bad I could taste it. The grooms brushed, fed and watered the horses, putting them away each evening. I saw myself a part of that blessed company.

After a year in solitary with no write-ups, I was placed in the general population at the Main Prison, determined somehow to join the world of Angola Rodeo. First, I had to cut cane and hoe rows in the fields. All the time, I was watched over by a man on a horse with a shotgun at the ready.

I graduated from working the fields to working the horse stables. Being a natural around four-leggeds, I got a shot at the precision riding team, the warden's pride and joy. Our team of riders always kicked off the rodeo competition. A rousing hand from the crowd went up as we galloped in the gate and put on a five-minute show. We were joined by youth horse riders from Baton Rouge. It was quite a sight—convicts and young kids weaving in and out, working together in harmony. The crowd loved it. Nobody got hurt in precision horse riding. No blood. That came later in the afternoon. It's what the crowd comes to see.

For a couple of years, I stuck to precision riding. I'd give tips to some of the young guys learning to ride bulls and broncos. With my shoulder, even I wasn't crazy enough to dive back into that pond.

But I had plenty of time to work with the weights and gradually got my shoulder to the point where I tried my hand at calf roping and barrel racing. I won a couple of buckles and a few prizes. They'd put $50 in your account if you won a single event. Inside Angola, any positive recognition is craved. The kind of recognition that comes with the rodeo—the brave, manly kind—is fought over like it was gold. So, I earned me a little gold here and there. What kept luring me deeper was the call of more gold and more glory.

I had been up about four years at that point. I signed up for convict poker. That afternoon, I led the precision team into the arena carrying the stars and stripes. I felt like a million bucks. It was a beautiful fall afternoon, and the crowd was primed and ready. I took second in barrel racing; didn't place in calf roping. No matter, I was planning to stick to the end in convict poker. My shoulder couldn't fail me there. God willing, with a little luck, the prize would be mine. My chances of winning were twenty-five percent. Hell, those were the best odds I had in my whole life.

As the afternoon unfolded, blood flow was on the rise. In the bust out, six wild bulls and riders were released at once. Convict cowboys were thrown every which way under stomping bulls. Two men were put on stretchers and loaded into an ambulance. Several convicts chased a mad cow around the arena, trying to get its milk into a pail during the wild cow milking contest. That was good for several stitches to the heads of the would-be milkers. Guts and glory came before us. A poker chip on a leather strap was tied to the head of a trussed and very angry Brahma bull. Twenty convicts chased the angry bull around the arena, trying to grab the chip without getting gored or trampled. Three had to be carried off. We were up next. What the crowd had waited for, convict poker.

Four of us knuckleheads carried our chairs out in the dirt of the arena that afternoon. Two were from Camp D. I didn't know them. I knew the young man who sat across from me. He was Joe Augustine. We lived in Ash 1 together. Bobby Dean was working as the clown. He wished us all well as he put the folding table in the middle of the arena. We unfolded our metal chairs and plopped down. The announcer explained the event to the crowd, which was building to a frenzy—blood lust.

The two convicts on either side were smiling and tipping their hats. Two real-life Southern gentlemen. I wasn't looking around. All I wanted was the prize. I was trying to focus straight ahead and not to look at my fellow knuckleheads or the crowd. That's what one of my buddies, an old rodeo veteran, told me to do. I focused until I locked eyes with Joe. We both saw our sinking fear reflected in the other's eyes. Just at that moment, the crowd roared as the gate flew open. I held on to the sides of my chair and closed my eyes.

I can't remember Joe or the others getting knocked into the air. I seem to recall seeing some of them rolling on the ground. In all the fear and dust, I didn't realize that I was the last man seated. I had won but didn't know it. I thought we were still in play. They tell me I sat there while the bull charged a final time, even though everyone in the place was yelling at me to run. Me and my chair went flying. I landed face down in the dirt, a familiar taste. The other riders hoisted me onto their shoulders like the guy who hit a walk-off homer. I remember the cheers of the crowd, the autumn sun on my face, and the feel of warm blood in my hair. Home at last.

My Week with Walter

I walked the Earth for sixteen years before I discovered the grand illusion that masquerades as reality—that even the people you love and admire talk to you from behind a very life-like mask. I know exactly when and where it occurred. The date was May 16, 1957, and the place was the office of Father Edmonds, headmaster of St. Stanislaus, a Catholic boarding school in Bay St. Louis. It was filled with rich, wayward New Orleans boys—like me.

During first period, I was called out of class to Father Edmonds's office. A recent admission to this place of confinement, this was my first such call. It was a bright, spring day only a week or so before the end of my junior year. A blazing sun shone down, and a nice stiff breeze was blowing west over Bay St. Louis, perfect for sailing. My father's sailboat lay at anchor across the bay at the Pass Christian Yacht Club. Just a few days more, and we would be cruising the Mississippi Sound together, just like old times. The secretary showed me into the empty office and pointed to a brown straight-backed chair across from a simple wooden desk. I tried to imagine anything positive coming out of this summons to see Father Edmonds but struck out. Not a good way to begin my stay.

The only office I had to compare it to was my father's, who ran our proud family business, Chandler and Sons Stevedoring, founded by my great grandfather. Although our headmaster was undoubtedly the king of his small domain, this office had nothing in common with William Chandler's. There were no sailing trophies or Mardi Gras crowns like those adorning my father's rich wood-paneled office on Canal Street, no photos with mayors and senators, no sheepskins from Ivy League schools. The only décor was a framed photo of Pope Pius and a statue of a Madonna cradling Baby Jesus in the corner. The walls were white, and the chairs were unadorned brown wood, seemingly hardened by the butts of unruly teenage boys who filled this *stalag*. The smell of pipe tobacco permeated the room. I considered all of my cleverly concealed offenses committed since my arrival and determined the nature of any charges he might bring against me. I had an appropriate alibi for each.

Father Edmonds entered with another brother. He handed me the New Orleans *Times-Picayune*, neatly folded. "Before you open that paper, Joseph, I need to tell you something. It concerns your father."

"What do you mean?" I asked. "Is he all right? Has there been an accident?"

Father Edmonds and the other brother glanced darkly at each other. The pause made me fidget in the hard, wooden chair.

"It seems," Edmond said, glancing again at the other brother, "there has been an investigation of Chandler and Sons, and your father is being charged with certain crimes. Well, go ahead and read the article."

I pulled the folds of the paper. The front page lay open across my lap, the banner headline in large black letters proclaiming *Chandler Firm Owner Charged With Bribery*. Below it were two images, one of William Chandler, the other of a man with an Italian name. I was fixated on the two images—one of a man I thought I knew, and the other of a man I had never met but who would change my life forever. My trance was broken by the loud ring of the telephone.

Father Edmonds handed me the receiver. "Your mother calling. She's coming to take you home. She'll explain more about what's going on."

"God, oh Joey, Joey! I'm so sorry all this is happening. I suppose Father Edmonds showed you the paper?"

"Mom, what the heck is going on? What is bribery? Who is bribing whom? What did Dad do?"

"Baby, they've been going before the grand jury for weeks, and we had no idea there would be charges. I can't believe this is happening. Daddy's going to fight it! You better believe it."

"Where is Daddy? Is he in jail?"

"Oh, God, no. Daddy's meeting with all our employees. I'm coming over there to pick you up. Father Edmonds said it was all right for you to leave now for the semester. We've got to have you back home with us, now!" My mother's voice cracked, her speech pattern, a rapid staccato.

"Mom, I just got here. Let me finish my classes. It's only another week or so."

"Oh God, I can't believe our lives are falling apart like this. First your wreck, the drunk driving charge and all this boarding school business. Now this. I can't take it, Joey. I can't take it. I need you here. I'll be there after lunch. I'm leaving now."

"But Mom—" She hung up.

I stood holding the receiver with my brain wiped clean and my mouth open. I wanted to vanish from the room and get as far away as possible from the newspaper and the business on the other end of the telephone wire. I handed the receiver to Father Edmonds. His face was as blank as my brain, his eyes downcast.

The other brother stepped behind me and gently placed his hand on my shoulder.

I rose and shuffled back to the dormitory to pack my possessions for the return to New Orleans. All the other boys were in class, and Father Edmonds assured me before I left his office that he would not discuss the matter with any of my classmates, to prevent any embarrassment. Before his assurance, I hadn't considered what others might think after reading this headline and looking at the photos. I had read newspaper clippings of my family in the past. As a girl, my mother was the queen of Comus. My father was a duke in Rex, someday to be king. When featured in the *Times-Picayune,* we Chandlers were often shown holding sailing trophies from the Southern Yacht Club or attending debutante balls. It started to dawn on me what this might mean for us in the pristine world constructed by my parents.

It had been to preserve their pristine world that my parents decided to send me to St. Stanislaus after my auto wreck and arrest for drunk driving. My thoughts of embarrassment and shame over my father gave way to panic and disorientation. My fellow inmates at Stanislaus would surely read about this scandal. How would they look at me? Joey Chandler, the son of William Chandler, the criminal.

Back in my dorm room, I grabbed at the framed photo of Dad displayed on the shelf above my bed. I tossed it toward my open steamer trunk, but I missed, and it fell to the concrete floor, shattering the glass. The photo was taken the year before at the Southern Yacht Club right after Dad bought our new sailboat. The boat was berthed no more than a mile from where I was standing at the time. It would be fueled and stocked with groceries and fresh water for our upcoming trip. I had thirty dollars in my wallet. Perfect, I'd get far away from all this mess, Mom's chattering and the shame that was bubbling inside my gut. I had not created this catastrophe, and there was no way I was ready to face it. An escape was in order. Great day for sailing out there. I knew the Mississippi Sound well. I'd head east.

I packed a duffle with a few clothes, a blanket and my Dopp kit. I left a note to my mother telling her that I was hitchhiking to my aunt's house in Atlanta, and I would call her when I got there. I told her that I loved her, but I needed some time alone. I dropped the note on my pillow and headed out for the marina just across the Bay St. Louis Bridge. I walked to the main highway and quickly caught a ride across the bridge. The fellow who looked after the marina had met me before. Moreover, I was Bill Chandler's son, so he didn't ask any questions. The engine fired up, and I motored into Bay St. Louis around noon.

An easy westerly was building that afternoon. After I got the sails up, I sat back at the wheel and admired the fine escape I had engineered. The west wind picked up as I moved through the green waters toward Gulfport. I lazily tacked my way southwest toward Ship Island.

My plans over the following days included snorkeling in various tropical lagoons, swimming and fishing in secluded bays off the barrier islands, roaming among the sand dunes and sea oats, and maybe encountering a race of beautiful Amazons who would welcome me with open arms. Magical thinking was now the order of the day for May 16, 1957— reality would have to wait.

Sitting back, I opened one of William's cold Falstaffs and smiled at this crazy day. They thought the wreck was shameful. Imagine that. It seemed absurd now, the whole damned thing.

I was now alone and deliciously so. No more daily masses with that bleeding heart of Jesus or whatever it was. I was apart from the panic in my mother's voice. I had transcended the stain of the car wreck and the nasty injuries to three high school friends caused by me and me alone. The wind blowing washed all those unpleasantries away from my face, out of my gut and out of my mind. For now, I lived only to relish this sailing life and the adventures it promised.

Piloting a vessel at sea, any sea, any time, was a serious proposition. Distraction could bring death. The man at the helm was forced to stay in the present, watching his sails, feeling the wind and the rolling of the sea beneath his beam. The future was suspended that afternoon, along with the chaos on the mainland. For as long as I stayed at sea, all would be well.

I passed by Cat Island, first in the chain of barrier islands. There was another sailboat anchored off the shore. The occupants were snorkeling and had pitched some tents for an overnight stay. Being a fugitive, I let the west wind carry me farther along the island chain. A few miles along, I passed Ship Island and the old Civil War fort. Tourist boats from Gulfport often visited during the afternoon, and all I could do was hope to sail past unnoticed. A place of respite and isolation was my goal.

I knew of a nice lagoon on Horn Island's north shore where I could anchor and probably not be noticed for days on end. I had never seen a soul there. I sailed on to the east throughout the breezy afternoon, reaching Horn near dusk. William's beer supply was slowly depleted. The wind was coming out of the south as I arrived off the mouth of Teal Lagoon. I pulled the sails down, secured the boom and motored into East Little Bayou, where I set anchor. After wading to shore in the still, blue-green bay water, I headed south across the island to the Gulf of Mexico. I plunged headfirst into the pounding surf and let the waves rush me back to shore.

I made my way across the narrow island, slogging through deep sand and huge bundles of sea oats. I found a path and noticed what I thought were human footprints. I knew of the occasional picnicking party, but there were a lot of footprints for what I believed was an uninhabited island. I stooped to examine them. They were all identical.

Was I alone on Horn, or did I have company?

I saw no one among the vegetation, and there was no other sign of human habitation in either direction. I thought of Robinson Crusoe seeing the footprints before he met the cannibals and his friend, Friday. I fancied myself as a runaway and adventurer in the mold of old Robinson. Would I have that same drive and determination that saw him through his troubles? Hell, yes, I would.

Approaching the south shore, I could now hear the roaring surf and smell the salt in the air from the churning green waves. The wind now blew strong from the south, which made for great body surfing. I ran a hundred feet into the water, turned and dove toward shore with the breaking waves. They carried me all the way to the beach if timed properly. Over and over, I rode waves into shore.

Winded, my legs wobbly, I staggered to the hard-packed sand on the water's edge and plopped down. I watched several batches of white and gray clouds slowly building into thunderheads over the Gulf.

The stress of the day and an empty stomach taxed my energy. The only thing I had to drink all day was my father's beer. My head was spinning. I entered the water once more to relax and revive by floating in a pool only two or three feet deep, very close to the beach, belly down, with my face in the water and my eyes open, searching for flounder, hermit crabs or other sea creatures. The tan sand bottom was rippled and dotted with tiny holes, portals to the homes of sea creatures living just below. Their world was a safer, simpler one than the world of Uptown New Orleans to which I would be obliged to return. I envied them their place of respite. How to become small and insignificant? To fade into nature with no burden of a shadowy future. I paddled lazily, not paying attention to my surroundings, eyes and mind locked on the tiny world below the sand.

The sandy bottom quickly became much deeper, and I raised my head to breathe. The tree-lined shore rapidly receded, and I realized I was caught in a current running away from the beach. My father had taught us about rip currents. Struggle was useless, he told us. One must wait it out and swim back to shore after the rip current died out. I floated and let the rip carry me farther and farther from the beach. By the time the current stopped, I found myself at least a hundred yards offshore. I set out with a strong breaststroke, swimming diagonally to the beach. I would ride the waves back in.

A sharp cramp in my calf nearly folded me before I reached the breakers. I tried again but gulped the salty Gulf water instead. I rolled over on my back, hoping to regain my form. Another sharp cramp grabbed my abdomen. I tried to take a deep breath but buckled with spasms and went under. My body sunk. Panic seized me, and I struggled to come up for air.

My body fought, but my mind seemed to want to let go. *Maybe this was the perfect solution.* Strange it had come to this so suddenly. I sunk deeper into the green sea.

Golden beams of afternoon sunlight filtered through the water. I did not want to die—not yet. I summoned all my strength and paddled toward those golden beams.

As I broke the surface, another spasm struck my abdomen, and I went back under. I felt a hand grab my arm and lift me up. My head popped up above the water, and I gasped, but no air rushed into my lungs.

"Son, are you all right?" a man asked. "Can you breathe?"

I coughed up saltwater and managed to say, "Yes, sir."

The man laughed. "No need to call me sir."

"I got bad cramps."

"Just relax," he said. "I've got you" He held me around the waist and shoulders until the cramps subsided.

I got my senses about me, and we both paddled to shore. I laid on my back in the sand, happy to have survived. A man in his fifties, about my father's age, but wiry, brown and bearded, he sat quietly looking out at the surf wearing paint-spattered overalls, a white undershirt and a St. Christopher's medal around his neck. He didn't seem in a hurry to ask what had happened. He simply sat by me, watching the western sun and the whitecaps coming into shore.

"Got caught in a rip current," I said. He just nodded and kept gazing at the orange sun filter through a far-off thunderhead floating over the Gulf. "Horrible cramps out there. Thought I might not make it. Thanks for coming to my rescue."

"I saw you get sucked out, and you were gone just like that," he said, snapping his fingers. "I took off running out in the waves, but you were gone. I swam out and couldn't see you at first. Then I saw your head bob up." He looked at me and smiled.

"Had a few beers on the way over," I said. "Can that cause cramps?"

"They say don't drink and swim, but they say a lot of crap that's not true, don't they?"

"Yes, sir."

"Call me Bob," he said. "Is that your boat over on the north shore?"

"Yeah, my school let out for the semester, so I'm taking it out along the barrier islands for a few days."

Bob cocked his head and squinted at me. "Some afterschool vacation, a forty-foot Hunter and all the beer you can drink. Need a deckhand?"

"Do I look like the kind of kid who'd cut school?"

"Maybe, maybe not. But you know how to handle a boat. Looks like it's in shipshape."

"Joey Chandler, sir." I stuck my hand out. He shook it and smiled.

"Well, Joey, if you're going to stay here on Horn Island, I guess I have to give you the tour. Come on."

We walked back toward the north side of the island. For a short time, I was just glad to be alive. But my feelings of simple gratitude soon gave way once again to the evil twins of anger and fear as I recalled the shrill desperation in my mother's voice. When I felt myself slipping into anxiety, I forced my mind to focus only on this beautiful and lonely place. What new things would I find here? I followed the man in the painted overalls through thickets of sea oats and scrub pines. The present became my best friend. My adventure must continue.

We crossed the island along a well-worn path, which rose and descended small dunes coated with fuzzy green cacti. I marveled at the variety and thickness of the vegetation springing from the sand. The island was alive. I saw it as a single thing; everything was connected. I felt a part of it all, so different from my Uptown world of great expectations. This world was ancient and existed separate and apart from any human activity.

Along the path, brightly painted tree trunks stood out in sharp orange, sky blue and yellow. Pieces of driftwood were painted to represent mythic sea creatures and screaming birds. We entered

23

a gallery under the Gulf skies. In a clearing stood a semi-circle of large papier-mâché jungle animals and a smiling circus clown, decorated as if in a child's playroom. Presiding over the group was a large, male figure from which sprouted angelic wings. He was bearded and wore a golden crown. In his hand, he held a golden orb. His angel eyes were black as coal, and I felt as if he stared into my small, fearful heart. I stood before him and touched the golden orb, transfixed; for how long I do not know.

"Do you know him?" Bob asked. "Maybe from church?"

I shook my head.

"Meet Michael the archangel. Here he is depicted before he took up the sword before the war with Satan broke out."

I lightly ran my fingertips over Michael's wings. "Did you make all these?"

"Yeah, it's my little menagerie and their celestial ruler," he said. "How do you like them?"

"That angel, Michael, those eyes. Is that what you are, an artist?"

Bob put his arm around the circus clown's neck and stood staring at the clown's ear. "Did you hear that, Chuckles? He thinks I'm an artist!"

"I mean that these are beautiful. The colors are so bright."

"Too bad others don't see them the same way. My family, and pretty much everyone in Ocean Springs, think I'm just crazy."

What did crazy mean? He was odd, but what was crazy? "Are you crazy?" I asked.

Bob patted Chuckles on the head, but he didn't answer my question. "Right now, you are my gallery's only visitor. So, you got all this to yourself." He made a sweeping circle, arms extended. "My wife and kids don't understand why I leave them for weeks on end to come out here and make this stuff. But something tells me that you might know. You came out here to be apart. Am I right?"

I nodded in agreement. After this day, I not only understood why a man wants to be apart but wondered if I ever wanted to return.

"Follow me," he said. "I'll show you my workshop. It's just over this last dune."

We walked to a grove of trees along the shore of Teal Lagoon. Inside the ring of trees, a small cabin came into view, nestled cozily in the very center of the small opening. I was surprised at the structure with its screened porch and even a porch swing. Bob lived out here, apart from the world. This island was his home, not just a painting destination. The cabin was sided with a shingle-type material painted to resemble bricks, a popular building material in those days. Bob ushered me inside.

"I've been coming out here for fifteen years or so," Bob said. "I got tired of sleeping under my boat, so I got some buddies to help me put this up. We scrounged whatever we could and brought it over from Ocean Springs."

The single room was filled with evidence of the labor of art—several easels, paint cans and half-used paint tubes. In one corner was a desk topped with piles of handwritten notes and writing pads. In another corner was Bob's small cot. On the ceiling and walls, Bob had painted what I took to be his view of the cosmos. Presiding over it all were winged angelic beings with golden auras surrounding their heads. Stars and planets illuminated the night sky. Celestial energy flowed down the wall from above, depicted as a river of fire running to the earthly regions where rainbows and peaceful animals awaited their blessings. My gaze fixated on the beauty of the whole scene. I wandered around the room, trying to identify each figure.

"It's my attempt to put it all down in one place," Bob said. "A pathetic attempt, but at least an attempt. I think that's what God wants of us—an attempt."

I staggered around with my head craned vertically, my eyes following the path of painted stars. "That's St. Michael, the one with the sword. And the one next to him, is that St. Christopher?"

"You guessed it. Are you Catholic?"

"No, we're Episcopalian, but I've been serving time at a Catholic prison in Bay St. Louis."

"Oh sure, know it well. Had some cousins sent there. Those Brothers of the Sacred Heart, whew! They beat the devils out of them both. Must've worked. They ended up solid citizens."

I smiled. "I don't think it's working with me. That sailboat, we call it Tranquilizer. It belongs to my dad. I stole it this morning. Not sure what kind of beating they'll give me for that, but if you don't mind, I'll stay here for a while, just until I figure things out."

"You're a pirate? Honorable profession. Long line of pirates has lived here on Horn Island."

I continued to admire his cosmos. Bob opened a couple of cans of beans and heated them in the fire pit outside the cabin. He answered my questions about angels and constellations, then heated water and poured us two strong cups of coffee. We sat on the porch and enjoyed our barbequed beans and French drip coffee. The sun finally set over the western Gulf of Mexico.

Later that night, we walked back over to the Gulf side of the island and sat on the beach under a full moon. Once again, the known universe unfurled itself for our viewing pleasure. We laid back and stared into the heavens.

We were silent for some time before Bob spoke. "God saw the light, that it was good. The light He called day, and the darkness, He called night."

That moment on the beach, I was at perfect peace. I was light-years away from the chaos in New Orleans, and it was evening on the first day. We returned back to Bob's cabin, and just before I slipped off to sleep that night, I realized that I hadn't thought of my troubles for almost two hours. Living in the here and now was proving to be a great way to escape. May 16, 1957 had finally drawn to a close.

The next day, after sleeping on a bedroll on the screened porch, I awoke to the smell of coffee. Bob was outside preparing to continue work on a large drawing of brown pelicans. I walked over to the fire and poured myself a cup. "Hey, I better go check on the boat," I said, looking toward the lagoon.

"She's fine," he said. "I walked over there this morning early. I like to catch the early morning sun just starting to filter through the mist. That's what Gauguin captured in some of his works in the South Pacific—that island light. Do you know Gauguin?"

"Is that the guy who cut his own ear off?"

He chuckled and shook his head. "No, but they were buddies."

I walked up behind him to watch him fill in the features of the pelicans. He worked quickly. The colors were flowing onto the rough paper from his colored pencils. I had never seen an artist at work. Bob did not have to think about his next move. His hand seemed to be guided by a source of which I knew nothing. A part of me wanted to know more.

"Can you tell me about this painter, Gauguin?"

"Gauguin scrawled an inscription on his last major painting. It contains the three great questions a young man like you needs to ask: Where did we come from? Who are we? Where are we going? Those are some good ones to start with."

"All I know is that I left Pass Christian Yacht Harbor yesterday. So, the first one I got down. But I don't have a clue on the other two."

27

We both drank coffee while soaking up the warm eastern sun. Later that morning, we took off in Tranquilizer for points east. Bob wanted to show me nearby Petit Bois Island, which had one of the few old-time, working lighthouses, complete with a full-time lighthouse keeper who Bob knew well.

We sailed the Sound toward Petit Bois a few miles away. In the ship channel leading to the Gulf from Pascagoula, a mammoth aircraft carrier departed from its huge shipyard. As it steamed by, I was in awe of the physical presence.

I pointed to the navy ship. "Chester Nimitz and my grandfather were classmates at the Naval War College. My father was an ensign in the Battle of Coral Sea. The admiral came to New Orleans for my grandfather's funeral. He ate dinner at our house."

Bob stared at the passing behemoth. "Fine man, they say."

His words hit me in the gut. Fine men, fine men all round, until the mask falls off.

"Bob, all that stuff about my ancestors and Admiral Nimitz is true, but there's something I should tell you."

"Should? There is nothing you have to tell me—if you don't want to."

"I want you to know. I need you to know," I said and paused. He nodded for me to go on. "What I need to tell you is that my father has been charged with bribery. It's all over the New Orleans papers. My mother was coming to St. Stanislaus to take me back home. I just couldn't face it. So, I stole the boat and came out here."

After my confession, I stared out across the Sound. So, there it was, out there at last. The words left a bitter taste in my mouth, but somehow, they had finally left my body, no longer plaguing my gut. Bob didn't respond with the usual adult fanfare. He just nodded as if I had just told him what I had for breakfast. I breathed a bit easier and relaxed back into my bright morning sailing.

"All that about your father," Bob finally said, "and the stuff about all the Chandler men, that's a story you've been told. It's all newspaper mythology. What I want to know is who are *you*, Joey? Who is it that's piloting this vessel? Who is he, and where is *he* going?"

"I got scared of what I heard in my mother's voice. I couldn't be with her. I couldn't go face my father. Guess I'm a coward."

"I'm an escapee myself. Once I used a rope of bedsheets to escape a looney bin. No one comes out here unless they want to leave something behind them. Hell, there's a little posse back on land that would like nothing better than to lock me up in another asylum and throw away the key. Son, you came to the right place, a refuge for escapees and seekers."

Bob told me the history of the Petti Bois lighthouse. He hoped to shoot photos of the huge blue heron population on the island. I listened to Bob and took in the beautiful seascape, but I couldn't shake the strong conviction that the pilot of Tranquilizer was a big phony.

We anchored off the lighthouse and waded onto shore. The keeper and his wife had left for a day onshore, so we had the place to ourselves. We wound our way up the tower's steps and were rewarded with the clarity of its huge, glass lens through which the guiding light poured out each night to passing ships. Bob pointed out the erosion near the base of the structure and noted the inevitability of the Petit Bois Lighthouse going the way of so many beautiful towers along the Gulf Coast. Apparently, Horn Island had a grand one for many years, but it was abandoned due to hurricane damage.

"In the end, man is just a visitor out here," Bob said. "Our domain is the mainland. The wind and waters control everything out here. Joey, this isn't land we're standing on—it's something in between land and water. Anything we humans build out here is like a sandcastle. It will soon be absorbed back into nature."

We trekked through the shifting sands, through chest-high sea oats and prickly cacti to the crest of a nearby sand dune. The sand was loose and the going slow. The morning sun gave way to a blazing noonday heat that seemed to singe my feet, step by step across the white-hot sand. I thought of returning to the soothing green water but followed Bob deeper into the dunes.

A huge throng of blue herons came into view. They were feeding in the green water of a tidal basin. I used my Brownie to snap photos of the rookery.

"What do you see through that lens?" Bob asked.

"Herons? Feeding herons?" I stammered.

"There's more. Look deeper."

I stared at the birds feasting on the small fish in the tidal pools, brightly feathered birds, male and female, with their delicate necks, plunging into the shallow pools. Crabs scurried along the edge of the basin.

"You're creating something with that little box," Bob said, "so take that seriously. What is it that you are seeing? What is it you are committing to your creation? It is *yours*; some would call it art, even if it is simply freezing a memory. Where do you fit into this creation?"

Opportunistic gulls dove at the herons' bony legs, trying to catch a dropped piece of their prey. In the distance, a line of pines along a ridge of Petit Bois stood like sentinels guarding the delicate spit of sand. The Gulf winds stripped the lower branches from the pines, leaving only a thin shaft of pinewood supporting a few boughs of pine needles, each fifty feet in the air. The lighthouse bore witness to man's attempts to claim all this as his own, and I wondered about the lives of the lighthouse keeper and his wife. I saw that there was indeed more to this vision. How could I possibly capture all this with my little black box? Would this be just another photograph that would be placed in an album and forgotten? I wondered if I could hold on to this moment and the vision my new friend was laying before me. How did I fit in? Who was the *I* that was Joey?

On the afternoon ride back to Horn Island, I pondered sandcastles—how the life my father built was being washed away. But what were its foundations? It was a life built on the opinions of others—The Mardi Gras krewes, the Boston Club, the home on Audubon Place—things that are cherished and admired in my small world of Uptown New Orleans. Over the horizon, squinting ever so slightly, I could see the curvature of the immense globe that was carrying us through space. Thunderheads miles high were building in the May sun. Here on the sea, I bore witness to the bigger world of nature, even archangels. Here was a man who seemed to take it all in, and he wanted to show it to me. I felt the puniness of my persona and the world from whence I had come. Hell, the biggest things I had done so far in my life were to put three friends in the hospital and steal my father's boat.

"Maybe this is where I fit in," I finally said. "Maybe this place is me, not New Orleans, not my family."

Bob just nodded, his chin tilted up to the sky.

The following day, I helped Bob carry a large piece of plywood along with a roll of coarse art paper over to the Gulf beach where he set up for the day to paint. I walked along the beach, picked up shells and plunged into the waves to ride them back to shore. It was yet another bright, white-hot day.

Later, I sat down on a log beside him and watched the image appear. He was working with watercolors, lots of greens and blues. At first, the sky appeared on the top of the large board. He washed

31

the colors over each other and change shapes and shades with each pass. He seemed to work quickly, using rapid strokes back and forth over the surface. When I asked him what he was painting, he simply told me he was painting the same thing he always painted.

"You see, there's just this one thing anyway," Bob said. "It's all one. This water, this sand, the gulls, me and you, all just one thing. I guess I'm just trying to keep convincing myself of that one thing."

I could not comprehend what he was saying, so I nodded silently in agreement.

After committing the sky, land and water to paper, Bob rested under a nearby tree. We sipped water from a glass jar. I asked him if he would consider painting those golden beams I reached for just before he saved me. Instead, he agreed to help me paint the scene. He would guide but wanted me to do the strokes. With absolutely no knowledge or experience in using watercolors, but with Bob as my guide, I set out to give form on paper to my recent near-death experience.

He handed me a large flat brush. "Dip that in the water bucket, and lather it on, get the top of the paper good and wet."

"You want me to wet it first?"

"All life starts with water. Trust me."

I streaked the large white paper with the wet paintbrush. "Now you're ready for some color. See that blue in the cup? I mixed it this morning. Use this smaller brush and create your sky, but not too heavy. Remember, it was late afternoon when you saw those rays. Stroke it from side to side."

I spread the blue pigment onto the wet paper, wavering streaks of afternoon sky appeared. He gave me a clean white rag to dab the blue paint. Clouds appeared. Under Bob's direction, I used a blue-green wash to create the sea. A slight scratching of the paper separated the sky above from the water below. Bold diagonal washes of ochre represented the sacred rays that had drawn me to the surface.

"These golden rays," I said, "they're like the beam from the lighthouse. You were my lighthouse tender. You saved my life."

"No, Joey. *You* saved your life. You saw the light and headed toward it. I just happened to be there. It was all part of *your* journey—not your father or your mother's journey, not my journey, but your journey. What will you bring back from your journey to Horn? Ponder that."

After our time painting on the beach, I rolled up my first watercolor and returned to Tranquilizer, where I slept that night.

Over the next few days, Bob began to talk of his travels, both on foot and bicycle, around the country and the world. He allowed me to read his travel logs, including one about his trip to China ten years before. In the pile of papers by his desk were hundreds of pen and ink drawings based on great works of literature ranging from *Alice in Wonderland* to *Don Quixote*. My imagination soared. He showed me more about how to work with watercolors.

One afternoon, we watched huge thunderheads building in the west over the Chandeleur Islands off the Louisiana coast. The wind and waves in the Mississippi Sound started to pick up. I checked Tranquilizer and made sure her sails were secure, and the hatches shut tight. I felt very sure about the boat, but I wasn't sure at all about Bob's cabin. This was a nasty summer thunderstorm coming out of Louisiana over the Sound. Bob seemed very relaxed.

"This is a real blow coming at us," I said. "Are you going to be okay in here?"

"I don't stay here during storms! This piece of junk—you think I'm crazy. The thing could collapse at any moment. We need to go out and drink it up, Joey. You don't want to miss a moment like this. Follow me."

He grabbed my arm and motioned to me to go with him. The rain picked up, and the wind's howl grew steady. Running toward danger was new to me. There was a thrill in my gut that grew as we crossed the island to the Gulf side. When we reached the beach, he told me to stand against a large pine tree and face west into the wind, and he did so himself.

The raindrops pelted my cheeks and bare legs. It felt like the pricks of tiny needles. Sand blew in my eyes and my mouth. Lightning flashed around us, jangling my nerves at first. But my fear was quickly expelled by the sheer rush of excitement coursing through my body. Bob yelled with unbridled joy. I followed suit. In a matter of minutes, the fast-moving thunderhead had passed over Horn and headed toward Petit Bois. I ran onto the beach, hooting and laughing.

Bob followed. "Goddammit! That was a good one!"

We stood and looked at each other, smiling. "Joey, I once rode out a hurricane out here. Tied myself to this tree right here. I learned more that afternoon than I did in all the different schools I attended. You just remember that hunkering down in a storm is sometimes the wrong thing to do. Sometimes, it's better to run out in it and stare it down—unless it kills you, of course, but then at least you tried!"

I knew at that moment that I would have to face my own storm, but I didn't yet know how or when. I didn't know if I could. We walked back to the lagoon and speared some flounder, which he served up that night as my last supper with him on the island. Afterward, I laid on the deck of Tranquilizer, counting the stars in the Milky Way. For the last several days, I had not once thought of what faced me upon my return to New Orleans.

I waded ashore the next morning and found Bob waiting for me. He held out a brightly painted papier-mâché object. "This is for you," he said. "It's the mask you wear to show the world. I want you to wear it today."

I looked upon the mask with curiosity and dread. "What's this mask for?" I asked. "Are we staging a ritual today?"

"Perhaps, if you are willing. Do you know what a rite of passage entails?"

"I've seen an article in National Geographic. It's for young men, to allow them to become warriors or something like that."

"Rites of initiation are practiced the world over," Bob said. "I have seen them depicted on the walls of ancient caves in France. I have witnessed them performed in the Far East. It is the process by which a boy becomes a man. If you are willing, I will help you go through a rite of passage here in our primitive society on Horn Island."

Could I stop running away from my life? Could I learn to face life on its terms? I couldn't go home as a coward. "Tell me what to do."

"Put on this mask. It's your boy persona, the mask you wear every day. I want you to take this jar of water and walk to the other end of the island. Take this sleeping roll and this box of matches. Stay there until tomorrow, and then come back to my shack. It's simple. You'll know when it is time to remove your mask. I'll have breakfast and coffee waiting for you."

I studied the mask. Three symbols were painted in purple over a base of fiery orange, a lightning bolt on the right cheek, a question mark on the left and a cross with the Sacred Heart of Jesus right in the middle of the forehead. I placed it on my face, and Bob helped me secure it behind my head. He hugged me and pointed the way down the beach to where the land ended. I took the jar of water and began walking, toward what I did not know.

The negative voices began as soon as I got out of Bob's sight.

Take off this stupid mask. What the hell can you gain from all this? You're just a stupid kid. He's an escaped mental patient. Why believe anything he says?

I kept walking and kept the mask on. The sand squeezed between my boney toes. I tramped west along the long spit of sand, which wasn't land and wasn't water. At the far end of Horn Island, I found a grove of scrub pines nestled together at the top of a grassy dune. There, I spread out my bedroll and sat in the shade of the green canopy awaiting further instructions from the universe. I leaned against a stout pine trunk and tried to imagine the storms that this living creature had endured here on Horn. I felt myself merging with the strong, resilient standing being. Some of my fears drained out of my gut and seemed to flow into the pine's weathered trunk and down into the earth. There was no Chronos there in my nest, no activities to mark morning from afternoon, or beginning from end. I was now on another type of time, Kairos time.

I awoke from a sleep that I had not planned. The sun was now slipping toward the western horizon. Over that horizon lay the eye of a hurricane, which had my family in its grip. Beyond the western sun were my three friends who were recovering from broken bones and lacerated faces. I had been whisked away to Stanislaus before I could face them and try to make amends. I knew a boy could not walk into a hurricane, nor could a boy repair the friendships rent asunder by my recklessness.

I removed the mask of boyhood and tied it to a tree, then walked in small circles around the grove. I cursed the tree that now became Joey, son, student, young hellion. But abuse did nothing, proved nothing but my own ignorance. I approached the wild orange mask and pondered the purple symbols. But I had no understanding, so they still lacked meaning.

With night approaching, I gathered a pile of dry driftwood for a fire. This would sustain me until I slipped into sleep and dreams. The fire evoked Bob's visit to the ancient caves in France. I imagined men dressed in animal skins sitting around ancient fires. I imagined half-naked young men being put out in the wilderness away from their villages. Each had found a way to bear the pain of the unknown. Why not me? I envisioned a long line of men—Bob, the Chandler men, grandfathers, great-grandfathers and others in my line whose names will never be known. This line reached back to the ancient caves and fire circles. All of them had found the way to manhood.

They were there behind me. I felt their rough hands on my shoulders, supporting me. With a wild pack of my own blood, I ran toward the breaking waves. There was no trail, but I was making my own. The cacti and thick brush of the dunes cut my bare legs, but no matter. Together, I ran with the shadow men of old. We ran through the dunes until I crashed into the shallow waters of Mother Gulf. I shook my head and howled, then broke into a cackling laugh. I gently rose and walked in silence toward the light of my fire.

Once back in my nest, I looked upon my Joey tree, the firelight flickering on the orange mask. I knew that I need not abuse that boy. Boy Joey was a part of man Joey. I could not run away from the boy. I would own him and face the fears he was unable to face.

"It's all the same thing."

From my perch above the darkened sea, I saw the lights of vessels transiting the Mississippi Sound. Men were going to sea and returning to land. They faced and overcame the perils of the sea and sky, just as the stout pine tree in my grove. I would take my place among those men. I stared at those tiny moving lights most of the night. Curiosity and a sense of wonder made me envy those mariners. I began to look upon my voyage with the stolen

Tranquilizer not as an escape but as a quest. Late into the quiet night, I slipped into dreamtime.

I was ravenous when I awoke. This had been the first fast of my life. Although I had not noticed hunger the day before, I craved food immediately. Gathering my bedroll and boy mask, I began my return. As I approached Bob's shack, he came outside and greeted me with a smile and a big hug.

"I see you have your mask, but you're not wearing it," he said.

"No need. I made peace with that boy. Don't need a mask anymore."

"What the hell happened to your legs and arms? Some of those cuts look nasty. I've got some iodine in the cabin."

"Just a short frolic down to the water with some close friends," I said. "I'm fine, just scratches."

"Come on in. I've got a treat for you. It's a soup I learned to make in China."

He gave me a cup of coffee, some crackers and a soup that tasted like the food of the gods. As the energy in my body returned, everything around me was brighter. The sky was royal blue, like I had never seen it, not a cloud to be seen on the horizon. The waters of the Sound were gentle and welcoming. Bob's face was radiant, his eyes bright and clear with love and blessing pouring out toward me, the returned initiate. For the first time, I felt like I was living on solid ground. Inside the cabin, the painted stars and angels seemed to twinkle and shine as I spread out my bedroll to sleep the sleep of the dead.

The next morning, I bade Bob farewell and thanked him for saving my life. He again humbly attributed my salvation from the surf to my simply letting go. He hugged me, wished me luck and put his St. Christopher medal in my hand. "He protects the traveler and the sojourner in strange lands. He's been watching over you, Joey. I want you to have this."

As I pulled away from Horn Island, Bob sat down on the beach and assumed the lotus position. For the rest of my life, this is how I would clearly remember him in my mind's eye—sitting cross-legged on that sunny beach, wearing his paint-splattered overalls, with just a hint of a crooked smile.

I sailed toward New Orleans to berth Tranquilizer at the Southern Yacht Club. As I motored back through the Rigolets Pass, I knew a hurricane was stalled over Audubon Place. I cleared the pass, set the sails again and started tacking back toward the yacht harbor. I felt no fear of the future or vicarious shame for what my father had done. After my time with the man whom I knew only as Bob, and after the lessons I learned on Horn Island, I felt strangely happy to be going back where I could feel some more wind in my face.

Those hurricane winds tore my family apart that summer and blew us in many different directions. My father ended up serving seven years in a federal prison in Texarkana. Mother sold our home on Audubon Place and left New Orleans for good. I went off to college, where I became fascinated with psychology and mythology. Years later, in an art class, I learned of an eccentric painter from Ocean Springs who became acclaimed in the world of modern art only after his death in 1965. His name was Walter Anderson, but close friends and family called him Bob. Today, I work as a Jungian analyst and regularly employ the tools of letting go, staying present and facing one's fears. On occasion, I tell my patients a story about a wild man in painted overalls who lived on a deserted island.

Lucinda

*L*ucinda knew it had to end, her time in heaven. Three days were three days. She knew this when she signed up for the meditation workshop. There would be an end as there had been a beginning. What was important was the in-between, what she would take away from this serene and safe paradise. She would return to Jonas and her glass tower, and that would be enough, safe and apart from the chaos of the world—not heaven, but enough. It would now be up to her to faithfully set aside time for the practice, up to her to repeat the mantra given by Maya, her guide and teacher. Maybe she could finally heal her tender heart and somehow excise the harsh memories of her childhood. She wanted the solace of sleep without the nightly hauntings of her long-dead mother and her punishing aunt.

The walled compound protected the mirror-like pond and beech groves from the busy city just outside. The scent of essential oils immediately put a new student at ease upon entering the ashram. She would miss this comforting smell. It was hard to believe such an exquisite jewel existed in the urban forest of steel and concrete just outside the wooden gate. She paused and turned back to cherish the place where she received the healing practice.

Maya embraced her one last time. "Go in peace, my friend.

"I can't—I don't have words. I feel free of her for the first time. Somehow, this is different. I don't want to leave. This place is so special. What you have done for me, I just can't explain my gratitude to you and everyone here."

"Lu, I want you to remember one thing when you feel fear or see the image of your mother."

"Just keep repeating my mantra, right?"

"Yes, dear. It's that simple. Just devote time to sitting in silence and fill that space with your mantra. Even a monster has no power against your mantra. Then, you will be free from the bondage of self and free of your past. Now, go in peace. Your husband is waiting to take you home to Dallas. He's just outside the gate."

Her mother—the monster—named her Lucinda, which meant beautiful light. At least she gave her a lovely name, if nothing else. Despite the name, Lucinda's life had been a struggle with her mother's overpowering shadow. What archetype had Jonas used for her when they first met? Yes, the Death Mother, where the victim is paralyzed by the shadow of a mother figure. Her childhood had been dominated by such a she-bitch. After being dragged from one California commune to the next, Lucinda was dumped on an aunt who deeply resented being forced to care for her sister's abandoned child. Death Mother? She could write a book about it. Maybe someday she would.

Thank God Jonas had taken her away from all the chaos. Now, she lived as the wife of a prominent Jungian analyst in a glass tower, protected, safe. She had the freedom to find a way to heal the soul sickness her mother inflicted on her psyche. Lucinda would stop at nothing to find a cure. At the ashram, she finally found one. Her hand pressed against the heavy wooden gate, and she stepped forward into freedom, so she hoped.

After dinner, Jonas and Lucinda settled into their respective positions, as if to begin a highly scripted Japanese tea ceremony. Dr. Jonas Wells lounged stiffly in his sleek black leather recliner, delicately holding the remote control. Alternating between resentment and cable news debates, he knocked back a second glass of scotch sitting in the chilled air of his white-walled sanctum, far above the hectic grind of the freeways, oilmen and bankers. Lucinda assumed the lotus position on the couch, gently stroking her Yorkshire terrier, Bo. She gazed through the massive glass wall at the nighttime skyline of Dallas. Bose headphones, which insulated her against any sonic intrusion, framed her shock of wild, red hair.

He used to love her red hair, the way it fell loose around her bare, white shoulders. Now, he resented staring at the back of his young wife's head, enduring her silence for hours. After a day at his busy practice, what he wanted to do was to relax in his recliner, sip his single malt scotch and have his lovely Lucinda rub his shoulders and ask him how he managed to help so many wounded people every day without fail. What he got instead was the pleasure of watching his Lucinda meditate in silence, constantly repeating her secret mantra for hours on end. He wanted to be Bo, pampered and fussed over, but instead, he was Jonas, the long-suffering husband.

"Lu, before you start tonight, I need to talk. It's been six weeks since your time at the ashram. Your nights, my nights, we're both alone. We never talk. I know this is helping, but can't you find another time for your meditation?"

"Baby, you know how hard I've battled these last five years. All the therapies you suggested, I tried every one of them."

"You only stuck with analysis for three months. I know I can't be your analyst, but Dr. Sternberg is one of the best. He studied under Edinger."

"I'm sorry," Lucinda said. "All that business about recording my dreams was just bringing my mother back to me every night. I felt triggered. And all the jargon. This mediation seems like it may be the answer and no meds. Mother is receding. I can feel it."

"It's eight already. You meditate at least two hours every evening. Then it's bedtime."

"Nighttime sessions help me sleep, and you know how much I need to improve my sleep. You remember that last therapist you sent me to? He said it was all due to sleep deprivation, all my mania and depressions. You sent me there, remember?"

"Yes, I know. You need sleep. We all do. But I need a wife to talk to. I need someone to show my love to, and I need to receive love in return, your love. Remember, Dr. Cartwright told us both we had to express our needs. That's what I'm doing."

She placed Bo gently on the cushion, left her perch over nighttime Dallas and walked over to his recliner. There, she kneeled before him, took both his hands in hers and locked eyes with him. "Baby, you know I love you. I owe everything to you. I'd be another lost soul in La La Land if you hadn't taken me out of Berkeley. You know my brain and my psyche aren't right. You knew it from the start. I want to be able to love you as a grown woman, a healed woman, an actualized woman. I know what I've put you through." Lucinda rose and picked up her headphones.

"This is the final piece of the puzzle. Maya told me it would take a few months to be fully grounded in the practice. She called it the point of self-forgetting. When I'm done, I'll be there for you. Fully there, better than ever." She kissed Jonas on the cheek and rejoined Bo on the couch, staring out over a thousand points of light shining in the darkness. She donned her noise-canceling headphones, and her evening session began.

Jonas sat back silently in his recliner and turned on the

television. Two thousand miles and five years separated the glass tower where Lucinda and Jonas now lived from where they had started out. Their journey together began following a magical encounter in Berkeley after his lecture at the university. He pegged her from the start, which lit a fire in both of them. Now, the fire had dimmed. He was more a caretaker to her than a husband, more a case manager than a lover.

Jonas quietly cracked his poached egg to keep from disturbing Lucinda. She ate berries from a bowl. Her red hair was pulled back, no makeup, but God, she was lovely.

Jonas placed his spoon on the glass table. "How was your sleep? I didn't feel you get up during the night."

"Much better. I think I got five straight hours in. No nightmares."

"Lu, I've been thinking about something this morning. How would you like to take a trip, get out into nature? A trip to the mountains."

Lucinda jumped up, ran to her husband and squeezed him with joy in her eyes. "What a wonderful idea! I think it will be great for us. How did you think of it? God, I can't believe we haven't gone before. I *love* nature. Did you know I was quite a hiker as a teenager? There was a wilderness area up in the back bay hills not far from where I grew up. I loved it up there. It was the only time I felt truly alive—and safe. Is that strange?"

Her enthusiasm had a hint of her young self when they first met. "Have you heard of the Ozarks?" he asked. "Just a few hours away. So green, full of rivers and waterfalls as I recall. My parents took us there in the summers. How's that sound?"

"Lovely. Just what the doctor ordered."

"Great, I have a friend, Jim Kelly. He owns a cabin up there."

Jonas was surprised by her seemingly newfound joy and hope. Maybe their life could be the way it used to be, the way they used to be. "By the way, you're not the only one who loves nature. Did you know that Jung loved nature? He wrote, 'Nature is not matter only. She is also spirit.'"

"Perfect," she said, "a Jung quote for every occasion."

Lucinda left to prepare for her morning session. Jonas managed a weak smile in response. He watched his wife walk away into her new retreat of silence. He rose to walk away into his work world of words and dreams.

The shrill squealing of the wild beasts died down, and the smoke began to clear. The smell of hog blood, urine and gunpowder filled the ravine. A few wounded razorbacks whimpered among the fallen. Rusty McClain locked the safety on the fifty-caliber machine gun he used to eradicate the feral hogs. He unlatched the holster of his sidearm with which he would dispatch the few that survived the initial volley.

This was his mission, to purge these mountains of an invasive species now destroying the natural beauty that he had grown to love as a child. No one else did what he did; no one had the nerve to do it right. Some thought he loved the killing and even the blood. His ex-wife certainly said as much to him. She was wrong, at least about loving the violence for its own sake.

After each of these eradications, the stench of smoke and blood singed his nostrils. The wolf deep inside him took over. His heart rate elevated, and everything in the bloody hollow slowed to a crawl. He saw and heard everything. Slow, almost still. The surge of adrenaline in his system made him giddy, even a little shaky. Rusty pulled a red bandana from his hip pocket and wiped the dusting of gunpowder from his brow and cheeks. A white noise descended on the mountain stream bed, muffling the whimpers of the dying beasts. Violence, yes, but was it something he really loved?

That's not how it was at all. It boiled down to how one viewed nature and how one should respond to an insult on the natural world. To Rusty, nature was once undefiled, and now man had unleashed a plague upon nature in the form of these wild hogs. It was his job to reverse that onslaught, to heal nature by removing the defilement. He had seen it all—the dead livestock and family pets, crops torn up, delicate ecosystems uprooted and polluted. At first, he tried to work within the Department of Agriculture, but there was no stomach there for what really worked. So, Rusty left and began to effectively address the scourge. His way worked.

He stepped down from his ATV and walked among the decimated pack of hogs. His four hog dogs ran among the dead and sniffed at their blood mixing with the clear water of the creek flowing through the ravine. Blood and water coated Rusty's steel-toed work boots. He dispatched the wounded razorbacks with a single headshot. Shortly, he would call for his helper to bring in the track hoe, and they would load the carcasses into a waiting dump truck for removal to his disposal site, where they would be incinerated. With the completion of each project, the Ozark Mountains were just a bit closer to their natural order. Job well done.

The adventure into the green mountains of Arkansas began with Jonas hopeful for a restoration of the affection and sexual energy they experienced after meeting in California. Perhaps a journey into the deep forests would rekindle those primal fires. But much to Jonas' chagrin, shortly after clearing the suburban sprawl of Dallas, her noise-canceling headphones came out of their case.

"Lu, do you have to do that now? Can't we just be in each other's presence? Those earphones make me feel shut out."

"I swear, I think it's helping. Have you noticed any difference?"

"Let's wait and see. You certainly haven't had any manic periods since you've been meditating, and I guess that's good. But it's a long-term thing, so let's wait and see."

"Thanks." She slipped the headphones over her ears. "It's just two hours."

Jonas often counseled his patients against the futility of resentment. It was simply reliving a trauma or grievance, which hurt only the resenter. This morning, as he drove deeper into the pine forests, he continually condemned his inability to heed his own advice. Those damned headphones, and that damned dog.

Bo slept curled up in Lucinda's lap, and she stroked his fluffy brown coat. Her eyes remained closed, her body relaxed.

Was he beginning to hate the small dog? Hating a dog? Sad, but true.

<hr />

Lucinda completed her meditation for the morning. The couple drove onto a scenic mountain byway known as Skyline Drive, running along high ridges for forty miles from eastern Oklahoma into western Arkansas. It featured panoramas of wooded valleys and lakes viewed from mountain vistas built as pullouts for motorists. She felt like a new person up in these mountains. Perhaps this journey was more than simply a getaway from their routine, certainly more than the romantic interlude Jonas was hoping to create. She had nothing to hide. Here she could truly step into her name—child of light. She rolled down her window and leaned her head into the wild and fresh mountain air. Her red mane blew straight back. Her pale white face welcomed the warmth of the morning sun. Bo wanted in on the action and jumped up toward the open window.

"Free and clean!" She gently waved her arm up and down in the rushing air. "This is amazing, Jonas. I had no idea there were real mountains so close. I feel like a girl again way up on my hill above the bay, away from the city."

"That's the idea," he said. "Soak it all in."

At one of the pullouts, Jonas stopped and prepared a light lunch for the two of them. They sat alone at a picnic table and gazed at the valley floor. A peaceful silence prevailed. They simply breathed together for a few minutes and drank in the serenity and simple beauty of the place. It was hard to believe they were merely four hours from their stuffy, wordy life in Dallas, devoted largely to chasing the very thing that apparently existed here in abundance.

Lucinda rose, took Jonas by the hand and led him to the edge of the canyon ridge. Embracing the mountain silence, she felt that there was something more out there. At home, when she was in quiet meditation, she could sense it, like a slight tug. But up here, in the mountain forests, she felt its presence all around her. What it was, she didn't know.

Jonas broke the silence. "This is what true mother energy is—the power of Mother Earth to heal, to absorb all our pain and anxiety and to restore us to balance."

She startled at the shattering of the spell of their serenity. Lucinda dropped his hand and headed slowly back to their vehicle. She said nothing. More words, not what she wanted. She wondered if Jonas had any idea of the deep mystery of this wild and unknowable forest. There was something here beyond serenity.

The something did not involve words. She felt a pull toward and not away from it.

Skyline Drive afforded dozens of promontories with panoramic views. Toward dusk, Jonas pulled out at one where an old fire tower gave tourists an extra hundred feet of view from its top. Lucinda scampered up the many steel steps, cradling Bo in her arms. Jonas trudged behind her, but at a steady, determined pace. They both entered the small vestibule at the top, where rangers once kept watch over the Ozark forests. The sun was barely above the distant horizon.

"Look at this," she said, "the light on the valley and the rolling hills. It's like a purple sea, and the hills are the waves. Have you seen something so serene before?"

"No, my family floated the Buffalo River, but this is something else."

"Maybe there's something out there," she said, "something beneath those purple waves, something just for me. From this tower, I'd dive right in if I thought I could find it."

"Better hand me the dog before you jump."

Lucinda smiled. She gazed upon the many shades of purple and gold the setting sun splashed across the horizon. Yes, she would find something in these mountains. She could feel it. Now she was sure of it.

The two stayed the first night at a mountain lodge perched on a rocky outcrop. In the morning, Lucinda awoke early and took Bo for a walk along the ridge. The valley was filled with white clouds, and above her was crystal blue sky and the warm morning sun. She was comfortable up here. But like the safety of her glass tower in Dallas, something was lacking. All her life had been an attempt to climb higher and higher, away from the dark depths, the domain of the Death Mother. More college degrees, more philosophies, more therapeutic practices. She gazed upon the opaque bank of clouds and wondered if the path of ascent was the correct one for her after all. Maybe what she needed wasn't up above the clouds. Maybe it must be found in the valley. She would have to take the path of descent, get her hands dirty, connect with the Earth. She would go down, not up. Lucinda sensed there would be risk involved.

Following a big breakfast, the two travelers resumed their trek deeper into the Ozarks. The GPS was set to guide them to a small town near the cabin—Kingston, Arkansas. The meditative silence of the day before was replaced with warm chatting. Lucinda snapped photos and quizzed Jonas about features shown on their roadmap. The route took them up and over Arkansas' highest peak, Mount Magazine. From there, Jonas drove north on a state highway proudly named "The Pig Trail" according to tourist markers posted along the roadside. Jonas explained that Arkansas used the razorback hog as a mascot for its university's football team. He had never seen one on his trips to the area and told Lucinda that they were probably akin to the buffalo—once very numerous, but now more of a historical relic.

While Jonas navigated the tight mountain turns, Lucinda searched the countryside for photo opportunities. Bo nuzzled in her lap. Jonas stopped occasionally to allow her a chance to photograph an abandoned barn, a sparkling creek. In one valley, he stopped abruptly to make way for a group of white-tailed deer crossing the road. After spotting the deer, Jonas pulled off the road in time to allow Lucinda to attach her telephoto lens and snap a close-up of a large buck. She carefully opened her car door and noiselessly exited the vehicle. Using the car hood as a stable platform, she firmly planted her elbow, cradled her camera in both hands and pressed the shutter button several times to capture the shot. She reentered the vehicle and leaned back against the seat, beaming at her husband, very satisfied with their teamwork in capturing the image of wildness in action.

Lucinda watched her therapist husband guide them through the mountains. She wanted to let him in on her interior journey and sometimes wondered why she could not open up to him, especially considering his expertise in such matters. For her, this trip was becoming about a new willingness to take risks. Why not?

"Vivid dream last night," she said. "Can you help me?"

"Are you sure? I'm kind of personally involved with the patient. Do you mind me bending the rules? Compromising my ethics?"

"No problem—just a quickie opinion—no long-term therapeutic relationship here. After all, you can't sleep with your analyst, can you? It's just a dream. Here it is. You and I were in the San Francisco warehouse district, and we were walking along the dock at night."

"Ah, San Francisco, the scene of the crime," Jonas said. "Please, go on."

"I saw an open door and ran into a darkened warehouse alone. There was only one light on in the far corner, illuminating a large bin of boxes wrapped in birthday or Christmas paper. I ran over to the bin and jumped in. I unwrapped box after box. Nothing was right. I was looking for a certain box, but I couldn't find it. I threw the torn paper out of the bin, making a huge mess. Some pirates broke into the warehouse, and they pointed at me and unleashed wild dogs to come and tear me to pieces. I jumped out of the bin and dove through a window. When I broke the glass, I fell out of the warehouse into the dark, freezing water. Then, I woke up."

"No evil mother after you? No, Aunt Mary?"

"No, just a pack of wild dogs. What do you think?"

"Well, if you really want to know what I think—the warehouse is your unconscious mind. The bin is your conscious mind. You're a seeker. Unwrapping the boxes may represent your efforts to heal from your past trauma. I don't always agree with your choices of which boxes to unwrap, but by God, you keep trying. That's what you do, Lu, strip away the onion skins." He squeezed her hand and smiled.

"Jonas, what about the dogs? And the plunge into the dark water?'

"It's just a dream. They usually end with some drama. Keep on unwrapping the boxes in your inner world."

God, he's good. The man could nail it every time. Her self-esteem inched up, and she relaxed into the drive. Jonas had affirmed everything she was feeling. This trip had been his idea, but now she was driving the bus. Somewhere in these mountains was an answer to all her questions, one last onion skin.

After a few hours, they entered the town square in Kingston and stopped to buy some last-minute items. They entered a general store on the square, which was jammed with foodstuffs, hardware, camping gear and a lot of junk labeled as antiques. The proprietor was very friendly and knew Dr. Kelly and his property well. He told them of two spectacular waterfalls—one deep into the property and one just off the gravel road leading there, maybe a hundred yards from the cabin. It was named Sweden Falls. Lucinda became excited at the prospect of falling water. She wandered outside onto the large covered porch and read the items posted on a community bulletin board. One flier read:

HOG PROBLEM?

Do you have a hog problem? Are hogs tearing up
your hunting lease or your crops?
Have you lost livestock? Do you need help?
If so, call Rusty. 1(800) KILLPIG. 1(800) 545-
5744. Rt.3 Ponca, Ark
I will help you and will take care of your hog problem.
Take a flier if you need help.

Lucinda took one and read it again slowly. Nature was in control here, not man. Finally, a place where man was the hunted. Wild hogs were on the prowl. One heard so much these days of man's dominance over nature and its ruination. Here was nature asserting itself against man. Yet, here was man offering a solution in the form of massive bloodshed. Somehow, the violent showdown intrigued her. She walked over to Jonas and handed him the flier.

"What is this, Jonas? Is this a real problem?"

"Apparently so. The razorback population must have made a big comeback—kind of like the alligators and the buffalo. I love it, that flier. Just love it, don't you? Razorbacks still stalk the land. The dire wolf still threatens the villagers. Nature has not been subdued after all, at least not in these mountains."

"Yes. It's good to know someone's there to help." Lucinda didn't understand the humor that had tickled Jonas. She took the flier back from him, folded it neatly and stuffed it in her shirt pocket. "Just in case we have a hog problem."

She sat down next to Jonas in their car and returned to stroking Bo's back on their way to the cabin. Dangerous wildlife, very interesting.

The Killpig convoy pulled into the small town, and heads turned. First came Rusty's Ford 250 diesel, pulling a thirty-foot trailer holding a 250 HP ATV, with a fifty-caliber machine gun mounted on the rear, plus a dog kennel containing the four canine members of the Killpig team. The gun case held two well-greased AK 47s, a .457 Glock sidearm and several large Bowie knives for cleanup duty. Following was a dump truck carrying the track hoe with a digging bucket for disposal purposes. When he stopped to get gas, three men came to admire the dogs. There was talk about the fifty-caliber and where he got the ammo. They asked about the noise and the blood—they always ask about the blood, how he stood it, the killing, the gore. He never thought about it, part of the work. They asked if he had ever been slashed by their tusks. He hadn't.

Rusty found most men secretly loved the thought of large guns and blood until they saw it themselves. Strangely, even a few women voiced their fascination with his work, but he had never met one who could bear to be near it. She would need to see the higher purpose in his work. She would have to see beyond the veneer to the depths. From what he knew, she'd be a rare find. As a hunter, though, Rusty remained constantly alert. There was always a chance.

After filling up, his cell phone rang. He reached inside his driver's door and took the call. Another complaint of a large pack of hogs in the Kingston area. Big problems, but no one had seen the pack. By the time the owners found the damage, the hogs had vanished. He'd have to wait to get a bead on them.

———◆◆◆———

"Jonas, let's go see Sweden Falls— the man said it was just down the road."

"We just got here. I'd like a little time to relax. Unpack, maybe read a bit." He pulled a large book from his backpack. "I'll be on the back porch trying out that rocker."

"Sorry darling, can't sit still today. You know me, maybe a little manic. You go ahead and relax. Bo and I will go exploring. I'll show you on my camera when I get back."

Lucinda and Bo followed the dirt road around the bend, and just as the storekeeper promised, there stood a tall and vigorous outpouring of white mountain water falling seventy feet, pounding piles of broken Ozark limestone. Although it was adjacent to the dirt road, the surrounding hardwoods formed a subtle covering, creating a green alcove in the hollow below, a hidden Eden. Lucinda had the place to herself. She found a smooth boulder on the top of the falls where she could comfortably sit and watch the white churning stream shoot over the edge. The sound of rushing and pounding water filled the space, seemingly forcing silence all around her. It was wild, untamed and unrelenting, so different from her glass tower in the sky, which separated her from the city chaos she found so threatening. She realized she had not yet meditated this day. Somehow, this wild country was taking her down another path entirely.

Bo busied himself, exploring all the new smells of the woods and water. Lucinda removed her hiking boots and splashed her bare feet in the cold water above the falls. She lay back on the smooth boulder and gazed into the green ceiling of leaves. Jung was right. Nature was both matter and spirit; she felt it deeply here. Her soul felt at home. *Poor Jonas, he may never be able to feel this.* But he had his books, and she figured they may be enough for him.

On the following morning, Lucinda stood atop the falls once again and cherished her solitude. She picked a sprig of white wild azalea blossoms and tied it in her mane of fiery red hair. She soaked up the sound of falling water. Her legs were strong and had a bit of color to them for a change. She felt rested and had not needed her regular sleeping medication since leaving Dallas. Although the view of the falls and the stream below were majestic, she decided to explore further. She grabbed Bo, stuffed him in her backpack and hiked down the side of the falls to the stream bed below. Once there, she put Bo down and walked among the boulders at the bottom of the falls to the pool formed by the falling water. Bo wandered off into the bushes.

Lucinda edged her way through the rocks to a small cavern behind the falls. She looked through the pouring torrent, down the stream bed. The noise was constant and overpowering. The water sprayed on her clothes and her bare legs. The morning sun glistened off the pool of water under the falls. She was all alone.

Lucinda slipped off her hiking boots, socks, shorts and t-shirt—naked in a hidden world. She paddled in the bracingly cold mountain water and stood up directly under the falling water, then raised her arms to the sky. Her snow-white body stood tall, leaning into the clear cold force pounding her downward. Her feet were firmly planted on the good Earth. In that moment, she belonged at Sweden Falls—at this place, in this time. She was a wild creature, unafraid, naked to the world. Death Mother had no power here. This place was life, and life here was supreme.

The cold falling water was bracing. Her heart pounded. The noise was almost deafening, silencing—but through it came a screech. It became desperate and constant. Maybe a bird, maybe a squirrel. Lucinda walked over to the edge of the pool and looked in the direction of the high-pitched noise. She saw two large, dark shapes moving in the bushes. The screeching grew louder. She attuned her ears. *Wait, that's not a bird; that's Bo.*

Four large barrel-shaped figures exploded through the bushes into the clearing next to the stream bed. Razorbacks! Their tusks were long and white. Their hides were black, the snouts armored with what looked like scales. There were more of them in the bushes. *Where's Bo?*

She was choked with fear, and the cries of her dog grew louder. No use screaming, no one to call. She scooped up her clothes and boots and backed slowly away from the pool. The four beside the pool continued to drink and ignored her as she dressed and donned her boots.

Lucinda edged a few feet toward the plaintive barks and pleas of her tiny Yorkie. Bo was cornered behind a large boulder by three more hogs with tusks like saber-toothed tigers. The hogs were rooting to get to him, and he barked in fear as they continued the siege. She dared not antagonize the beasts. Her only choice was to run for help. She had to take the chance that the hogs would either give up or be unable to reach Bo until she returned. She scrambled back up the side of the hill and sprinted up the road to the cabin. Rage rose in her gut. Her intention was clear.

Lucinda flung the cabin door open. Jonas was on the back porch reading. She ran to him. "Where's that fucking flier? Where is it?"

"What's going on, Lu? Why are you so upset?"

"Jonas, we've got a hog problem. Where's that flier? Now! I need it!"

Rusty, his dogs, and his equipment arrived at the Kelly cabin later that afternoon. They were met by a manic woman who ran immediately to the open window of his pickup. "Mr. Rusty. I'm Lucinda Wells. I called you. My dog Bo is trapped down at the falls. Those hogs are trying to kill him. Oh, God, I'm so glad you're here. Come, I'll show you the place." She ran around to the other side of his truck and was opening the passenger door to jump in when Jonas walked up.

"Hello, Mr. Wells. Rusty McClain." Rusty turned to Lucinda, who was already sitting in his passenger seat. "Let's go inside and talk before we go down to the falls. I need to get some information. You need to calm down to help me with these hogs. If those hogs hadn't got him by the time you left, he's probably still safe. Either they could get at him or they couldn't. So, calm down and let's talk."

The three entered the cabin. "How did you two come to be here?" Rusty asked. "Is this your cabin?"

"I'm a friend of the owner, Dr. Kelly, in Dallas," Jonas said. "We refer patients to each other. He loaned us the cabin for the week. Please sit down. Can I get you something to drink?"

"Sure, some water. Mouth's always dry before an eradication." Rusty sat in a small wooden chair beside the kitchen table.

Jonas and Lucinda joined him.

Two opposites here, the redhead and the professor. "You a doctor?" Rusty asked.

"No, Dr. Kelly and I are both therapists."

"Like a physical therapist?"

"No, we are both Jungian analysts, kind of like psychologists."

"I'll need to speak to him," Rusty said, "get his permission to do an eradication. Do you know what I do?"

"Judging from the machine gun on the back of your ATV, I suppose you kill hogs."

"Yes, sir, kill, remove and dispose. We clear the property of the immediate threat and prevent any more potential damage. We might disturb things, tear up the ground a bit. It's loud. There's blood involved. We'll need to get our equipment down there. I'll need to discuss the price with him. Two hundred per carcass. Can you get him on the phone?"

"Please hurry," Lucinda said. "Every minute may count. My poor Bo. Rusty, those fucking beasts deserve what you are going to give them."

"Mrs. Wells, they do a lot of damage, true. But remember, they're wild animals. They run on instinct. It ain't personal. It's the humans that brought them here and sustain their presence. People are to blame for the damage done up here. Those hogs should never be here in the first place."

Lucinda rode next to Rusty down the road to Sweden Falls. She sensed the presence of a man whose focus and purpose were sharp. He was bound firmly to the Earth. She didn't have to guess. There was a slight smile on his face. She knew in her heart that the chances of finding Bo alive were slim, but she also felt the assurance that the man driving her to the killing fields would know exactly what to do when they arrived. She felt giddy, fully present. Her breaths were rapid and expectant. She wanted to be part of it all. Rusty stopped the truck on the road near the falls.

"Please," she said, "let me go with you down to the falls. I have to know if Bo's still alive."

"Can you handle it? I just want to be sure you're okay with all this. There'll be a lot of noise and blood. But you'll be far enough away—at a safe distance. They're down in the ravine. We'll be able to hear if your dog's still barking. Come along with me, if you want."

"Thanks," she said. "I want to go with you."

They pushed through the briars and scrub pines to the edge of Sweden Falls. Below were eight large black razorbacks splashing and drinking in the pool below—no screeching or barking. Lucinda peered through her binoculars to look for any signs of life. She saw nothing. Her face fell; her shoulders slumped.

"I'm sorry for your loss, Lucinda."

"Please, call me Lu. Thanks for trying. Thanks for coming so soon. I had to try. I loved that dog so much. He saw me through some very lonely times. All he wanted was my love." She sobbed softly.

He put his arms around her. Her tears poured down her cheeks onto his chest, and his rough hands patted her back.

After a good cry, she picked herself up. "What happens now? There's nothing down there to save."

Rusty gently grabbed her by both shoulders and looked her straight in the eyes. "Lu, there's still a hog problem. This property is infested. I'm trained and licensed to solve that problem. Those hogs don't belong here at these beautiful falls. You deserve to be safe and secure. I want you to be able to walk around Sweden Falls again. I'm going to see that you remain safe and secure. How's that sound? Let me do my job. You just sit back and watch if you want."

A smile came across her face. "Rusty, I'd like to help. Can I do something for you? I've never been around guns. I've never even heard a gun fire. So, all this is new to me. I find all this exciting, don't know why. Is that strange?"

"You can help me with the hounds. They're from Louisiana. Call 'em hog dogs. Catahoula curs. You like dogs, right? I'll show you how to help me handle them, get them in position to release on the hogs. Don't worry, they're very well trained. I've made sure of that."

Back at the truck, Rusty prepared the ATV for use and placed his portable firearms in a rack next to the machine gun. Lucinda made friends with John, Paul, George and Ringo, attaching a massive four-dog leash and harness to the pack of hog dogs. The plan was to take the ATV and the dog pack down into the ravine a hundred yards down. The hogs would then be at the end of a box canyon formed by the sides of the hills and the hard rock of Sweden Falls.

"Ready little lady? Got your earplugs? Just follow me with those dogs, and I'll let you know when to release them."

Lucinda followed Rusty, walking purposefully into a green hollow of violence and death, which he would soon unleash. The dogs pulled a bit, but they were well trained. Rusty positioned his ATV in the stream bed entrance to the box canyon leading to the falls.

"Lu, you release the dogs when I signal. Let 'em go and scurry back up to the promontory overlooking the falls. Keep a safe distance from the side. I don't want you to get excited and fall, so watch your footing. Keep your earplugs in. There's going be a ruckus down in that pool."

Rusty checked his weapons one more time and turned back to face her. "Okay? Let 'em go!"

She released the hog dogs from their harness, and the four Beatles ran at Rusty's command down the streambed into the space that would soon become a killing ground.

"Let's roll!" Rusty yelled, starting off toward the falls on the ATV.

Lu climbed back up to the cliff overlooking the falls. The barking of dogs and grunting of hogs overcame the roar of falling water. She heard the ATV approaching. The dogs methodically herded the hogs into the area formed by the pool. The hogs were trapped in a limestone box full of cold, clear water.

Rusty positioned the rear of his ATV toward the pool. The dogs stood back behind the ATV, snarling and barking. Rusty stood with an AK-47 strapped over his shoulder, his pistol on his side and a Bowie knife in his belt. His strong, rough hands gripped the machine gun. Lucinda inserted her earplugs.

Fire and smoke poured out of the gun into the clear pool where she had stood naked before a peaceful, loving world earlier that day. She felt shock waves from the concussive sounds in the ravine below like Rusty was operating a jackhammer rather than a .50 caliber. Blood splattered the limestone walls and turned the creek water red. Swine squeals penetrated her earplugs. Dust and chips of rock drifted up into the air. The bitter scent of gunpowder stung her nostrils. The razorbacks perished in a hail of bullets. All but three were dispatched by the machine gun burst.

An energy deep in her solar plexus warmed, then spread through her body. What she had seen and heard was not repulsive after all. It had drawn her in, the power and raw justice of it all. Violence could be righteous, even virtuous, when meted out for a good cause. Rusty knew this. Now she knew it. She needed to understand more. She must know this man. She must remain with him. He was what she came to find deep in these mountains.

Lucinda made her way back down into the green alcove of Sweden Falls. Rusty was standing among the fallen hogs, blood covering his boots and trousers.

She had taken her boots off and stepped with her bare feet into the flowing red stream, frigid on her white legs. She approached him as he dispatched another wounded hog. "Can I shoot the last one?" she asked.

Rusty held out the gun before him with one hand and pulled her to his side with the other. He placed the pistol in her hands and placed his hands over hers to ensure a proper grip and trigger position. "Hold it with both hands, and place the barrel behind its ear, about eight inches away. Then brace your arms for the recoil and gently squeeze the trigger."

Lucinda did as he told her. The Glock exploded. The hog's head jerked. Blood surged from the wound, spattering along Lucinda's arms and chest. She felt a release of a dark poison from her deep inside her young girl's heart. This was beyond therapy. A direct pipeline had opened, and all her rotten past drained out. Death Mother? It now had a new meaning to Lucinda. She didn't understand what had happened, but it didn't matter. She felt it, way down in her gut.

She gave Rusty the handgun, which he promptly holstered. She took both of his hands in hers, staring into his eyes. "Thank you. I needed that," she said quietly. She walked over to the boulder that had sheltered Bo and gently lifted his lifeless body to her bosom.

Rusty approached her and touched her shoulder. "I know you told me to call you Lu. But can I give you a new name? Just between us? Can I call you Little Red?"

"I love it. No one ever gave me a nickname."

They made their way up the hill. Little Red clutched Bo's body and gently laid him in the bed of Rusty's pickup. Rusty packed the truck and trailer. The dogs jumped into their kennel. As Rusty started the truck for the drive back to the cabin, Little Red placed her hand on his. "When you get to the cabin, don't stop," she said. "Please, you won't be sorry."

He looked at her, his gaze following all that red hair hanging about her ample breasts. She knew he couldn't refuse.

Rusty's truck and trailer drove slowly by the Kelly place en route to nearby Ponca. Jonas heard the gravel crunch as the truck drove by and looked up from a journal article on PTSD, expecting that his wife would shortly walk in the door. She didn't.

Lee and Me

You know him as Lee Harvey Oswald, the crazy assassin who killed President John F. Kennedy. We just called him Lee. I met him in 1954 on the corner of Canal Street and Jefferson Davis Parkway in New Orleans. We were on what is called the neutral ground—that's the land between the traffic lanes on big boulevards. I've never figured out why they call it neutral ground because there wasn't anything neutral about it. It was more of a battleground—boys and men fighting all the time. Lee and me, we met during a fight.

A bunch of us ninth graders was hanging out at the playground, and five hoods from Warren Easton High School came up and jumped us. There was about eight or nine of us, but those boys were older, and one of them wrapped his belt around his fist and started whaling away on Lee. Lee was this skinny kid just assigned to my homeroom class. I felt sorry for him. I grabbed a fallen limb from one of the live oaks and whacked that hood upside his head. He fell off Lee just long enough for the two of us to take off running toward Bayou St. John a few blocks away. The hoods took out after us. The boy with the belt looked like a charging bull, with crazy eyes and a little streak of blood coming from his ear. As we neared the bayou, I yelled to Lee, "I'm Murray. What's your name?"

"Lee. Thanks for helping! What the hell we gonna' do?" We both stood breathless on the bank of the bayou as the hoods drew nearer.

"Can you swim?" I yelled. "We gotta' swim the bayou—let's go!" We dove into Bayou St. John and started swimming for the other side. The hoods stopped at the water's edge. We made it across the dark green water and ran toward City Park, where we hid in thick bushes until after sunset.

Lee looked at me and smiled. "Man! You saved my ass! I owe you. Why'd you do it? Those guys coulda killed both of us."

"I dunno. I just reacted. I saw that limb. I always take up for the underdog."

There, among the bushes, we traded our histories, short as they were at the time. Lee's daddy died before he was born. He and his mom had moved around a lot, just returned from a stint in New York where he got thrown in the can as a juvenile delinquent. The two now lived in a tiny apartment in the French Quarter above a pool hall on Exchange Alley. He told me he could get me into the pool hall because his uncle knew the owner. He could teach me some pool shots and how to throw darts. He seemed like a cool kid, the kind of kid I wanted to get to know, especially the part about the pool hall. I had never met a real juvenile delinquent.

At that time, my folks and me was livin' in the Faubourg Marigny neighborhood, right off the Quarter. My daddy worked the docks as a longshoreman, and my momma cooked at Antoine's, so I had a lot of time on my own. The next Saturday afternoon, I walked down to Exchange Alley to meet Lee. His mom wasn't home. She was never home when I was there. I figured she worked somewhere.

Lee took me downstairs to Angelo's Pool Hall. He whispered something to the three-hundred-pound bouncer at the door who let us in. It was early afternoon. Two men sipped beer at the bar and read their racing forms. A large Negro woman was mopping the floor, spreading vapors of Pinesol throughout the joint. All the tables were empty.

"They know my Uncle Dutz," Lee said. "They let me play for free when there ain't no payin' customers. Can you rack 'em?" I smiled and gathered up the balls. We played eight and nine-ball for a couple of hours on a professional slate table in a real pool hall. Lee showed me how to jump balls and how to use reverse "English" to get better position after a shot. He sure knew his way around a pool table. At Beauregard Junior High in 1954, playing pool and fighting were prized skills. I guess you could say that Lee and I were riding high, fresh off our big fight, strutting around a real pool hall.

The 54-55 school year ended in May. To remove me from the juvenile delinquent scene that summer, my old man sent me to my uncle's horse farm up in Folsum, Louisiana. Lee worked for his Uncle Dutz at his shipping company on the docks, and at a gambling joint he owned in the Quarter, the Lomalinda. Lee was just an errand boy, but he got to rub shoulders at the gambling joint with all the big shots of that time, including ex-Governor Earl Long and all his boys, and the Mob boss—Carlos Marcello. Me, I got to shovel horseshit and carry hay bales all summer. When summer sentence finally ended, I was chomping at the bit to get back to town and find some trouble as soon as possible.

A few days after I returned to the city, I ran into Lee at J&M Records on Rampart Street. Lee had a record player back at his apartment and always liked to talk about the new 45s coming out each week.

"Hey, Murray. Where you been, man?" Lee asked.

"I been shovellin' shit, working at my uncle's place north of the lake. Lee, you got any idea how much shit a horse can turn out overnight? It's unbelievable, man."

"You want to go out to Pontchartrain Beach tonight? They're having this big back to school bash with a band and all. Big outdoor concert. My uncle got me four tickets."

"Sure. Who's playin'?"

"Guy named Elvis Presley and his band. It's like a caravan of stars, the Louisiana Hayride. Bunch of bands."

"Oh man," I said, "that sounds too country and western. What a name. Elvis? You got to be kidding me. Who's he sound like, Hank Williams?"

"No, he's more like that rocker, Bill Haley, a cool cat. But hey, the tickets are free. You got somethin' better to do?" Lee smiled, flashing the tickets from his pocket like they were a magic wand. We crossed Rampart down into the Quarter. I remember stopping by his apartment so he could change into his Civil Air Patrol shirt. He had joined a few weeks back and was really proud of it. He had a pin with wings and a nameplate. To someone who didn't know better, it kind of looked like he was USAF.

We went downstairs, played a couple of games of pool, and then headed for Bourbon Street to troll for girls. Hell, we had nothing better to do. The concert wasn't till eight o'clock that evening. After a couple of trips up and down Bourbon, all we had chased up was a few prolonged stares through the open doors of strip joints up and down the street. The bouncers would let you get a peek, but not much more. I think they had a five-second rule. Any more than that, and they figured you were stealing something you should be paying for. We were getting hungry. I offered to buy us some grub since Lee had the tickets. We walked to the corner of Bourbon and Toulouse, where this huge red-haired fellow ran a Lucky Dog cart. The guy had been there for years. Everyone knew him. The man was a raconteur, a real Quarter character. Not only did you get a great hot dog, but you got entertained. As we approached his cart, he spied us, and his eyes lit up.

"Ah...what have we here? Tweedle Dee and Tweedle Dum? Or is it Tonto and the Lone Ranger? One of 'em got a uniform on! Or perhaps two hungry juvenile delinquents lookin' for trouble? What'll it be, men?" he asked with eyes buggin' out.

"Two Lucky Dogs with chili and relish," I said.

"Two? Just two? How would you young men care to make a dent in world hunger? I have these two young waifs over here who have appealed to the better angels of my nature, but alas, we couldn't find any." He turned around and gestured toward two brown-haired girls wearing blue jeans and dingy white blouses. One was tall and slim, and the other was short. Both were stacked. The short one had a bandaged forearm. They smiled sheepishly at Lee and me.

"Men, these two girls are stranded in our fair city and have fallen on hard times. Can you spot them two Lucky Dogs?"

Lee stepped up on the sidewalk and asked them, "Where you girls from?"

"Chicago," they said in unison, smiling sweetly.

"I'm Lee Oswald, and this here is Murray Blank. He's a friend of mine."

The tall one said, "I'm Connie Sanders, and this is Betty Dean. We started hitchhiking from Miami, trying to get back home before school started, but we're having problems. We ran out of money a few days ago. We've been bouncing around the Quarter trying to raise some money to get back home. We'd sure appreciate your kindness."

"How old are ya'll?" Lee asked.

Connie replied, "We're both nineteen. We're supposed to be enrolling in beauty college, but by now, I'm sure our parents think we're missing. I don't know what we're gonna' do, but it's not going to be pretty when we get back home. So how old are you guys? Can you buy beer?"

"We're seniors at Warren Easton," I said, lying out my ass. "We're almost eighteen, not quite, but we can get beer if we want some. I know a place down in Faubourg."

I stood next to Betty. "What happened to your arm?" I asked.

"Got shot last night at the Seven Seas. But it's not bad. They told me at Charity they'd take the bullet out tomorrow," Betty said without even a trace of concern. I tried to imagine what it was like walking around with a bullet in your arm and what the hell these two could've been doing with all the low life at the Seven Seas.

"You girls like chili and relish?" Lee asked.

"We'll have whatever you guys are havin'," Connie said. She sidled up to Lee and grabbed his arm.

Betty smiled and looked at me. She was the kind of girl who you understood was accustomed to taking whatever was leftover.

"Four dogs with chili and relish—and four Cokes," I said. We walked to Jackson Square and sat on the grass for our evening picnic. As we sat and ate our feast, I could see these girls were more than a little hungry, that they probably hadn't eaten in a while. Lee was trying to impress them with stories from the pool hall and the gambling joints, claimed he knew the mayor. They seemed more interested in the hot dogs.

After falling flat a few times, Lee pulled out his tickets and said, "Hey girls, how'd you two like to catch a rising star? I got four tickets to a concert tonight out by the lake. You wanna' go?"

Betty asked, "Who's this rising star?"

"Name's Elvis," Lee said. "They say he sounds a lot like Bill Haley and the Comets. You know, 'Rock Around the Clock.' Like that guy."

"Bill Haley! I love him!" Connie said.

"Hey, trust me—this guy's good. Someone said they heard him on the radio. He's on a show each week. They call it Louisiana Hayride. You girls wanna go?"

"Sure, but how we gonna get there?" Betty asked. "You guys have a car?"

"Hey, we got tickets—that's a starter, but no car," Lee said. "We're city boys. We don't need no car."

I chimed in. "We'll catch the Elysian Fields bus. It takes us right there. You girls ever been out to Pontchartrain Beach? They got rides and a midway. Look, I got some money from my summer job. How 'bout it?"

"Can't go to a concert without some beer," Betty said.

"Follow me," I said. "Know just the place." I started off toward Faubourg Maringny. After I sweet-talked the clerk at Domino's Grocery, we all sat down on a bench in Washington Square to drink the four Dixies meant for my father. Lee was playing the stoic type, and nothing was going to happen without me taking the lead. Connie quietly exuded an animal lust but seemed remote and shut down like Lee. Betty held out vague possibilities. Her red hair dropped gently onto her freckled shoulders. Her gunshot wound and her presence at the Seven Seas just hours before led me to hope that she didn't give a damn about morality or the company she kept. For a boy who had never kissed a girl, this set the bar where it needed to be set. She smiled warmly at me, batted her lashes, and thanked me for the beer.

"So, tell me about your road trip," I said to her.

"We made it to Miami Beach, saw the sights."

"We both got sunburned," Connie said. "I'll be peeling for another week."

"Met some cute boys. Met some assholes," Betty continued.

70

"Ran out of money, so we're stranded here for now. And you two fellas are feeding us and taking us out tonight. No gunplay, nice and proper. Two real Southern gentlemen."

"I ain't a Southern gentleman," Lee blurted out. "I'm down here from New York City."

"I thought you sounded different," Connie said. "I can tell a big city accent. What you doin' down here, Mr. Big Apple?"

"Cop trouble," Lee said. "I could see where it was going. Served time in juvenile hall. So, my mom and I moved south. Her people are here."

"Yeah, I know what you mean," Connie said. "The fuzz are always rousting my brothers and cousins." Her interest suddenly aroused, she clicked her beer bottle against Lee's. "Here's to outlaws." Lee smiled and put his arm around her.

On the bus ride out to the lake, the four of us crammed into the last seats in the very front of the bus with the other white riders. The Elysian Fields bus was packed that evening with folks going to the concert. There must have been something going on that night at Lincoln Beach since the colored section was also full. I was jammed next to Betty, so I gingerly put my arm around her shoulder. No resistance! She smiled at me; all was well.

Connie asked Lee, "Are you in the Air Force or something?"

"It's Civil Air Patrol."

"What's that?"

"It's for guys who want to fly someday," Lee told her. "They teach you about aviation—how to fly a plane. There's a lot to it, you know. It's really cool, but I'm havin' problems with our supervisor out there, so I might have to go straight in the service next year. Follow my big brother. He's in the Marines."

"Oh, the Marines are cool," Connie said. "I saw that movie

Flying Leathernecks—with John Wayne. So cool! But you're a little young yet, huh?"

"Yeah, I got a year more," Lee said—lyin' through his teeth. I had to admit, the shirt looked pretty official. I was impressed with his bullshit.

Between the two of us, we had enough money for a couple of rides along the midway and some cold drinks for the four of us. First, we went straight to the Zephyr, the largest roller coaster in the South. After standing in line for twenty minutes, we piled in and were treated to the ride of our lives. We all damned near lost our Lucky Dogs on that one. Next, we went through a place they called Laff in the Dark. It was kind of a haunted house with mechanical spooks, and smoke from dry ice, that sort of thing. There was a twist at the end. They sent you through a hall of crazy mirrors with a tilting floor thrown in to really disorient you completely. When you came to the mirror, which reversed whatever trait you hated about yourself, that was the one you wanted to stay and stare at. Betty yelled, "Connie, come see—I'm finally tall and skinny!"

Lee stood by the same skinny mirror and kept calling to me, "Murray, come see—I'm ten feet tall! Come see!"

Sure enough, Lee towered over me; but it was just a mirror trick. "Don't worry, Lee. You'll get there for real someday soon—you just ain't had yer' growth spurt yet."

The next stop was a ride into horror on the haunted house ride. Betty and I climbed into a small cart behind one occupied by Lee and Connie. We were all pulled into darkness to be scared and thrilled by mechanical spooks for a few minutes on a journey through the netherworld. When we entered into total darkness, I placed my arm around Betty and pulled her toward me. She placed her head on my chest. This was an uncharted world I was entering, a far cry from slow dances at the CYO. Without a clue, I moved my face and waiting lips toward where I thought Betty's might be. Her moist lips met mine, and a surge of joy filled my chest and head. Then, something strange occurred. Her tongue slipped into my mouth, and her hand slipped into my crotch. Not knowing how to respond, I grabbed her other arm to embrace her more tightly.

Betty winced in pain and pulled away. "Don't grab me there. It's the bullet."

"So sorry. I kind of forgot," I said. "I didn't mean to hurt you."

"Sorry to scare you. It's just painful when you move a certain way. It'll be gone soon. You want to feel it?" She grabbed my hand and slowly moved it along her forearm until I felt a small hard lump near her elbow. "That's the tip of it. The doctor wanted the swelling to go down first."

Just about that time, a bloody werewolf appeared overhead, eliciting squeals from our fellow cart riders. Between Betty's encounter with real violence and the fake horrors now unfolding in the tunnel, any magic moment of my first kiss had vanished. I caught a glance at Lee and Connie kissing in between scares. I sat in confusion, a teen with blue balls. My arm still hung limply around Betty. We drank sodas and had some laughs about my encounter with the embedded bullet.

Folks were already packing the area around the outdoor stage. It was a simple concrete promenade with a raised stage that resembled a boat deck. Lake Pontchartrain provided the backdrop. The crowd was so thick, and the four of us so far away. I didn't think we'd get much of a view. I was content to just hang back and listen, but Lee insisted we weave our way through the crowd to get a better view. He led the way and was working forward like a halfback picking his holes. I followed him for a while, but we got separated. Pretty soon, I couldn't see the girls. It was like Canal

Street on Mardi Gras Day. So, I just stopped and decided to stay where I was for the concert. Standing room only.

Elvis and his band came out right after the sun went down over the lake. I couldn't see Lee anywhere. He'd squeezed upfront. I last saw the girls talking to two tough guys wearing leather jackets. But that didn't bother me—not after the music started. Elvis started rocking and shaking his hips, and the girls started squealing. Rebel yells went up after each song. People were stomping and clapping. I had never heard anything like it. When he sang "Love Me Tender," the girls went wild. He ended with "Hound Dog," which left the crowd stomping and yelling for more. They clapped for five minutes, but no encore. Elvis and the band were already off on their bus to somewhere else to play the next night. The crowd left grumbling, but knowing they'd seen something special—an hour of Southern rockabilly, only the word hadn't been invented yet.

The crowd flooded back toward the midway and carried me along. I stood by a giant clown head until Lee appeared a few minutes later. "Where's the girls?" he asked as he walked up to me.

"Last seen with two greasers, whereabouts unknown," I replied with a smile. "I guess they didn't like being abandoned. Hope you got a good view. How was it down front?"

"I got one of his guitar picks—" Lee held up a small brown pick. "He tossed it into the crowd, and I caught it!" He admired the prize in his palm. "Maybe he'll get famous, and this'll be worth a lot of dough. They say he's got some records comin' out. Damned, he's good!"

We walked down the midway back toward the bus stop. "To hell with those girls anyway," Lee said. "They're just some runaways moochin' off guys in the Quarter. Ain't no tellin' where they been. Besides, we had bullshitted them about as far as we could. They had to be three or four years older than us, right?"

"Yeah, we had run out of bullshit. At least I ran out—but you, man, you're the master—with that shirt and all. It really looks official—what is this CAP stuff?"

"It's just a club I joined," he said. "I really like the other cadets, and the stuff they teach us is cool. We have meetings out at the airport, study real airplanes, drill, and learn about rifles. But there's this one faggot out there, and he's one of the sponsors. The motherfucker is sweet on me, I think, and I might have to hurt him if he tries anything. They say he got kicked out of a Catholic seminary, and he got a cadet killed last year in a plane crash. He's fucking creepy; he's got no hair on his body, and he paints in his eyebrows."

"What's his name?" I asked.

"This is the shit, man—" Lee smiled a crooked smile. "His name is Ferrie—David fucking Ferrie. Can you believe that—a faggot with the name of Ferrie?"

"So, speaking of runnin' out—I spent my last dime on those Cokes. You got any bus fare?"

"Negative. Maybe we can thumb back into town. If not, we can always walk back. Come on; let's get going."

We caught a ride as far as Broad Street and walked back toward the fairgrounds race track where the defeated horse pickers and bookies were just shuffling out onto the street from a night of racing. We walked on to Esplanade and turned back toward the Quarter. When we got to Rampart Street, we went our separate ways—Lee back to his perch above Angelo's Poll Hall, and me, back to the longshoreman's pad in Faubourg. Lee and his mom moved to Fort Worth soon after school started. We lost touch with each other.

This night I told you about was the last time I saw Lee before I saw him on TV on the afternoon of November 22, 1963. By that time, he had become the kingslayer. I shall never forget the night when the kingslayer crossed paths with the king. One would die in a Dallas basement on live network TV, and the other would die while sitting on a toilet in his Memphis mansion.

I sometimes wonder if Lee hung on to that guitar pick he caught that night in 1955. Like a whole lot of other things about Lee, I'll never know.

Find Franny Now

She knew it was wrong, but she did it anyway.

Lydia pulled her autistic son across the steaming asphalt parking lot of Children's Hospital. The pair moved in fits and starts toward the dose of radiation that would be shot into the center of his brain. Taking Justin anywhere in public was a contest of wills in the form of a sporadic tug of war. Justin broke away, crashing into a chain-link fence surrounding the parking lot. Coating the fence were row upon row of missing person posters, all for the same missing person. The posters read, "Find Franny Now!" Franny's face smiled out from each poster at passersby.

Lydia corralled Justin and pressed him against the fence to regain control. Stepping back with Justin in hand, she stared at the ubiquitous pleas for help by the grieving parents of a missing teenager. Did these people really believe somehow that plastering these posters all over the city would bring their daughter home? Justin continued to tug on her arm. Sweat trickled down her temples. She ripped down a row of the posters and quickly stuffed them in a trash barrel before anyone could see what she had done.

The missing teenager's bicycle had been found the day before in the swampy land on the other side of the levee, along with some of her clothes. Lydia couldn't understand people's mania with these goddamned posters. Franny wasn't coming home, and Lydia damned well knew it. She accepted it, just as she accepted the fact that her son Justin was dying from brain cancer and that her husband, Paul, was living with another woman. Oh, she had wanted to run, wanted to crawl into a bottle. But no, she was trapped. Mothers don't run, at least not in her family. So, Lydia accepted all of it—she had to. It was real. She had no time these days for anything but reality. She knew now the rest was bullshit: no Easter Bunny, no happily ever after, no 'till death do us part, no welcome home, Franny. People who could not accept reality were fools, and she had no use for fools.

The oncology waiting room at Children's was tiny and cold. The room featured fresh flowers, and there were soft couches and leather armchairs for the families, simulating a faux hominess, but the place was freezing. Lydia took a seat with two sets of parents whose children were undergoing procedures that morning. She felt obliged to exchange stories with them, something she resented, but it seemed that such recitations were socially required here at Children's among parents bearing the unbearable. Somehow, it seemed to help, at least for others.

"He's having his first radiation session," she answered in response to a question by one mother. "They're using a fluoroscope to target the cancer. They're trying to hit his brain tumor."

A brief silence ensued.

The inquiring mother finally replied, "Lord have mercy on you, sweetie. Sam and I are just dealing with leukemia. They're optimistic about a remission. We got lots of prayer warriors praying for him, lots of rosaries around the clock. We can feel it, the love of Jesus, in our bodies. My husband and I believe prayers work when nothing else will. I sure wish you the best. You just keep praying. You'll see."

"Thank you. You know how it is. One day at a time," said Lydia. Perfect, another platitude. Conversation ended. This was why she hated to talk to other parents. Prayer warriors? Let them take on fucking medulloblastoma. What else could she say? The lady didn't want to hear her truth. Hell, her kid had leukemia. They got a cure for that. But nothing personal; it was just small talk, like in a long elevator ride.

Lydia's name was called to come to the nurse's station. "Justin did fine," the nurse said, "but he's heavily sedated on account of his autism. He won't wake up until three at the earliest. We're watching him in recovery. You go ahead and get some lunch. I got your cell number if he wakes up earlier."

"Do I have enough time to catch the streetcar to Camellia Grill?"

"Honey, you go and take you some time. Your little man's sleeping good now. I'll be with him. See you when you get back."

Lydia walked out of the front entrance of the pediatric center into the oven of a New Orleans summer afternoon. She headed for the wide walkway along Audubon Park called Exposition Place. It was lined with huge oaks and Victorian homes that had survived wars, floods and hurricanes for well over a hundred years. Today, the trees and homes would provide her shade and a few moments of respite from the frozen atmosphere of the oncology unit. No more talking. She couldn't bear talking to another parent. There was nothing left to say to those people, and nothing else she cared to hear. She wanted to walk by herself, walk and think. She headed toward St. Charles Avenue to catch the streetcar. She could easily make it back for three o'clock, pick up Justin and beat the rush-hour traffic to the causeway and back across the lake to her mother's house.

She approached a newly renovated Greek Revival framed by towering live oaks and surrounded by a black wrought iron fence. Brand new wicker furniture graced the front porch, and brocade drapes were pulled back from the newly installed windows to exhibit the smart furniture in the front parlor. A pair of baby-blue tricycles sat unattended behind a large Mercedes in the driveway near a huge azalea bush. Did the matriarch of this fine uptown home have twins to care for? Did their brains function normally? Maybe they had a Downs child? Maybe one was autistic, like Justin. No, not likely. The families in these exquisite homes were probably immune from such a plight. If only she could slip through a breach in the heavy metal barrier separating her from what lay on the other side, maybe she too could enter a world where fate was not such a cruel tyrant.

Lydia approached Magazine Street, walking toward the front of Audubon Park and the St Charles streetcar stop. She had wanted to be out of the hard cold of the oncology unit, but now the tropical heat pulled the sweat out of her chilled body. Only one block and already her blouse stuck to her back. She wiped her brow and stopped to clean her glasses. A New Orleans city bus zoomed past her, belching black diesel fumes, its passengers seemingly locked in place and staring blankly into the abyss immediately before them.

As she continued along Exposition, an unexpected light breeze off the river cooled her back. The oak canopy brought her temperature down. She stopped at a raised Creole cottage painted a very subtle lime green. The house dated from the mid-nineteenth century. What type of families had lived, loved and fought within its walls? Were they people who kept their word? The men, did they love their wives and keep their vows? For better or worse, that's what she and Paul had promised each other. *Fuck him.* He came from a fine home like this a few blocks away. The Wilsons were a good Episcopalian family. She had given him everything he asked of her—a son, a home and her trust. She had given him a flower. Paul had thrown it in the trash. *What is wrong with him?*

The heavy footsteps of a jogger approached from behind. He

ran past and stopped at the cottage's front gate, then looked back at her and asked, "Do you like it? My wife picked the color. Kind of wild for my taste."

"Oh, yes. It's lovely. I studied design at Newcomb a few years back. Nice modern color. Crisp."

"Hmm, that sounds like lettuce," he said. "But you ladies know what works, don't you? Hell, I'm color blind. What the hell do I know?" He ambled up the steps to his front porch.

"Say, what is it like having Audubon Park as your front yard?" Lydia asked.

"Great for jogging and walking, but you got to watch everything you do. Lots of break-ins down here. Some violent crime as well. We make sure we set our alarm at night. I guess you've heard about that Franny girl. Right across the levee, they said. So sad."

Lydia lowered her eyes. "Sure, posters everywhere, and it's all over the TV. I'm sure the whole city knows about it. I've never seen so many posters before. They're all over Uptown." Like that's going to bring her home. *Fools.*

"Can you blame them?" asked the homeowner. "I don't know what I'd do if someone grabbed my little girl. Maybe they figure one of those posters reaches that one person who knows something. I guess you do what you got to do. That's what we parents do for our children, whatever we got to do."

Lydia smiled, nodded knowingly, and proceeded on toward St. Charles. She was doing what she had to do, but there were no fairy godmothers involved and no rosaries. A Find Franny poster was attached to an oak tree along her way. She ripped it down and stashed it in her purse.

She fingered six quarters for the fare while standing in the neutral ground at the St. Charles stop. The streetcar's ancient doors screeched open, and she dropped her coins in the conductor's glass box. One window seat remained open toward the rear of the car. She made her way back. The streetcar lurched forward, its metal wheels squeaking along the rails. The hot breeze from the open window did little to cool her from the bright furnace of the New Orleans summer afternoon.

She got off at the first stop after the turn onto Carrollton and crossed the street to Camellia Grill, where she and Paul had spent so many Sunday mornings. The lunch crowd of tourists was dwindling, and she was able to grab a seat at the section of the long counter served by her favorite waiter, raconteur and ancient seer, Harry LeBlanc.

"What's ya havin' today, Mrs. W? Cheesecake? Coffee? With or without chicory?"

"Yeah, Harry. You know what I want. Oh, without the chicory. How're the Yankees doing this summer?"

"Oh, baby, that damned A-Rod. All those women up there are killin' him. Man's worn out. He can't hit the side of a barn these past two weeks. My bookie laughs every time he sees me. How you, my baby? Hadn't seen you in a while. Ya doin' all right?"

"You don't have time, Harry. Long story. Paul's been gone for three months, and I moved back with Momma in Abita Springs. Justin's down here at Children's. That's why I'm down in the city today."

"Children's? Is it bad?"

Looking straight at Harry, Lydia nodded slightly but said nothing. "Do y'all have a Times-Picayune around?" she asked. "I haven't read the paper in weeks."

Harry walked to the end of the counter and scooped up a paper left over from the morning crowd. He handed it to Lydia and reached over the counter to squeeze her forearm. "Let me get your pie and coffee."

Harry returned with the cheesecake. *The best anywhere*, she thought. Paul had introduced her to the wonders of Camellia Grill. As Lydia sipped her coffee, she thought back to their time together at the camelback on Upperline. Weekends spent laying around reading the Sunday Times and making love on the sun porch. As an indulgence, they strolled down to Camellia Grill for Harry and his cheesecake. Another world, another time. A time before the cruel hand of fate began to steal children like Justin and Franny, before the wine and the fights, before the redhead, before the load fell on her, and her alone.

Harry watched Lydia eat her cake, arms crossed and smiling down at her. He leaned over the counter and whispered to her, "Did I tell you that Ellen and I lost a child?"

Lydia looked up and shook her head.

"It was after the war. She died in the polio epidemic—1949. She was our first. I didn't know if I could make it after she died. I couldn't get out the front door, much less deal with other people. But baby, you just hang on. You can make it through whatever it is that you are going through. You see all the people in this grill? They all got a story. I hear them all day long, a thousand stories. They all finding their way through that swamp."

"Maybe some don't make it," Lydia said. "Maybe they get lost. Maybe the gators get them."

"True, Mrs. W. True enough. But I got a hunch you gonna make it through."

Lydia's vibrating phone interrupted her conversation.

"Where *are* you?" Paul asked with an edge. "I'm here at the oncology unit, but you're not."

"I took a walk to grab a cup of coffee. The nurse told me three o'clock."

"Are you downstairs in the coffee shop? I'll meet you."

"Actually, I'm at Camellia Grill. Harry just fed me cheesecake. He says hello."

"Jesus, Lydia, that's over a mile away from here. What if something came up with Justin? It's his first radiation session."

"Everything is fine. I just talked to his nurse, Paul."

"Are you sure *you're* fine?"

"Do you mean, have I been drinking? Is that what you're asking?" She turned to Harry, held out her phone to him and mouthed the words *motherfucker*.

"Wait, wait. Let's calm down," Paul said.

"Don't you dare!" Lydia hated it when Paul became calm and assumed control, hated even more when he told her to calm down.

"Look, I'm here at the unit. Take your time. Tell Harry 'Hi' for me." He hung up without saying goodbye.

She opened her purse with shaking hands and grabbed her vial of Xanax. Her doctor gave it to her to get her through the next few months, with Justin's cancer and all the mess of living with her mother. She promised to take it at night to sleep and not while driving. But having to deal with Paul this afternoon and driving her Justin back across the lake—these seemed like good enough reasons to make this one exception. She felt like she could breathe better when she took it. After all, it was an anti-anxiety medication. Fear rolled over her right now like a huge wave from a busted levee. The children of New Orleans were being stolen in the night. She needed help.

"Harry, can you bring me a glass of water? I need to take my vitamins."

She swallowed the pill, bid goodbye to Harry and walked across the side street to a grocery store where she picked up two wine coolers. She allotted herself two each day. She would drink one on the way back to her mother's and one after supper while watching TV. At the checkout counter, she reached back into her purse for her wallet.

"That's the girl from River Ridge," the checkout girl said, noticing the Franny poster stuffed in Lydia's purse. "I saw her momma and daddy on the news. So sad. You never know what can happen these days. So pretty, but that's how they like them, isn't it? Some sick weirdo. They lookin' for the pretty ones. She was just out for a bike ride on the levee."

"It's terrible," Lydia said and paid for the wine coolers. "I'm taking a poster to put up in Abita Springs. Maybe someone over there saw her. You never know." *What the hell did I just say?* There wasn't a chance in hell of finding Franny alive. On the other hand, they hadn't found her body, at least not yet, so maybe there was hope. It was possible, wasn't it? In a way, she envied Franny's parents. What Lydia would give just not to know. Right now, she'd give anything not to be so goddamned certain. Maybe she *would* put that poster up in Abita Springs. You never know. Just no more talk about rosaries and prayer warriors. She clenched her pursed close to her side and walked out of the store.

The oncology unit's automatic doors opened to release a blast of super-chilled air against her warm and sweaty body. Three pairs of pensive parents gazed up at her. Paul stood talking with Dr. Rainwater, who extended his hand to her as she approached. She shook his hand. It was cold and limp, like the unit itself. He was driving the bus on this wild goose chase of radioactivity and false hope. He looked like a child wearing Coke bottle glasses to guide his path.

"Justin's still sleeping," the good doctor said, addressing them both. "It'll be about thirty minutes until he comes around, and you can take him home. I was just going over things with your husband, what to expect tonight and tomorrow. That's when he'll start feeling it—vomiting, nausea. He might have a fever. Do you have far to go after you leave here?"

Lydia slid down on the couch a safe distance from Paul. "I'm staying with my mother across the lake. She's helping out."

"That's great. Help is good. He'll be down for a couple of days, then he'll gradually feel better. Before you know it, you'll be back here next Tuesday again, and we'll see him for his second treatment. After six more weeks, we'll scan him, and hopefully, we'll see some tumor shrinkage. That's our hope. So, you two take care of the little man. He's going to need a lot of TLC. That stuff is pretty nasty for a kid."

"Well, I'm afraid it's going to be Lydia and her mom. I'm staying in the city, near my work. But he'll be in excellent hands." Paul reached over and patted Lydia's knee. "Both of them are born caregivers." His hand remained—cold, disembodied, like the unwelcome hand of a stranger. Lydia withdrew her leg reflexively.

"Doctor," Lydia said. "You took him off his Risperdal. What can we expect with his autism? Will the radiation slow him down until we come back?"

"This is a first for me—medulloblastoma and autism. I haven't seen the combination here or in my residency. There's no literature I could find, but frankly, between the radiation and the tumor in his cerebellum, he should be moving slowly. Most kids simply don't feel like doing a lot after a session, so I think Justin will probably spend a lot of time in bed or on the couch. We'll just have to see if a child with autism is any different. Just love him."

She knew this radiation mess was a vain and useless act, and Dr. Rainwater just confirmed her view. Even the doctor didn't know. It made her furious, not at him, but at Paul and his parents. All this effort was for them; it wasn't going to change a goddamned thing.

"Maybe he'll actually want a hug," Paul said as he smiled and shook hands with Dr. Rainwater. "Thank you, doctor, for at least trying to help him. That's all we want, just to give him a chance. We just want to know we tried."

Precisely, they want everyone to know they are good people, the kind of people who don't give up. The kind that keep on fighting. Not like her, a weakling and a drunk.

Lydia turned to Paul as soon as the doctor took leave. "Why did you use *we*? You know I wasn't for this. I just want him to live until he dies. You know the stats on this disease. It was you and your parents. This was *your* idea, and I'm the one who has to deal with it, so next time use *I*. Okay?"

She got up to leave. Paul grabbed her arm and pulled her down to the couch beside him. "Look, Lydia, I'm sorry. I was just trying to tell him I appreciate him as a professional. Sorry, but those are my feelings."

"And what was all that crap about you staying 'near your work?' We're divorcing, Paul—you left me, and you left Justin. Now, you have Ricki. I live in one place, and you live in another. Or is that not something you care to admit to our good doctor?"

She sprang off the couch to walk away, but he grabbed her arm again. The bottles in her purse clinked together. She stared directly at Paul, who looked at the source of the noise and then directly at the face of his soon-to-be ex-wife. "Those are two wine coolers for after I get home. Two, okay? And I don't need any advice from you."

She walked briskly out of the waiting room and took the elevator down to the first-floor coffee shop. A few minutes later, the call came that Justin was ready. She drove her car around to the emergency room door, where the oncology nurse delivered Justin to her in a wheelchair. Justin's thin seven-year-old body was practically limp, and his eyes were barely open as she and the nurse eased him into the backseat of her car. Lydia laid him down for more sleep. She covered him with a quilt her mother had given her for her wedding eight years earlier. Justin made no noises, and as usual, did not acknowledge her presence.

"He'll need to keep cool," the nurse said. "He'll run a fever and may kick the covers off. Just keep him cool. Make sure he drinks as much water as you can get down him. He'll probably sleep well into tomorrow."

Lydia drove away from the hospital and got on the expressway at the Carrolton onramp, beating the rush-hour traffic. She got on the Pontchartrain Causeway at four o'clock and set the cruise control. In forty-five minutes, she'd be back at her mother's home. It was a straight shot for twenty-five miles, and the traffic was flowing smoothly. There was only light and water, nothing too difficult.

She reached into her purse and pulled out one of the wine coolers. The first two swallows gave her that click inside her head that she had wanted since earlier that afternoon. She opened the vial of Xanax and swallowed another pill. Soon, she would feel that familiar sensation, and then a brief respite. There would be no one to question her tonight. Her mother would be working on an afterwork cocktail by the time she got home. She sure as hell wouldn't question Lydia, what she drank, or how much. Justin would sleep all night, the doctor said. She would just lay back and enjoy the water and the summer sun, try to forget that goddamned frozen place where they shot poisonous rays into her dying son, try to forget that bastard who left her alone, try to forget the nervous city desperately searching for its lost child. She would enjoy the drive and lose herself in the bright emptiness over Lake Pontchartrain.

After eight miles on the northbound span, Lydia entered the stretch on the world's longest bridge where she could no longer see the south shore of the lake in her rearview mirror. She would not be able to see the north shore for another eight or nine miles. Lydia felt deliciously apart from both worlds. Maybe living in this space was something she might want to make a way of life. Liminal space. She wondered what things would be like for her after Justin died. How would she feel? Where would she live? There was nothing evil or wrong about thinking about such things, the future and all that. She had to look after herself—no one else was coming to the rescue, that was for sure.

Lydia lost focus on the roadway and stared over the horizon of the bright empty lake. She approached a slow-moving vehicle from the rear and jammed her brakes, returning her to the present. For now, she couldn't live in between. Next Tuesday, she would bring her dying son once again to that frozen theater of the absurd. Lydia couldn't run; she was trapped. It had been decided. All the crap on the south shore was real. Children were lost; children died. It wasn't going away no matter how many rosaries were prayed, and she and only she would have to deal with it. She continued north, this time inhabiting the present.

A black Suburban zoomed by on her left. Inside, the male driver gestured wildly at a passenger in his backseat. After passing her, he cut sharply to the right and violently struck the concrete rail of the causeway. Reacting sharply, Lydia jammed on her brakes. The Suburban careened back into the left lane, struck the left bridge rail and then flipped hard on its right side. Metal ground into the concrete roadway sending up a fountain of sparks. The SUV slid to a stop on the concrete roadway only a short distance from Lydia and her sleeping son. She called 9-1-1 and reported an accident at mile ten northbound. Smoke oozed from under his hood. Her heart pounded and her mouth was bone dry. Somehow, through all the chaos, Justin was still asleep in the backseat. He hadn't moved. Near the rear window of the black Suburban, a child was moving.

Lydia acted on instinct. She ran to the rear window of the crippled vehicle. The back glass was covered with Find Franny posters. Goddammit! Just below, the tailgate bore the name of River Ridge Methodist Church. A small girl lay next to the window screaming, crying for her daddy, blood dripping off her forehead. Lydia motioned for the girl to move back. She dropped to the ground and kicked the poster-covered back glass with all her might. Nothing. She kicked it again, and the glass collapsed. Lydia carefully pulled the small girl through the opening. Her little, boney body was stiff with fear, and she continued screaming for her daddy. She scooped the girl up into her arms and cradled her briefly to her breast, then hurried back to her car with her precious cargo. Lydia wiped the blood off the girl's forehead with her blouse and made her sit in the front seat of her car.

She ran back to see about the driver. Flames broke out along the bottom of the overturned truck. This fire was growing. Fear sprung from her chest. Her car was close to this emerging inferno. *Where were the firefighters?* Lydia's pulse pounded in her head. The driver wasn't coming out. Trapped.

Another car stopped, and a young, muscular man came to help. "Anybody hurt here?" he yelled.

"The driver," Lydia said. "He must still be inside. Give me a boost."

The man cupped his hands and lifted her. She hopped on the upturned driver's side of the disabled vehicle. The belted driver hung sideways, twisting in his seat, yanking at his seatbelt with one arm. The other arm hung limply from his shoulder. His head was bleeding.

"I can't get my seatbelt off," the driver said, his voice cracking. "My arm's broken or something."

"Stay calm, sir," Lydia said. "We're going to get you out."

The driver looked up at her, his eyes glazed with panic. "Where's Jenny? Is she safe?"

"Stay calm; Jenny's back in my car."

She glanced over at the hood. The flames shot out of gashes in the crumpled metal. She bent over toward her fellow helper and extended her arm. "Hey, let me help you up. We can't wait for the cops. Help me get this door open. We gotta get him out."

His strong, sweaty hand clasped onto her right forearm. He bounded up on the driver's door next to Lydia.

"He can't get to his seatbelt release. Here, let's pull." The two lifted the driver's door to a nearly vertical position.

"Is that a fire I smell?" the driver said.

Lydia dropped to her belly and reached in to release the driver's' seatbelt. Black smoke filled the inside of the vehicle and stung her eyes and nostrils.

"You're free. Can you move? Can you crawl out?" she asked.

Lydia and her helper stepped back and extended their hands to pull the young father out of the driver's door. The three scrambled back down to the super-heated concrete. The fire in the engine compartment continued to burn. Just as they got clear of the wreck, the fire erupted in the passenger compartment. The blaze roared, rupturing the stillness of the bright summer surface of the lake. A firetruck and two police units screamed to a stop, horns blaring. In a blur of activity, the firefighters pulled their hoses and sprayed the inferno with white foam.

"Where's Jenny?" the driver asked. "She got out her harness in the back seat, and I turned around and was lunging backward to try and get her back into her car seat. I lost it and hit the side rail. My Lord, I almost killed us both! Is she okay?"

"Calm down. She's in my car with my son." Lydia's voice trailed off as the adrenaline in her veins subsided. She and the young father ran back to her car, where he embraced Jenny.

Blood was still dripping down Jenny's forehead. Her father kissed her wound and pulled off his shirt to stem the bright red flow. Lydia straightened her white cotton blouse and noticed Jenny's blood smeared over the top of her breasts and down her belly. She knew that the father and his child had passed through the valley of the shadow of death. But so had she, and they were all very much alive.

Lydia opened her rear door and checked on Justin. He was cool to the touch and sleeping like a newborn. His eyes twittered in REM sleep, and she wondered as she always had what was going on in his world. Lydia hoped that it was a peaceful world, a kinder place than she could ever give him. She hoped that it was a place where he felt at home and that it was a place where everything he found welcomed him. Just for a moment, amid the smoke and elation of those yanked from the jaws of death, Lydia knew it was so. She pulled up the old cotton quilt, tucked her son in snugly and shut the back door.

The father had stepped from the front seat and embraced her with a long hug as they stood by her car. She felt tears running down his face onto her neck. Holding both of her shoulders, he extended his arms and gazed into her eyes. "Thank you," he said. He released her and addressed both she and her helper.

"Ev Miller," he said. "Assistant pastor at River Ridge Methodist. You two are something! God blessed you today. He put you in the right place this afternoon. My daughter and I owe you our lives. We were both trapped, as good as dead, and now we are alive."

Her helper stepped back and wiped his forehead with a red bandana. "It wasn't me, man. This lady here told me what to do. She pulled your daughter out the back by herself. I just did what she told me. Lady—you're frigging Superwoman!"

Lydia began to laugh. *Superwoman! Yeah, Momma will like that one. Hey Paul, I'm Superwoman! Did you hear that? Superwoman!*

After the firefighters had suppressed the blaze, the police gathered the three witnesses together for their statements. They wrote out their versions of the crash using the hood of a state police cruiser for a table.

"How did you do it, Lydia?" Ev asked. "How did you compose yourself in the face of the fire? You ran into the danger, not away. That's extraordinary."

"I didn't think, pastor. I just acted. I don't really know why. I had to go into and not away from it. Maybe the god you worship had a hand in it." Lydia leaned back against the state police car and looked over the carnage. She was no longer trapped. She had a choice of which way to run. It was her choice alone, and there was no fear involved.

Two EMTs arrived to clean and bandage Jenny's wound. Lydia was able to wash the blood off her hands and face. She felt her body assume its normal pace.

Lydia glanced at the burned-out Suburban. Most of the Franny posters were burned beyond recognition. She turned to Ev. "Those Find Franny posters are all over Uptown. "I'm going to put a poster up in Abita Springs," Lydia said, and she meant it this time.

"The family are our fellow church members," Ev said. "My Jenny is in a Sunday school class with Franny's little sister. We're all so powerless, so this is at least something we can do, besides prayer, of course."

The investigating officer broke in. "Franny? You know the family? I just heard it on my unit's radio they found her. Some scumbag had her in a seedy hotel in Gulfport, but she got away from him. Suspect in custody. So, good news, pastor. Lots of miracles and happy endings today for a change."

Lydia took it in. Thirty minutes ago, she was in a different world. She was trapped in a cage of expectations, hers and those of others. Thirty minutes.

She stared out across the water. Suddenly, Lydia was lost in the beautiful flat surface of the lake, only silver water and sky and light. Standing next to the concrete bridge rail and leaning over the water, feet from her sleeping son, she spread her muscular arms out from her body and swayed ever so slightly, even though there was no breeze. She thought of children lost and children found. She knew she was meant to be here from the beginning, and there was no why, only a beautiful mystery.

Lydia raised her hands to the sky. Tomorrow, she might awake and hear Justin ask her to go to the beach down in Mandeville. He always loved the water. They would fix a picnic. There would be no tug of war. Her mother would come along, and they'd spread the food out on her old cotton quilt. The sun would shine, and the breeze off the lake would keep them cool while they watched Justin swim.

Lydia turned and walked back toward the others. She said her goodbyes and headed north. It would be seven or eight minutes before she saw land.

Slab City

For Julia Lewis, life was a constant struggle between order and chaos, serenity and agony, light and darkness. Wasn't that what the Tao taught? Even the Bible. Jesus divided them between the sheep and the goats. Father Cooper preached on it last Sunday. Part of keeping the chaos at bay in her life was constantly tending to her spiritual home, Saint James Episcopal Church. Tending demanded work, and this Sunday afternoon following mass, work came in the form of a prolonged vestry meeting, in which the voices of Father Cooper and the vestry members competed with the rumbling of Harley Davidsons just outside the church conference room.

Julia jumped to her feet, interrupting the vestry meeting, and stomped to the window. "If those damned motorcycles don't stop, I swear I'll start throwing prayer books at their fat heads!"

"Julia, please sit down," Father Cooper said. "You know a lot of people call that the sound of money here in Eureka Springs. Fall used to be a much slower time until those motorcycle clubs started coming up for the leaves."

"But they just won't stop. I can't hear myself think. It's like they're coming through the door."

All those doctors from Memphis and lawyers from Dallas, playing like they're rebels in their leather, with their chubby wives on the back, their butts hanging off the seats. It made her neck muscles spasm, her nerves taut. It was unsettling.

Father Cooper motioned for Julia to come away from the window. "Take a deep breath," he said, reaching out and gently squeezing her hand.

She shook her head. "I can't take the racket any longer."

"Let's try a little charity. You remember—strangers in our midst? Okay? Let's get back to our air conditioning problems."

She heaved a sigh, then looked around the table at the nods and smiles of her fellow vestry members. Affirmed, she took her place at the table. "Sorry, y'all. They have me on edge today."

Julia had been a doer and planner all her life, and now she was paying the price: a third term on the vestry, interminable meetings, every air conditioning in Saint James Episcopal had failed last week. She was in the middle of it, all the talk, all the well-meaning folks and their opinions. She longed to return to her hilltop sanctuary, the Arkansas home she and Roger built for them and their three boys. The boys were all gone, leaving it even quieter and more serene. She wanted to sit on the veranda overlooking the city and listen to her babbling creek, sip a cocktail, and watch the red and orange leaves float in the afternoon breeze. It was a place far away from the pathological business of meetings and set apart from the rumblings of rich men's Harley Davidsons. Separation from the pathologically busy world outside had been assured with the construction of a huge stone wall around their compound and the rerouting of a nearby creek. Her Zen group met there once a month for mediation sessions.

Julia left the vestry meeting late that Sunday afternoon. The leaves were falling along the tree-lined streets of Eureka Springs after a spectacular fall showing. Large patches of burnt orange and yellow blew up behind her red convertible. Roger was out deer hunting at their camp. He was probably three sheets to the wind by now, yelling at the television screen along with the rest of his buddies during the fourth quarter of the Cowboys game. He would be home Monday morning, shaved and smiling. For what remained of this beautiful afternoon, she would be deliciously alone, sitting on her back deck, watching the red and yellow colors floating in the air.

Julia mixed herself a bloody mary. The phone rang. She picked up the receiver and was met with a crisply posed question by a grim male voice. "May I speak to Mr. or Mrs. Lewis, please?"

"I'm Julia Lewis."

"Mrs. Lewis, I am Deputy John Martinez of the Imperial County Sheriff's Office in El Centro, California. Are you a relative of Zachary Thomas Lewis, age 26?"

"Yes. He's my middle son. Is there a problem, officer?" Julia sunk into the familiar dread she always felt when she got a call about Zach. She had received many over the years—since he was fifteen. There would probably be a petty charge of some type. A lawyer would be required, promises would be made and ultimately nothing would change. She took a deep breath to await the description of the newest annoyance.

"There's been an accident, ma'am."

"Is Zach injured, officer? Is my son all right?"

"Mrs. Lewis, I am with the Coroner's Division of the Sheriff's Office. I am sorry to tell you that your son was found dead this morning in his VW van."

Julia's ears filled with a whirring static. Her legs buckled. She grabbed the barstool, pulled herself onto the seat and leaned on the bar. Something like a knot formed in her belly, and she struggled to get air into her lungs. Complete silence fell upon her hilltop sanctuary, just now breached from without. A strong breeze blew fiery-red and burnt-orange leaves through the open glass door, disturbing the stillness.

"Do you know what happened?"

"He'd been staying up at a place near the Salton Sea, called Slab City. Some friends found him dead in his sleeping bag. He died from a gunshot wound. We believe it was accidental. There was no indication of foul play or suicide."

"Did you say something about a gun?"

"Mrs. Lewis, we found him dead in his sleeping bag along with a .38 caliber pistol."

Zach knew nothing about guns. "Was there a crime? Was my son shot by someone?"

"We were told he slept with it every night. There was no indication of a forced entry . . . or a fight. No indication of suicide."

"What do you mean, 'slept with it'? Zach, sleeping with a pistol? That's crazy! I don't understand." She paused. There was no reply from the deputy. She struggled to pull in a breath. "Where is his body?"

"We have him here at the county morgue in El Centro. If possible, we'd like to offer you the chance to come and identify the body. If that's not possible, we could arrange for a viewing online."

"You mean by computer? God no. I'll come get my son's body and arrange to have him sent home. He has a dog—Chester, a bloodhound. Is he there?"

"I don't know who has the dog now, but I'll check on that for you. I know his van is still up at Slab City. He had a few friends up there. He'd been camping there for a couple of months, from what they told me. They checked on him this morning when they heard his dog yelping. Mrs. Lewis, they're good people, knew your son pretty well and are all broken up about it."

"Slab City? What kind of place is that? Such a name."

"Slab City is about fifty miles north of here in the middle of nothing. It began a few years ago when a group of people started living there year-round. It's an abandoned military base, so there's lots of concrete and old slabs around—perfect for RVs and trailers. Attracts a lot of drifters, lots of retired folks who just live on the road. It's quite a place. But we rarely have problems up there. They kind of self-police the place. You'll see—nothing to fear, that's for sure."

Julia entered the study of the spacious home she and Roger had built and wrote down the deputy's name and number, thanked him and hung up. On one wall of her study were photos of her older sons, Josh and Aaron, along with their wives and young children. The adjoining wall displayed a large map of North America, which had come from a *National Geographic* magazine. The map was tacked to a bulletin board, and taped on the map were a series of Polaroid photos Zach had taken of himself, Chester and the old Volkswagen Westphalia van in numerous locales around the US and Mexico.

She slowly ran her fingers across photos of Zach and Chester posing at the foot of the Golden Gate, attending a Mardi Gras parade, singing with a mariachi band in Mexico City, standing on a dock in Key West at sunset, looking out at Niagara Falls. Zach wrote short, usually cryptic, notes on the small paper strip at the bottom of each photo—things like "Two against nature," "Wish you were here," "Happy, happy, joy, joy." In each photograph, Zach proudly wore his bright-purple LSU jersey with bright lettering, his single memento from his one year of college in Baton Rouge. The notes and Polaroids were all she had from Zach in the last four years. Neither she nor Roger had seen or talked to him since.

Julia knew Zach was a wanderer. She knew he was troubled. He drank way too much. God knows what type of drugs he had done. He had scrapes with the law. She and Roger had been with him through the psych clinics, two drug rehabs, and a stay at a halfway house. But there had never been any mention of guns.

What in the hell could have gotten into him? Sleeping with a pistol? This was *not* supposed to happen, not in her life. She had devoted her entire life's work to building a safe container for her family. Now it was violated. The chaos Zach courted had won out. Her sanctuary had been breached.

Julia rose to her feet, freshened her drink, and walked slowly onto the veranda. She sat on her chaise lounger surrounded by an otherwise epic fall afternoon. She was on the top of a mountain overlooking Eureka Springs. No bird sang. The wind had died, giving way to a vast silence that filled the chasm below. But now, there was no comfort in the quiet.

Josh and Aaron had taken the path she had prepared for them, and both were well on their way toward lives filled with love and meaning. What had gone wrong with Zack? Why did he feel he had to run away from what she and Roger had to offer? She remembered all the smiles in the Polaroids. Why wouldn't he share his adventures with them? She and Roger would have gladly gone to meet him. Had she driven him away? No, that's something they had sorted out in rehab. The counselors told all the parents this wasn't about them. It was about choices their children made, and it was the children who had to make different choices. She was powerless, or so they said. She wanted to believe it wasn't her fault. But Zach was dead. Now those questions were back with a vengeance.

But wait; calls had to be made. Roger, how would she tell Roger? Cell coverage was sketchy at best out at his hunting camp. Better tomorrow when he returned, in person. Julia, the fixer, must be summoned. Arrangements must be made. She downed her drink. Every step back to her study to begin her work was a chore. So far, she had not shed a tear.

It was decided the next day that Roger would stay in Eureka Springs to make funeral and burial arrangements. He would await the arrival of their two sons. Julia drove to Fayetteville and boarded an early flight that would take her to Dallas, and then on to San Diego. There, she would rent a car to drive to El Centro. She managed to put one foot in front of the other, thinking that she had to do what was required. She could collapse later. She needed to get Zach and Chester and bring them home. Only she could do it.

From her window seat on the plane, Julia stared down at the brown and barren landscape of the American Southwest. This had been a favorite haunt of her wandering son. He sent Polaroids from Taos, Flagstaff and Thousand Palms. He was drawn to the desert, particularly during the last two years. What was it that drew him? The emptiness? The silence? The solitude? Julia felt no such draw. She wondered how people could live with so little greenery, so little water, no lakes or rivers, no waterfalls.

She followed a lone truck as it wound its way down a snake-like ribbon of road in the Sangre de Cristo Mountains. It was traversing a brown wasteland, nothing for miles around. She wondered what the life of the driver was like. Was it overrun by chaos? Was the driver fulfilling a mission in his journey, or was he merely wandering around the desert with no sense of purpose? Julia thought of her mountain sanctuary. Could it ever be restored, or was chaos now a permanent occupant of her beloved home place?

She slept for the last hour of the flight and arrived in San Diego just after midday, a bit more refreshed. After leaving the airport, she turned the car east on I-8 and drove through the dry coastal mountains into the white-hot desert. Julia arrived at the office complex housing the Imperial County Sheriff's Department and was directed to Deputy Martinez's basement office. She passed deputies escorting a small group of young men wearing hand and foot chains. The deputies barked short exhortations to the group to keep in line and move forward.

The prisoners made no eye contact, said nothing, but the sounds of clinking chains and their heavy breathing rang deeply in Julia's ears. She drew back against the wall as they passed. That could have been Zach, trudging toward a lonely cell with other sad young men, his hands and feet bound. A large gray metal door opened, and the prisoners were quickly herded out of the hall. The heavy steel door shut behind them with a hard clang, and she flinched.

She made her way down to the basement. Her heart racing, fear building in her gut.

In a small foyer, she sat in a gray metal chair. cold and hard, it squeaked as she twisted to look at the walls adorned with anti-drug posters and applications for a bootcamp for wayward youths. There she waited for the man who would lead her to the body of her son. In the rational part of her mind, she knew that Zach's death was part of a larger story. The posters bore stark witness to the scourge upon the land. Her son was only one of thousands who died in this scourge. She tried to tell herself that she and Roger were not alone, that thousands of parents, just like them, had suffered the same fate.

But this wasn't supposed to happen—not to them. Zach had been getting better, or at least he looked that way in the Polaroids. Now she had to face every mother's nightmare. She had to see and touch the dead flesh that she had struggled to bring into this world. The urge to run out of this damned office with all its sad posters came over her, but the office door opened, and she slid back in her seat.

"Mrs. Lewis . . . I'm Deputy John Martinez."

She stood up, and in silence, she offered her hand to him, raising a weak smile.

"The county morgue is located at the county hospital. Let me drive you over there."

"Thank you, Deputy Martinez, but I have a rental. I can follow you."

"Let me help make this as easy on you as we can. I'll drive you over, and then we can drop you back here." He smiled and opened the door to the hallway. Julia followed him out into the glaringly bright afternoon to his police unit. They headed for the morgue.

Julia broke the silence of their drive. "Deputy Martinez, how do you get shot while you're sleeping?"

"Ma'am, I can show you better when we get there, but the bullet entered from above the shoulder blade. It punctured the central artery coming from the heart, and he bled out. We found the discharged weapon under the pillow. The powder stains on the sheets and pillow confirm it discharged in that position. It looks like it was just a strange accident. People make all kinds of moves in their sleep. Believe it or not, we've seen similar things."

An image of her precious son, curled up in his blood-soaked sleeping bag, lodged in her mind. "I asked you before, why would anyone sleep with a gun?"

"Ma'am, if I had an answer why folks do strange things, I'd be happy to tell you. No telling what or who he encountered out on the road. We probably won't ever know, unless his friends have some idea."

They entered the coroner's suite and walked through hallways past autopsy rooms and offices. Women wearing white masks were busy working in their labs, and they called out results in Spanish to each other. The scent of formaldehyde hung heavy as she and Martinez approached the morgue. Martinez opened the door to a chilled room in the county morgue where bodies were kept after autopsies, awaiting either a funeral by their loved ones or burial by the county in an unmarked grave. Julia took a deep breath to steady her nerves and walked through the door. A technician in a white lab coat met them. He escorted them into the refrigerated room containing several drawers where the bodies were kept.

Martinez touched Julia's arm and whispered, "Please remember that Zach has gone through an autopsy. I say that just to remind folks."

She nodded and steeled herself. They stood in silence as the technician pulled out the drawer containing Zach's body. He solemnly pulled back the sheet exposing Zach's face and chest.

She ran her hand across the side of Zach's face. What had her little boy gone through? "He looks so much heavier," she said.

"Mrs. Lewis," Martinez said, "blood pools in a corpse at an accident site, or a crime scene, in the hours after an incident when a body sits in a certain position for several hours. Here, the blood pooled in Zach's face. He just appears heavier."

The poor child. God help me through this. "Can you show me where the bullet entered?"

Martinez lifted Zach's left shoulder and showed her the entry wound. "You see, the bullet entered right here, just above his left scapula, and it went downward through his chest cavity and nicked the aorta. Lots of internal bleeding. Not a lot of pain." He lowered Zach's shoulder.

Julia leaned over and kissed her son on his forehead. She reached under the sheet, held his hand and kissed him again on the cheek. The two men stepped back and quietly left the room. Julia was alone with only the present moment, as awful as it was. Time was suspended. There was no internal dialogue in her mind, only the overwhelming reality presented by the sudden halt of human breathing in a being one has come to love. Jesus, help me bear this. I need you now. She ran her finger over the entry wound behind Zach's left shoulder. She stared at the post autopsy scar around the crown of his skull, which allowed the examination of his brain. She needed no further persuasion that this was real. It was indeed happening to her, the consummate planner and organizer of safe lives.

After she finally stepped back, the deputy entered the room and covered Zach. He closed the drawer. The two returned to his office at the Sheriff's Department.

There were details to discuss. Roger joined them on a telephone conference. A local funeral home was called to embalm Zach's body and make arrangements for his transport home to Arkansas for a funeral and burial. All this would take several days. They agreed that she would meet Martinez the next morning and drive with him to Slab City to pick up Chester and her son's belongings.

The morning drive to Slab City took them north through the Imperial Valley. They drove through untold acres of vegetable farms made possible by the waters piped from the Colorado. Martinez turned off the main highway at a small town near the Salton Sea and headed out into the desert.

"Deputy Martinez, what more can you tell me about these friends of Zach's who are watching after his dog?"

"Another couple with their old RV, I think maybe mid-twenties. They have a couple of girls. They met Zach a few months ago and traveled together. Where, I don't know. Very nice folks, the girls are well cared for. You'll see. They have the dog. They say the girls are crazy about him."

Julia had been shut out of her son's life for years. Zach met these friends roaming around the desert, dragging two little girls along. What Martinez found nice about them was hard for her to imagine.

"Tell me more about Slab City."

"The place is like a city, but without a government. Somehow, they make it happen, look after one another. I think El Centro could learn a few things from Slab City, maybe America as well."

Julia rolled down her window and hung her head out into the rushing desert air. Perfect desolation surrounded them, the clean nothingness of this place. There was no clutter here, no chaos. The only sound was the rushing air. Julia imagined the luxury of self-forgetting. She envisioned what complete silence would mean to her here in the sandy flats of the northern Imperial Valley. Perhaps that truck she saw in the Sangre De Cristos was driving toward this desert solitude. Perhaps this is what drew Zach to this place.

They approached a low-slung depression in the lightly vegetated desert sands. It was bordered by some low hills in the background. The depression was filled and overflowing with RVs and aluminum-sided trailers. A colorful sign welcomed visitors, asserting happily, *God Never Fails*. Back in the morgue, she had felt as if she stood alone in the middle of a swirling set of chaotic events. But now, there was only the powerfully real present.

They passed a huge painted hillside with all manner of scripture and symbols on its slopes. Next to it was a large commercial fishing boat painted a bright blue and white, sailing on a sea of painted sand, rather than the waters it once worked. "What in the name of heaven is that?" she asked.

"That's what they call Salvation Mountain. Here . . . I'll pull over and let you look at it." Martinez stopped the car next to a brightly painted antique panel truck with the word *REPENT* plastered across both sides.

A slender white-haired man wearing paint-splattered overalls shuffled up to greet them. "Howdy, officer! God bless you this glorious morning! Just come to see the site?"

Martinez smiled and nodded to him.

The man took off his gloves and extended his hand to Julia. "Leonard Knight. I've known your police friend here for years. Glad to meet you."

"Is this your work?" Julia asked.

"It's really God's work, but he's kept me busy here since '84. Well, not just me—anybody and everybody who wants to help. Would you like a brush and paint can?"

"Thank you, but we've got business in Slab City," she said and looked up at the huge painted mound, the slopes of which were covered with religious slogans and visionary images of angels and flowing rivers. "Is all that concrete?"

Leonard nodded proudly and looked back at his holy mountain. At the summit stood a white cross at the base of which were the words *GOD IS LOVE* written in huge concrete letters. The whole structure had to be fifty feet tall.

Julia stared agog at the conglomeration of spiritual encouragement and color rising out of the baking scrub brush. She looked at the smiling face of the artist and envied his enthusiasm. "Mr. Knight, did you know my son Zach? He had a dog, always with him."

"Was he your son? Yes, I heard about his death. I'm so sorry for you and your family. May God bless you all. He had come by a few times and helped me paint. The boy with that bloodhound? Of course. A fine young man, but I didn't know him well. But he contributed some to this holy place."

"He did?" Zach had not spoken to her and his father in years. Zach stayed away from his entire family, his brothers as well. The Polaroids from his wanderings was the closest they got to him. To be here felt as if she could touch him somehow.

"He sure did."

"It means a lot to hear he helped out on your monument."

"He and his dog. That dog's special—so loving. Dogs become like their owners, you know. Well . . . I'll get back at it before it gets too hot for an old man." He donned his gloves and walked off toward the mountain with his brush and can.

They continued into the warren of dusty RVs and beat-up travel trailers. Many residents favored bright signs and flags identifying their allegiances. American flags and large peace symbols were popular. One hand-painted sign proclaimed Slab City as the last free place on Earth. Abandoned cars were parked outside many trailers. An aluminum house trailer served as the Slab City Christian Center. Martinez stopped the car outside a cluster of trailers with a large sign out front identifying the place as L.O.W. Community Center.

"L.O.W.," Martinez said. "That's Loners on Wheels. We're meeting Zach's friends here."

In the courtyard area, framed by four RVs, a large plastic tarpaulin stretched overhead, providing shade. The common area contained several sets of folding tables and chairs. A pot of coffee was set up in the corner. Martinez poured them two cups. They sat down to wait for Zach's friends.

Julia looked over at the week's activities posted on a nearby bulletin board. "Looks like folks stay busy out here—movie night, dancing night, shuffleboard. They don't sound too much like loners, more like a summer camp."

How many times had Zach come to this place? Did he watch their movies? Did he dance here? How could he fit in with all these strangers and stay away from his own blood, the people who truly loved him?

"It's autumn right now," Martinez said. "Temperature's more

tolerable, so the population grows a lot. They stay busy in the fall and winter. Lots of older folks down here, lot of retirees."

They sipped their coffee and awaited their scheduled meeting.

Shortly, a young woman walked up accompanied by a man with long graying hair. "Deputy Martinez? I'm Stephanie Long. This is my husband, Dennis. We spoke to your officers the other day, told them what we know, and how we found Zach." She turned to Julia. "Are you Zach's mother?"

Julia extended her hand to greet her. "Yes, he was my youngest son. We hadn't heard from him in quite a long time."

Stephanie took Julia's hand. "We are so sorry for your loss."

"Thank you for taking care of Chester."

Stephanie still held onto Julia's hand. "Can we sit down? I'd like to talk to you here before we go over to our place and the van."

Julia nodded. How is it that these people were the last to see him, speak to him? Did they sit down and eat dinner together? Did he tell them his dreams and hopes? Did he still have dreams and hopes?

"Mrs. Lewis, we knew Zach well, and he was very special to us. We met him up at Joshua Tree National Park last spring, and we had camped and hung out together since then."

Dennis stepped up and offered his hand to Julia. "Zach was like a brother to me these past few months."

Like brothers? Did Zach tell them he had two brothers? Did he ever mention us?

"We hiked these mountains and all over the desert up at Joshua Tree: me, him and Chester. My wife and I are both from Alabama, so Zach and I had that Southern thing in common."

"What did Zach tell you about his life back in the South? Julia asked.

"Canoeing the Buffalo River with his father and brothers, said it was paradise. He always mentioned a certain valley. What was it, Steph?"

"Boxley Valley," she said. "We had a hunting camp there."

Stephanie patted Julia's hand. "He loved y'all so much," she said. "He told us all about Eureka Springs. We want to come there someday. Zach painted quite a picture for us."

Dennis nodded, flashed a full-gum smile. "He told us about him and his daddy, hunting, fishing. Zach loved those Ozarks."

Their kind comments seemed to stab deeper. Why did he stay away? Why couldn't he have called? What did these kind strangers offer him? Sounded like they knew her son well, maybe better than she knew him, at least during the last few years.

"He'd send us postcards," Julia said. "Polaroid pictures. But we haven't spoken in years." Julia let out a shallow sigh. Her eyes teared up. "You two folks seem like good people, and I'm glad Zach was around you and had two friends who cared about him."

"Yes, ma'am, we did care about him," Dennis said. "Do you want to follow us back to our campsite?"

"Sure," Martinez said. "We'll follow you over."

After a short drive down a warren of concrete streets and then a dirt path over a small rise, they came to the slab on which Zach's Westphalia was parked alongside an old Winnebago. As soon as they pulled up, Chester barged out the door of the Winnebago followed shortly by two young girls—a towheaded blonde nearing adolescence and a small red-haired girl who looked to be two or three years old. Julia bent down to catch the full embrace of the happy hound. She hugged his neck and buried her face in the loose folds of red fur. She couldn't help but cry for joy and sorrow at the same time. Chester whined and slobbered all over Julia's face and arms. She held him even tighter. The warmth of the happy hound was a restoration of something of hers that had been lost.

Part of her tribe was home again. She smiled and gazed upon the two children.

"And who are these beautiful young ladies?" she asked.

"These are Sara, my oldest, and Juliette," Stephanie said. "Say hello to Ms. Julia. She's Zach's mother."

The older girl extended her hand. The younger one looked down and brushed the sand with her bare feet.

Stephanie leaned over to Julia and whispered, "She's been really quiet since all this happened. She knows something bad happened, but we kept her inside while the police were here. We've tried to keep her calm and not talk about it a lot. She really loved Zach and knows he's not here."

Julia nodded and walked toward the van. "This van belonged to Roger and me. We would pile all the boys in it with our sleeping bags and a cooler of cold drinks. We traveled all over the Ozarks and the Smoky Mountains. I can still hear that gang of boys—Zach and his brothers—laughing, teasing and fighting with each other. I was constantly running to the back to put down some ruckus. That's been twenty years ago."

Julia opened the panel door and stepped inside. She opened the cabinets and the drawers in the kitchen and sat down on the pull-down seat, imagining all the drawers stocked with their provisions. Her family together and well cared for, on the road to look for America.

"I can't believe it's still running," Julia said. "It looks great. Zach really took good care of it."

She sat on the folding bed. Martinez stepped in and walked to her side. He gently touched her shoulder.

"I guess he was sleeping here when it happened," she said.

"Yes, ma'am. We removed the bloody sleeping bag."

Dennis stepped in the open door. "Zach was sleeping there,"

he said and nodded to the mattress. "He was turned over on his left side. I heard Chester baying. We were having our coffee that morning, and we got up from the table and walked out here and found him. Never heard the gun go off. Must've happened during the night."

Julia reached where his pillow would have been—some small bloodstains remained on the thin pad. She touched the dried blood and again was struck by the image of her son curled up with a smoking gun, his life draining slowly out of him in the middle of a dark desert night.

Martinez tapped her shoulder as if he had been trying to get her attention several times. "Mrs. Lewis, if this vehicle belongs to you and your husband, we could hold it for you in our impound yard down in El Centro. Whatever is easiest on you. Just let me know."

"No. . . . I'll drive it back tonight to El Centro. Roger and I will figure out what we will do with it. Thank you so much, Deputy Martinez. You are so kind. I'll sit here and talk to Stephanie and Dennis some more. I'm sure you've got things to do. I'll call you tomorrow."

Martinez wished them all well and departed.

The three adults sat around a tiny fold-down table in the old Winnebago and drank cups of coffee. Outside, the two girls played tug of war with Chester using a string made of old white cotton socks. Such red hair on that little one, and so strong.

"So . . ." Julia said, gazing out the window at the two little girls. "Zach must have been close to your girls. You said Juliette really loved him. Did he play with them often?"

"He was so tender-hearted," Stephanie said. "Played with the girls all the time. I think he wanted a family, one like y'all had when you raised him, but somehow it was a mystery to him how to start one."

A family?

"Did he ever have a girl in his life?" Julia asked. "Did he talk about that?"

Stephanie glanced at her husband and said nothing at first. Her face took on a serious affect. "Mrs. Lewis, we need to tell you something, and we wanted to wait until we were alone with you. We didn't want the police involved."

Julia continued to stare at the two little girls, now tumbling in the dirt with Chester.

Dennis leaned in closer to Stephanie and whispered, "It's best to just come out and say it."

"I'm getting to it," Stephanie said. "Juliette, we believe, is Zach's daughter."

Julia gasped. "Good Lord!" She looked at the little girl, running in circles with Chester—that red hair.

Julia swooped out of the Winnebago and trotted to Juliette. She stooped down and cupped her small round face in her hands. Of course, those are Zach's eyes and Roger's hair. "Dear Lord!" She clutched Juliette to her bosom. Chester wanted in on the loving and covered both she and Juliette in bloodhound slobber.

"Juliette, I should have known, but my mind is spinning." Her heart pounded. Once again, everything seemed to settle down. She heard nothing but her heart in her chest. The gravity of the revelation sunk into her psyche.

Julia felt like she was floating above the scene, that her spirit was drifting out of Slap City and into the blue desert sky. Her mind dashed back to her Arkansas hilltop, to Roger and the boys. They were all supposed to be in mourning.

"How?" She wasn't sure if she asked it aloud or not. How, who, when, where—these thoughts pierced her numbness. Chester exploded with a booming bark, and he dashed for the socks, then brought them to her to play tug of war. Julia's attention bounded back to the urgent now.

"Stephanie," Julia said, letting her hands drop from Juliette's little face. "What do you know about the mother?"

"Only what Zach told me. He had Juliette with him when we met. He said Juliette was born in Tacoma. Her mother was a drug addict. Zach claimed she died in Mexico. He had raised Juliette for a couple of years."

Julia closed her eyes and said nothing for a few seconds. The chaos that had killed Zach was unrelenting. It had brought her to this dry land to touch the corpse of her youngest son. Now, news of a grandchild, somewhere a drug-addicted mother, or maybe dead. Where would this chaos end? Could she endure it? She straightened her back. "I've got to get away, just to think."

Juliette snuggled deeper into Julia's lap. Julia kissed her on the top of her head, then held her so she could gaze into her blue eyes—Zach's blue eyes. "Honeypie, I'll be right back. I promise."

Juliette lunged into her, clutching her tightly. Chester once again intruded into their embrace. But Julia gently disengaged them and rose to her feet.

Stephanie took Juliette's hands and gently coaxed her to her side.

"I'm sorry," Julia said to Stephanie. I've got to get away right now. I've got to think, maybe talk with Roger. I'm just lost right now. I'll be back shortly. I promise."

"Ms. Julia. We'll be right here. She's fine with us. Sara loves her so much. You go do what you need to do. We're right here." She looked to Dennis, who nodded his affirmation.

Julia pulled the VW Westphalia van up to the stop sign on the main highway. A sign pointed to the Salton Sea State Park, a sea in the desert. How absurd. She must see it. It was eight miles to the north. Instead of returning to El Centro, she turned right, heading north toward the desert sea, thinking maybe she would see a boat that floated on water rather than painted sand.

The green vegetable fields ended, giving way to the southern tip of the Salton Sea. Julia traveled along its southwestern direction, past broken-down vacation venues and the rotting hulks of automobiles and pickup trucks. A sign attracted her attention: Bombay Beach 2 miles. She turned into the seaside hamlet of a few dusty houses and trailers and followed the arrows to a public beach next to a marina berthing a few pleasure boats and a couple of larger fishing vessels. Not a human soul was in sight. She walked along the pathetic shoreline composed of gritty brown sand and ample trash from weekend picnickers. The "sea" was a very pale gray, and the midday haze made the distinction between the anemic beach and the water ambiguous.

Julia kicked off her sandals and waded into the water, pulling her skirt up to avoid getting it wet. Entering the water, she could feel a marked difference between her wet feet and the rest of her body above the water. Her feet, ankles, and calves tingled in the waters of this dead sea. She walked deeper. The welcome stimulation crept up her legs. Dead was only her opinion of this sea, formed in advance, based only on her surface observations.

Julia had been so wrong. She dropped her skirt into the water and waded in up to her waist, then scooped the salty water in her hands and splashed her face and bare shoulders with the new-found elixir. She stared out over the plane of water, extending to infinity. Blue mountains floated in the air at the edge of the horizon.

Magnificent desolation, yet life persisted. Zach was dead, yet not completely. Was she woman enough to accept this new life her son had created? Could she accept that chaos and order were the Siamese twins of which life was made?

Standing in the living water, she was alone, yet not. Something moved on her periphery. A single mallard duck swam from behind her and crossed her vision. It made the only ripples in the water off Bombay Beach. She watched it for a couple of minutes, and then turned around toward the shore.

Sitting on a bench under a tree on the edge of the beach was a small white-haired Mexican woman with a little child. Julia walked through the water toward the shoreline in her soaked skirt and sleeveless blouse. She picked up her sandals and slid them on her feet. As she approached the old lady, the little girl ran behind the bench and hid.

"Senora," the old lady said, "you should know that the waters here—they're not good for you, Mrs. Our sewer system isn't good, so the Health Department, they say no swimming here at Bombay." She turned around and pointed behind her. "You missed the sign, Senora."

Julia looked over at the sign and laughed. "Well, I don't know what the sign says, but the water was wonderful. I feel clean now. Can I sit here with you?"

"Please, sit with us here in the shade while you dry," the old lady said. The little girl eased from behind the bench and crawled into her grandmother's lap.

"She's beautiful. How old?" Julia asked.

"Her name is Maria, and she's three. She is my oldest son's daughter. I live with them in his trailer over there. He works down in the valley. He's a tractor mechanic. He's alone now, so I help with Maria. It's hard sometimes, no mother around. But she's a blessing, this one."

"I have a granddaughter about the same age," Julia said. Julia smiled and sat still with her thoughts in the dry desert air, moving gently across the Salton Sea.

No doubt she would bring that little redhead home to Roger and the boys. That was who she was, a woman who got things done. She no longer needed a place away from the noise of the world. Now, she wanted to hear the hustle and bustle she knew as a young mother.

When her clothes were dry, she bade the pair farewell and headed south in the VW toward Slab City.

Stephanie and Dennis packed Juliette's clothes and her teddy bear. Hugs and kisses were exchanged. Sara sulked, and Juliette cried as they started to leave. They promised to visit Eureka Springs in the spring.

Julia pulled out from the slab with a fully packed VW Westphalia van bearing a slobbering bloodhound and a fiery-haired little girl. She called Deputy Martinez to arrange for her rental car's return, and then they headed out of the last free place on Earth. Salvation Mountain came into view. Julia pulled up to the painted truck and was greeted once again by its paint-splattered creator. She rolled down the window. "Mr. Knight, do you still have a paintbrush for me?"

"Why yes, ma'am, I sure do. I see you acquired some new friends and a new car during your short stay here in the slabs. What color would you ladies like?"

"Purple, Mr. Knight. Do you have purple? I hear that God is partial to purple. And some gold paint as well, if you have some."

"Absolutely correct, ma'am. God told me that He loves purple. Absolutely loves it! Come with me, and I'll fix you up."

The three of them exited the van. Julia laughed for the first time in many days. Juliette and Chester ran straight for the paint-splattered holy man for hugs and kisses, which he bestowed generously.

The traveling companions climbed the concrete mountain and sat near its summit. Julia and Juliette sat down next to a painted version of a wild, raging river of life. Chester peed on a nearby red-lettered version of John 3:16. There, grandmother and granddaughter painted a purple heart with the letter Z in gold in its middle. Julia snapped a photo of Juliette sitting by the purple heart. Holding hands, the two hiked back down the holy mountain.

Stolen Kisses

A boy, a girl, a time, a place.
The boy was sixteen. He lived in a bubble, a very thick bubble. The boy was White.

The girl was sixteen. She lived outside the bubble. The girl was Black.

The time was one of change and violence. The girl's hero had been shot down in Memphis. Murder and the smoke of burning cities hung in the air. Cracks in the bubble were beginning to show.

The land was rich, the topsoil thick. The Red River flowed nearby. The girl lived on a bayou covered by cypress trees. Her father and brothers farmed the land and stood watch over her.

The boy saw the girl through a crack in the bubble. She was beautiful but forbidden. He knew that. They met at a school bus stop along the bayou where the girl lived. He was there in his car to pick up his sister, who was going to school with the girl. His sister was nowhere to be found that afternoon. But the girl, she could be seen, heard and touched. The boy wanted all those things.

The girl wondered about the White devils who killed her hero. Were all White people devils? No, she thought. At least one wasn't. She knew the boy's sister. They talked on the bus, even laughed together. The sister wasn't like the devils who killed her hero or the ones who spat on her in the halls at her school. Now, the boy was talking to her at the bus stop. He made her laugh. Would it be okay to talk back? No one was around. The boy was offering her

119

a ride home. No one would be there when they arrived. No one would see them together. Sure, why not? A ride was better than three miles of hot dirt road.

The time was late spring. Her fathers, uncles, brothers and cousins were in the fields planting until dark. Her mother, aunts and older sister were all working late at the big house. It was laundry day. The house would be quiet and empty. As they drove home with the windows down, the boy and girl couldn't help but smell the turned-up earth that yielded their daily bread. It had been this way for as long as anyone could remember men and boys turning up the earth, planting cotton in the deep red dirt, battling weeds and weevils over the summer, and picking come the fall. Bubble or no bubble, blood or no blood, murder or no murder, the cotton would be picked, and all would be well in the Red River Valley.

The place she stayed was down a shady road lined with cypress and water oaks. The road ran along the bayou, which flowed into the Red River. Her home was one of several sharecropper cabins built long ago and still occupied by the families working for the Dutch farmers who owned what was left of the old plantations. While the bubble may have been cracking in town, and more so in the big cities, it was still thick and strong along the bayou. No way a White boy should be giving a Black girl a ride home, even talking to her. Both were doing wrong, and they knew it, but neither knew why. It was just that the boy thought he smelled something sweet, and the girl thought the boy was funny. He wanted to touch her hair. She wanted to show him their shrine to the Virgin Mary, maybe hold him.

The boy parked his car in some bushes down the road from her home. He was leaving the bubble. He might be seen. He didn't want that. The only soul who could see him was the girl. He wanted to be seen by her and heard and touched. He entered the threshold of her home, his eyes wide open, his heart pounding. Above a wooden chest was a statue of the Virgin. Her skin was Black. A Black Baby Jesus sat in her lap. Two small candles burned in colored jars. Left of Mary was a saint he didn't know. Right of her statue was a photo of their fallen hero. He looked like the grown man Jesus, staring over the horizon, straining to see something better. The boy was a Baptist, so some of this was lost on him. He whispered to the girl that it all was nice. She had a really nice home. He was trembling inside and out. He had never been outside the bubble. He didn't know how to act. The girl bade him sit on the couch.

The girl sat next to the boy. She pulled her dress down, properly. She could see the boy was still nervous. She wasn't scared. She knew her people wouldn't be home for a couple of hours. He would be long gone by then. She told the boy as much. They smiled at each other. The girl rose and went back to her bedroom to get a record. She placed it on the hi-fi and returned to the couch next to the boy. The hi-fi played songs by Marvin and Tammy. The girl could see the boy ease back and relax. Instead of looking googly-eyed around her living room at every object and family photo, he was now gazing at her, into her eyes. She took his hand and stared down at their hands intertwined. Zebra hands, she thought, and laughed inside. It tickled her.

It was a time for something special to take place. She felt it. There would be an uncovering, an apocalypse, like what John saw on Patmos. Something would be revealed to her. Had she invited a White devil into her home? She was ready to find out. Would this destroy them both? Fear and desire ran hot in her veins. The zebra hands parted as he drew her closer.

The home was now silent. The record stopped playing. They heard nothing now except the crickets in the woods and the frogs in the bayou. The creatures formed a rising cacophony from those dark realms. A soft breeze blew through the windows carrying that smell of turned-up dirt from the fields. A small trickle of sweat ran down the boy's neck.

The boy gently grasped the girl's shoulders and pulled her closer to him. He bent his face to hers. Their lips met. Withdrawing his face, he looked into her eyes. Finding peace there, he kissed her again, this time tasting her sweet mouth for what seemed a very long time. His heart pounded in his chest as he drew her close for an embrace. The taste of fruit lingered in his mouth. He knew not where it had come from. He was sure of what he tasted and would remain so even as an old man.

The girl knew the answer to her question. He was just a boy, not a devil—a boy much like the others she had kissed. Just a silly boy, but with zebra hands and zebra lips. She liked that. She pulled down the hem of her dress again and smiled, telling the boy she was glad he was just a boy. She stood by the hi-fi to play the opposite side of the record. Then, she heard a truck coming down the road. It was her daddy's truck. She could see her brother driving. Running to the back of the house, she kicked open the screen door and told the boy to run, quick!

It was time to run. The boy didn't know what was chasing him, but he knew he better not let it catch him. He ran through the fields behind the girl's home, through the tall grass to where his car was hidden. He heard someone yelling after him—curse words. He was sweating, panting, more afraid of being exposed than being beaten. He fumbled with his keys as he neared his car. The boy started his car and backed out onto the dirt road. He heard a huge crash from behind. Glass splinters flew around his car from his shattered back window. A rock landed in his backseat. He pressed the gas and sped down the road along the bayou.

The bubble received the boy once again. No one had seen him, except the girl. No one could testify he had been there, outside the bubble, kissing a Black girl. The back glass could be replaced. The taste of fruit would remain forever.

The girl argued with her brother. This wasn't the first time he'd chased a suitor out their back door, and it wouldn't be the last. She smiled when she thought of their zebra hands and lips. She kept her secret to herself, even as an old woman.

Report to Mrs. Roosevelt

I paced the plush waiting room, examining the modern art, the bronze sculptures, the leather-bound books. I thought of war, or in my case, the lack of it. Lately, I regretted having gone to law school. Now I was stuck working as a lawyer on The Hill. My big brother, Paul, was driving a tank under Patton's command in North Africa. Little brother Billy was busy sinking U-boats on convoy service in the Atlantic. Me, I was stuck in the Executive Office Building in Washington, D.C., nervously waiting to find out why Eleanor Roosevelt wanted to see a young congressional staffer.

"Mrs. Roosevelt will see you now," her secretary said. She pushed the door open and waved me forward into the first lady's office. "Ma'am, Mr. Broussard from New Orleans."

"Mrs. Roosevelt—" My throat was suddenly dry, and I struggled to utter her name, "—I am honored to meet you. I'm a great admirer of you and your husband."

"Please relax, Mr. Broussard. I'll do most of the talking. In fact, I'm just wanting one word from you today—a 'yes'—after I explain why I asked you to come." She lifted a manila folder off her desk and looked inside. "Your name is James. Is that what you go by?"

"Most folks call me Jimmy." While she read over the folder, I noticed the photographs on her credenza—family shots of her children and the president, their wedding photo, one of her and Will Rogers. She looked up again.

"I understand you recently took a job with Senator Truman's subcommittee probing war profiteering. Most needed. I take it you like to investigate corruption?"

"I suppose so. It's all I've done since law school."

"You helped convict your Governor Leche down in Louisiana, correct?"

"I was on the trial team for the Department of Justice. Mainly tracked down witnesses, poured over boxes of documents and worked with our accountants at the trial."

"Job well done," she said. "We can't tolerate corruption in the middle of a war."

"Still plenty of corruption back home, but it started a long time before Hitler or Tojo got the idea to overrun the world. Frankly, I'd rather be fighting them with a gun than pushing paper here in D.C."

"I have another important job for you, and it doesn't involve pushing paper," she said. "Harry Hopkins thinks you are the man for the job. He's arranged for you to take off from Senator Truman's committee. In a way, it may involve corruption, but there's much more than thievery. What do you know about a so-called riot that occurred near a military base in Alexandria, Louisiana January of last year?"

"I recall reading about an incident in North Louisiana. Negro troops on weekend leave from a training base got rowdy. Gunfire, some troops were wounded. With all the war stories coming out each day, it's hard to keep up with all the details."

"I want you to read this, Jimmy." Mrs. Roosevelt rose from her chair, circled around her desk carrying a letter and sat beside me. She handed the letter to me. "It's a plea from three Baptist ministers in Alexandria. I received it last week."

"They claim here that twenty soldiers were murdered," I said. "How could that be? How could they cover up twenty bodies?"

"That's what I need to know, so I can tell the president."

"What do the police reports show?" I asked. "Did the Army investigate?"

"There was a report done, but it concludes no deaths occurred." She reached to her desk and handed me a report marked *Top Secret—War Department Personnel Only*. "We don't think we're getting the straight story."

I opened it, read the introduction and then looked back at her. "It says it was prepared for General Benjamin Davis. Isn't he the only Negro general?"

"Yes, correct. This report was authored by a prominent Negro lawyer, Judge William Hastie, for the Army—former federal judge. He was acting as a special advisor to Secretary of War Stimson on race matters. They asked him to do the follow-up report on the incident, or should I say, they asked him to sign it. Recently, he resigned from his post as special advisor. He's now back running Howard Law School. I'm writing him a note and asking him to talk to you candidly. I think you should start there."

"Mrs. Roosevelt, I'm honored by the fact that you would choose me for such an important investigation. But this is the Bible Belt. My name is Broussard. It's a French Catholic name. I'm a Cajun in their eyes. They distrust Cajuns. Anybody asking questions makes them jumpy. Down there, they shoot first and ask questions later."

"Jimmy, that's exactly what we think happened here." She walked around her desk and sat in the other visitor's chair, just a few feet away. "I promised those ministers that I would find the truth and get it to the president. That's my job, you know, digging up the truth for Franklin. You would be shocked how he's lied to every single day, even by trusted advisors who want only the best for us."

"With all due respect, Mrs. Roosevelt, I'm just some young lawyer from Washington. I can't stroll into the police station and start asking questions."

"Mr. Hopkins will get you a badge and papers from the FBI. You show them your badge and say you are there on behalf of President Roosevelt. I'll see that you get a stenographer and a couple of men from the Bureau to help. Should you have any problems, or need anything at all, you call my secretary, and she'll get you what you need."

I squirmed in my chair, then looked out her window at the sun-drenched Washington Monument. I wanted so much to join my brothers in the great fight against our mortal enemies. This was going in the wrong direction, back to Louisiana.

Mrs. Roosevelt reached over and touched my hand. "Each of those boys had a mother somewhere in this country. They need to know what happened to their sons."

I rose and walked to her large office window. Down the Mall, I could see the summer sun lighting up the Lincoln Memorial's white marble, which portrayed in stone the better angels of America's soul. It was clear to me that the work Lincoln had begun was not complete, not by a long shot. My people still stood in the way. If not me, then who? Mrs. Roosevelt got her, "Yes."

———◆———

I hailed a cab to take me to my Georgetown apartment. My cabby was a middle-aged Negro who smiled in his mirror and said, "Coming from the EOB. I got a real-life VIP in my cab this morning."

"Na, just a staffer on The Hill, I'm sad to say. Nothing special. But hey, what a beautiful spring day."

"You bet, my first day driving this beauty. Straight eight. She's smooth. White guy drove it for two years, but he got shipped out to the Pacific, so I moved up to a nicer ride."

On the ride back to my Georgetown apartment, I watched young men in uniform step sharply across the sidewalks, satchels under their arms, walking with a purpose previously unknown in this most northern of southern cities. The women who typed and filed their papers moved decidedly, fulfilling the tasks assigned to them. There was no longer room for dawdling or frittering away one's time. The country was at war.

Even the cherry blossoms forming a garland around the Jefferson Memorial seemed to point the way to a glorious undertaking by all citizens. Where did I fit into this collective effort? I was being asked to pry open the sinful and infected wound of racial terror. I was going backward, south toward my home. God knows what I would find or who would have to bleed because of my prying.

My family had a history with racial violence. My grandfather had been a member of the White League, and the mere mention of anything associated with the Republican Party would send him into a near tantrum. He bragged that during Reconstruction, the White League ran the Union troops and the Republican carpetbaggers out of New Orleans at gunpoint.

In my immediate family, we were always made to refer to the other race as "Negroes," the proper and polite word. Jim Crow laws were firmly in place, and we all took separation for granted. But I never heard race hatred at home. Whites and Negroes each had their separate and rather grand Mardi Gras organizations. Whites and Negroes danced to the same jazz and ragtime music down in the French Quarter. While there was no thought in our city of equality of the races, there was no lynching or cross burning in the city. That went on in the countryside.

Back at my apartment that night, I read the Army report on the Lee Street incident. It was a damned turkey shoot, ninety guns blazing. No deaths it claimed. I took a walk down by the Potomac to clear my head and maybe lose the queasy feeling in my gut. I knew the danger and possible futility of the undertaking Mrs. Roosevelt had given me to accomplish. An FBI badge meant nothing to people who would murder soldiers wearing their country's uniform.

———————

I was shown into the office of the dean of Howard University School of Law and shook hands with a distinguished Negro gentleman. Dean Hastie asked me to step with him to a worktable near his desk. On the table, he pointed to an open volume of the *United States Reports*, containing the Supreme Court's rulings.

"Mr. Broussard, you're a lawyer from New Orleans; that's what they told me."

"Right sir, Tulane University. Class of 1936."

"You recognize the case I have open here? It's out of your hometown. *Plessy v Ferguson*, the legal keystone of Jim Crow."

"Right, read it in law school."

"This business with racial murder doesn't just come out of nowhere. It's not just a momentary reaction to hate or prejudice. There's a long history here, plus the legal sanction of our highest organs of government." We sat at the worktable, the law book between us. "Mr. Broussard, I hope you get deeper than I did in Alexandria."

I handed him the ministers' letter. "Mrs. Roosevelt gave me this letter from local ministers who claim more than twenty were killed that night."

"There is no question in my mind that men died that night. How many remains to be seen, but there was definitively a cover-up here by the Army. Perhaps out of genuine concern for overall war morale and to prevent damaging news falling into the hands of our enemies, but a cover-up."

"But Dean Hastie, you authored the Army report. Help me understand why you said in the report that there were no deaths."

"This was supposed to be a preliminary report for the press, based only on what the Army gave me at the time. You may know General Ben Davis?"

"I've read about him."

"He's a dear friend from way back. He came down with me to Louisiana and acted as my liaison with the Army. He personally assured me that there were no deaths, gave me his word, so I took it. I was not allowed to do an independent investigation. I was whisked in and out of there in a couple of days. Talked to the Chief of Police and to General Davis. Spoke to a couple of wounded Negro soldiers in Ben's presence. We found that the gunfire by the police was wild and indiscriminate. The shooting knocked out the power in the area; think of that. Businesses were damaged. Civilians were wounded and sent to local hospitals. The local police chief claims they just shot in the air. Shit...."

"Is that why you quit the War Department?"

Rather than answer, he stood up and walked to a nearby bookcase. "Mr. Broussard, you're from Louisiana. Do you truly know what you're being asked to do down there? Do you understand the homicidal rage among the Whites toward anyone questioning their right to kill or lynch anyone challenging their system?"

He pulled down a binder and brought it back to our table, then opened it to reveal numerous photographs of public lynchings of Negro men. Thousands of Whites stood watching Negro men swing in the air. Women and children watched, as well. "This is what you are dealing with. Apparently, neither the fact that our country is under attack nor the wearing of our country's uniform makes any difference to these people."

"Being from Louisiana, I think I know something about race terror. I won't lie; I'm scared. But as you know, when this president calls, you say yes."

"So, to answer your question, I didn't quit over the report. For me, the final straw was another race murder in Alexandria this past November when a state trooper named Dalton McCollum murdered a Negro MP in cold blood. Shot him in the back in front of several credible witnesses, including Whites. Our Department of Justice refused to prosecute this murder of an active member of the military. The case was referred to the local DA, where it died. That's why I quit."

"Where do I start? The first lady wants to know what really happened on Lee Street, how many died, even where they buried the bodies. So, I'm White, and you're Black. How's that going to change anything? We're both outsiders. No one's going to talk to me, not if they value their life."

Hastie pushed a manila folder across the table to me. "Start with James Lafourche, with the NAACP in New Orleans. He sent me this letter with detailed allegations based on eyewitnesses from the community. He claims as many as ten were killed. You're not trying to put anyone in jail—that clearly won't happen. You're just looking for the truth, so I'd start there. The Negroes who live there know what happened. Keep a low profile, very low."

He rose, walked back to his desk and pulled a letter from his drawer. "There's another concern brewing in Alexandria. Read this." He handed me a small envelope containing a hand-written note:

Judge Hastie, please act now. Justice must be done. If not, there may be an uprising. A group called the Easter Avengers is arming and is prepared to act.

"Where did this come from?"

"A Negro janitor gave it to me at the police station. I slipped it into my coat. I have no idea what it means, other than that vengeance is a possibility. The McCollum case can't have helped matters. Last thing we need now is a full-blown race war in the South. Axis Sally and Tokyo Rose will have a field day, not to mention the rivers of blood that will flow."

I looked once more upon the Plessy case and the mob violence that it helped to create. Feeling shame for my fellow Southerners' acts, I closed both the law book and the binder. "Thank you, sir, for both your assistance and the reminders." I shook his hand goodbye.

"Tread lightly, and God be with you."

<hr />

My next stop was the Department of Justice, where I was given my badge and investigative credentials along with a folder containing press clippings from around the country covering the Lee Street incident. I was joined in a small conference room by Roger Steadman, one of the department's seasoned stenographers in federal courtrooms and law enforcement agencies. The middle-aged man had the bearing of an athlete, tall and raw-boned. His green eyes flashed at me before lighting a bowl of tobacco in the burl pipe, which would be ever-present during our work. He laid his steno pad on the table and shook my hand.

After introductions, I asked him, "How were you chosen for this suicide mission?"

"They blew a bunch of smoke my way and told me I was

their best man. I was between assignments. I personally think it's because I'm a bachelor and don't have a wife and kids to worry about. Plus, I'm from Georgia, so my accent won't be a problem. Frankly—" He drew a few puffs, "—from what I heard about this situation, I can understand how things got out of hand. I know what would happen in Macon. The least resistance from a Negro, out comes the gun."

"Have you done fieldwork like this—witnesses outside a courtroom?" I asked.

"Most of my work has been in federal courtrooms. It's been twenty years now. I administer the oath. I have my pad and pencil. No matter where we are, I'll get it all down right here in shorthand." he tapped his pad. "Later, we transcribe it through the typing pool here at DOJ. My question is: Where is the transcript going after that? Is there a grand jury involved?"

"Negative. This is an investigation requested by the White House, the first lady actually. We're going to Alexandria. I hope—" I pulled the Army report from my briefcase and handed it to him, "—to locate enough witnesses to give her and the president the straight truth of what happened on January 10 of last year. Also, what the Army did to cover this up. What they do with this information afterward is up to them."

"So, these Klansmen get to kill our soldiers and go on living their lives," Roger said. "Is that it?"

"Won't be the first time. Come on, you're from Macon. Would that shock you? Look, we have a job to do. All we can do is all we can do."

Roger and I read the press clippings, all of which depicted a major clash between the combined military and civilian law enforcement and hundreds of unarmed Negro trainees from local bases. I handed him one. "Look at this—front-page editorial from the Alexandria Daily Town Talk, January 13, 1942. 'Don't Believe the Worst,' is the title. They're backing the Army's version one hundred percent."

Roger held out another article from the New Orleans *Times-Picayune*. "Here's one that says eighteen were killed. What the hell is a Picayune?"

I smiled. "It's a near-worthless Spanish coin. Don't ask me how they chose that name."

We finished our reading and parted until meeting at the train station the next afternoon. Our first stop was New Orleans.

The train arrived in my hometown early the next morning. Roger and I walked the few blocks to a building in the Central Business District where the local NAACP offices were located. James Lafourche met with us in his office. We spoke over the sounds of dockworkers, cranes and an occasional passing streetcar that drifted through his open window. "Mr. Broussard, does your family run Broussard Stevedores?"

"That's my uncle's business. My father is a marine insurance broker, so we're all about shipping and trade."

"Several colored friends work on the docks with your uncle's company. They tell me good things. Judge Hastie asked me to help you. Is it true you are here for the president?"

I pulled my wallet from my coat and showed him my FBI credentials. "The first lady asked us to investigate. We have your letter to the judge; it mentions ten deaths. Who can verify this?"

"The Negroes who live in the area saw it all. I spoke to several witnesses right after this massacre."

Roger opened the clipping file and handed the Picayune story to

Mr. Lafourche. "Says here eighteen were killed. Your letter claims ten. Where do these numbers come from?"

"I based my number on what a Negro undertaker told me," Lafourche said. "He embalmed ten for the Army. So that's a minimum as I see it, maybe more."

"Ten bodies!" Roger said. "Where did they stash ten bodies?"

"God knows. Maybe you'll be able to bring them home. Ain't no telling where they hid them. But I can tell you the Army wants this case kept closed. Ben Davis' handprints are all over this one."

Lafourche scribbled on a piece of paper.

"You start by calling this gentleman," he said. "He's the preacher at a nearby church, and several of his people were on Lee Street that night." He gave me the note with the name and number of Reverend J. W. White.

"What I want to know is this," I said. "How could police empty their guns into a group of unarmed US Army soldiers just a few weeks after Pearl Harbor? I'm having a hard time understanding why, even though I grew up down here."

"Jimmy, trouble had been brewing up there for a couple of years. All the colored troops piling in from up North. Hell, they got a nigger-killing unit up there on that police force. They proud of it. You call Reverend White. He'll line up some witnesses for you. And you be very careful and keep that badge handy. The FBI might carry some weight up there, but don't count on it."

Roger and I stayed overnight in a cheap motel near the train station, relieving me of having to discuss my purpose here. We took the morning train north to Alexandria. We were met there at the train station by two FBI agents from the Shreveport field office who were to serve as our security and assist us in the investigation.

They were Bob Bannister and John Lewis, both North Louisiana natives with years of FBI service in the area.

They drove us a few blocks to the Lee Street location of the shootings. The four of us stood on the sidewalk in front of a colored theater, the Ritz. This was the alleged site of the scuffle that sparked the massacre.

"They call this area Little Harlem," Bob told me. "On Saturday night, this place will be jumping. You got your movie house, a meat market, all these bars, a café. On the second floor of that building over there and the one across that side street, two brothels for the Negro soldiers."

"Understood," I said.

The sight of four White men in suits looking and pointing drew long glances from the Negroes coming and going in their daily business. I felt a trespass of sorts as we inspected the bustling street for signs of a massacre. Little Harlem was a prosperous business district, which closely abutted the heart of the city—the parish courthouse, post office and federal courthouse, the White business district and the stately Hotel Bentley. All were no more than three blocks away. I examined the façade of the Ritz Theater and noted numerous chips and holes in the brickwork caused by the barrage of bullets unleashed on unarmed soldiers out to have a good time. Something had happened that Saturday night that ripped apart the delicate co-existence of the two communities.

We drove to the Rose of Sharon Baptist Church and posted Bannister and Lewis outside in their car while Roger and I went in to meet the witnesses. We were ushered by the church secretary, Susannah Wells, to a large Sunday school room in the back of the church. The sounds of a children's choir boomed down the hall. "Practicing for our Wednesday night prayer meeting," she said. "Sister Johnson does a wonderful job with them, don't you think?"

"Amazing," I said. "Beautiful voices."

"You gentlemen, please have a seat. Reverend White will be here to meet you before you leave. He's visiting a sick church member right now. There's one thing for you to keep in mind here—" She paused, and her gentle expression changed. "—all these people are scared, bad scared. They're only talking to you because their pastor asked them to."

I positioned a straight-backed chair for the witness and then turned to our hostess. "Mrs. Wells, we both grew up in the Deep South. We understand their fears and will use our utmost caution and discretion. Mrs. Roosevelt knows this as well. We have no intention of getting any of your members hurt or harassed in any way."

"Mr. Lafourche told us this. I'll show the first one in."

Our first witness that day was a very young man, Earl Sullivan. A student who evidently had come straight from his afternoon baseball practice, he placed his books and leather gloves beside his chair and swallowed deeply. He was visibly quaking. I introduced Roger and explained how he would record on his pad everything we said exactly as we said it.

Roger lit his pipe and pulled his steno pad from his briefcase. He swore him to tell the truth, and I began.

Q: State your full name and age.

A: Earl Sullivan, age fifteen.

Q: Earl, are you a member of the Rose of Sharon Church?

A: Yes, sir. I am in the youth choir and junior ushers.

Q: Are you here with the permission of your parents?

A: Yes, sir.

Q: Were you an eyewitness to the Lee Street shootings on the night of January 10, 1942?

A: That's right, sir.

Q: Why were you there that night?

A: Me and a buddy went to the Ritz Theater that night to see a western—Apache Trail. It started around seven. Seems like halfway through, we heard guns going off outside, so we ran to the front door. First, we felt the tear gas in our eyes and mouths. Everyone was running and shouting. Bullets were hitting the front of the theater and some of the bars and other businesses on Lee Street. Glass breaking, people yelling. We was scared like crazy and ran to get away. I saw seven or eight colored soldiers lying on Lee Street bleeding. One had been shot in the head, and he was face down. I ran by another man whose chest was open, and he was staring into the sky. His eyes were blank. We ran away from the Ritz toward the parking lot at the A&P. Once we got over Ninth, we were safe and ran to our homes. There was a line of police and other White men with guns, just shooting, one after the other. One man had a Thompson submachine gun. They were lined up along Ninth Street, and some others were on the other sides of Lee Street and on the river side as well, just firing into where the bars and all the colored soldiers were.

Q: Did the shooting continue as you were running home?

A; Oh yes, sir. It went on a long time after I got home. I was so scared and upset at what I seen. I couldn't sleep that night.

Q: Were you or your buddy hit or injured in any way?

A: We just got bits of shattered glass in our face and our arms, but other than that, we were okay.

Q: Can you tell me the name of your buddy? We'd like to talk to him.

A: He say he didn't want anyone to know he was there. Made me promise not to say his name.

Q: Earl, do you know anything else about this? Anything else you can tell us?

A: Sir, I ran so hard toward home, I was just grateful to be alive that night. I wasn't gonna be like Lot, turn back and die. We got away and kept running. I ain't ever gonna forget that man's face, sir.

Q: Thank you, Earl. You're a brave young man to come here, and I want you to know that the president thanks you for telling your truth.

The next witness was Ellis Henthorne. He wore dusty blue jean overalls and roughed up leather work boots. His work gloves protruded from his front pocket. His eyes darted back and forth between Roger and me. After reassuring him, and swearing him in, we began.

Q: State your name and age.

A: Ellis Henthorne, age eighteen.

Q: Are you in school or employed?

A: I work for Martin Lumber, in the yard, but now I'm eighteen, I'm going in the service. Signed up last week. Supposed to learn where they gonna send me any day now.

Q: Do you attend Rose of Sharon?

A: Yes, sir. My family's been here since before I was born. I told Reverend White what I saw, and he asked me to speak to y'all. Y'all really workin' for the president?

Q: Mrs. Roosevelt asked me herself. Tell me where you were and what you saw.

A: Yes, sir, glad to help. I was meeting my girlfriend down at the Ritz to see the Saturday night movie. I was walking past a bar on Lee Street. It was like a parade or something, all the colored soldiers in the street. They was talking loud like they was liquored up good. Joe Louis had beat Buddy Baer the night before, and they was saying Joe was the greatest fighter ever, better than Jack Johnson. They was so happy and loud. I was about a block from the Ritz, and I saw a big commotion, yelling, like someone getting thrown out of a bar. This wasn't far from the Ritz, but out in the street. I saw a colored MP grab the colored soldier, and then two White city police jumped in and started in with their billy clubs on the MP and everyone nearby the fracas. Next, I heard some gunshots, and I got scared. I knew my girlfriend had to be near there, or maybe inside the theater. The gunfire hadn't started, but more police were pouring in, and bottles started flying from the soldiers.

Q: Did you find your girlfriend?

A: Yes, sir. I went around to the back entrance to the theater; a buddy worked there. So, I ran around back of the Ritz and got to the lobby. She was behind the counter with the staff. We was all scared to death. I took her out the back way, and by then, they was using gas on all the crowd on Lee Street. Everyone was running, and I saw a line of police a couple of blocks away. They started firing their guns into the crowd. I saw a couple of White men with no uniforms on roofs, shooting rifles. As we ran toward Samtown, I heard a machine gun, continuous firing. By then, they had the strip surrounded, and everyone in there was fair game."

Q: By the strip, you mean Lee Street? And, where is Samtown?

A: Yes, Lee Street. They call it the strip 'cause all the bars and such. Samtown is what they call the colored section, south of town. That's where we both live. We ran and didn't stop.

Q: Did you witness anyone get shot?

A: Oh, yes sir. I saw several soldiers down and bleeding from bullets. I saw a lady being carried away, bleeding from one of her legs. Bullets were flying everywhere, broken glass from the businesses along the strip.

Q: Did you see any dead people?

A: I'm pretty sure one soldier was dead. He was shot in the

back of the neck and wasn't moving. I think he was about a block off Lee Street, toward the courthouse. I had to cover my girl's eyes. Didn't want her to see him.

Q: Can you give me your girlfriend's name? We'd like to hear what she saw.

A: Sir, I came because Reverend White asked me, and when I heard it was for the president, well, I'd do anything for Mr. Roosevelt. But we're scared to talk otherwise. I can't ask my girl to speak. She's gonna wait for me to finish the war. I got to have her here, sir. I can't afford no violence. You know what I mean?

Q: Sure, Ellis, I understand. Both Mr. Steadman and I are from the South. He's from Georgia, and I'm from New Orleans. We know the risk you are taking. Thank you for your courage coming here.

Roger slowly shook his head. "Hard to believe you can hate so hard that you'd kill one of your soldiers trying to save your country."

"These kids are scared to death," I said. "They must think the world of their minister, willing to help us and maybe put their ass on the line."

The final witness secured for us by Reverend White was a Negro woman who came into the Sunday school room limping noticeably with the aid of a cane. She stared at the wall, making no eye contact with either of us. She nodded for me to start my questions.

Q: State your name and age, please, ma'am.

A: Mary Frances Scales, age twenty-seven.

Q: Are you married, ma'am?

A: I'm married to James Scales. We live here in town, a few blocks from here. It's called Samtown, but it's part of Alexandria. The police sure act like it is.

Q: What do you mean by that?

A: You see me walk, sir? My cane? That's what I got from the city police that night, just walking to a meat market, shot down like a dog. They got what they call a nigger-killing squad, the Alexandria City Police. Act like they God, but they not, not by a longshot.

Q: So, you were shot that night by the police, is that what you are saying?

A: Yes sir. There was a line of them. Some used their revolvers. Some had shotguns. One had a machine gun on his hip and was just firing it into the crowd of soldiers. I was crossing Lee Street on my way to the meat market to get some chicken for Sunday dinner. First, I saw some men fighting and some MPs. Next, all hell broke loose. Guns started firing, and next thing, I got hit in my right hip, like a hot knife. I went down, couldn't walk. I was lying on the street bleeding. Then, they let gas go on us. I couldn't breathe, but I couldn't move. Stayed there the whole time. Must have gone on an hour or more. I didn't know if I'd make it or not. I think I went in and out. When I came to, saw maybe ten of our colored troops dead and lying in their own blood all around me. The police were coming through with their billy clubs, chasing the soldiers away from the strip, clearing out the dead and wounded. They seen I was alive and put me in an ambulance to Charity Hospital in Pineville. Doctor took the bullet out of my hip, gave me something for my burning eyes.

Q: Are you certain you saw dead soldiers?

A: They were lying beside me on both sides, sir. Yes, I am certain. Must have been ten. They was stacking them on the side of Lee Street, outside the Ritz, when they was putting me in the ambulance. But I saw some more dead men at Charity.

Q: Tell me what you saw at the hospital.

A: I was on a stretcher waiting for the surgeon to finish and get to me. They gave me a shot for pain, but doctor was in the room operating on wounded soldiers. I waited for a long while, watching the stretchers come and go from the surgery room. I saw several stretchers wheeled out with sheets pulled over the bodies. Maybe four or five. They were taken away by other soldiers, White soldiers, not nurses. There were several soldiers keeping people and even nurses away from the area. It felt like a military hospital. My eyes were feeling better by then, and the shot had taken away the pain. Finally, they wheeled me into the surgery room to remove the bullet.

Q: And all this was at Charity Hospital in Pineville, across the river?

A: Yes, sir.

Q: Did any of the soldiers speak to you, Mrs. Scales?

A: Yes, sir. About two weeks later, a very nice young colored soldier came to see me. You see, they put my name in the Town Talk as being wounded in the shooting. He said he was an assistant to General Davis. He asked me on behalf of General Davis not to talk to anyone about what happened to me or what I saw. He said it might hurt the war effort and that General Davis was asking this as a personal request on behalf of our troops. I told him I greatly admired the general, our first colored general. So, I haven't said nothing to anyone. But when Reverend White told me you were here for the president and Mrs. Eleanor. I knew I had to help. I ain't mad at the Army. They didn't shoot me. It was those White devils with the city police, and that's the truth.

Q: Is there anything else you can tell us about what you saw that evening? Any more conversations?

A: No, sir. That's what I saw. I do know that some soldiers who were shot and wounded, they crossed the tracks into Samtown and *hid under houses. A lady told me one had died under her house, and they came and pulled his body out and took it to Mr. Lacoste to embalm. That's what she told me. I didn't see this myself.*

Q: Who was this that told you about the dead body? Can you tell me her name?

A: Sir, she's a friend, and she's scared of the police and the Klan. My name is already known, and I haven't talked to anyone but you, and only because my preacher asked me. You understand.

Q: Of course, Mrs. Scales. This is all going in a report to the president, so you needn't worry. Thank you for coming.

The door shut as she left the Sunday school. A choking silence descended between us. We started at each other, both trying to comprehend what type of monsters created and maintained this toxic brew of violence and fear. The thought those monsters might be watching us raised the stakes of our investigation considerably.

<hr />

Mrs. Wells appeared and took us to Reverend White's office. Reverend White looked at us gravely as we sat before him. He gave me a folded newspaper. "Read this. It's from the *Pittsburgh Courier* from 1921."

"What is it?" I asked. Grainy photos of burned corpses laying along destroyed streets jumped off the yellowed newsprint page.

"Do you two know about Tulsa 1921? Hundreds murdered. The entire colored section of town burned to the ground."

"No, I can't say I know the details. How about you, Roger?"

"I've heard it mentioned," Roger said. "Never seen photos like this."

"Gentlemen, I hope these witnesses this afternoon were illuminating. January 10 was a tragic event. More may be on the way. That's what I'm trying to prevent. We don't want another

Tulsa here. We in the colored community need to see that some sort of justice comes out of these murders. Just knowing that Mrs. Roosevelt has sent you is a start."

"Reverend, we can't thank you enough. What the first lady wants from us is the whole truth about what happened and what was covered up. Looks like the Army did a good job of squelching the story. They have people thinking it is their patriotic duty to remain silent."

"General Davis used this approach on Mrs. Scales," he said. "I expected better from him as one of our race. From what I hear, he puts himself on a high horse and looks down on colored troops."

I pulled out the note given to me by Dean Hastie and handed it to Reverend White. "Can you help me with this? Do you know of a group calling itself the Easter Avengers?"

Reverend White read it. I saw a look on his face that read, "This is trouble." He closed his eyes, paused and returned it to me. "Fellas, let's go for a ride. I need to give you some history lessons."

We left the church, and the three of us got into his large, black Buick. Agents Bannister and Lewis followed behind in their unmarked unit. After a short drive south, he turned his car into a vast area of worn out shotgun shacks. The dirt roads were bordered by deep open ditches filled with weeds and sewage. Children played baseball in the streets. Adults sat in rocking chairs and fanned themselves in the thick, warm April air. Samtown, I had seen plenty of places like this in the South, but usually in rural settings.

Roger stuck his head between us from the back seat. "Reverend White, Samtown—is this in the city limits?"

"Yes and no," he said. "Yes, in the sense that the city police keep a close watch and tight rein on Samtown. No, in the sense that the city furnishes no services here. These folks are clearly a part of the city, but other than a couple of water wells, they have nothing here—no sewage connections, no electricity. Even got another name. This ain't Alexandria; this is Samtown."

"What do folks do for work around here?"

"Only thing good happened here lately is all the military bases being built. Gave some of the men jobs for a while. But that's petering out. One reason so many folks went north. I bet we lost twenty families, left for Chicago, some for California. A couple of those men were my deacons. Between getting lynched and halfway starving, I can't blame a man for leaving. Would you live here?"

It was a question that needed no answer.

"You said we need a history lesson," I said. "We're all ears."

"What would you say if I told you that the South won the Civil War?" Reverend White asked us.

"How's that, Reverend?" Roger asked. "I'm from Georgia, and we still remember Sherman's torches. That don't sound like winning to me."

"Depends on when you think the war ended and what the South was really fighting for. What do you say, Mr. Steadman—1865?"

"Sure, when Lee and Johnston surrendered. Jeff Davis was captured. It was over, and the Yankees won. Reconstruction started."

"What if I told you the war didn't end in 1865, that battles occurred throughout the South between White militia and Union forces. These continued until 1877, when Hayes withdrew the Union troops. These battles resulted in the massacres of hundreds of Negroes, both civilian and military, and the White militias won for the most part."

"He's right, Roger," I said. "My grandfather was in the White League in New Orleans. They ran the Union troops out of the city three times. He was very proud of that."

Reverend White pulled the note out of his pocket. "The Easter

Avengers in this note—that's referring to the Colfax Massacre on Easter Day in 1873, just twenty miles from here in Grant Parish. Ever hear of that?"

"Never heard of it," I said. Roger shrugged and shook his head.

"Big battle between White militias and some colored Union troops and volunteers. Fighting over a courthouse after a disputed election. Ended with surrender of the Union forces, and over a hundred colored men were executed with a bullet to the brain. Some Easter morning, huh? It made the national papers, big hurrah. Congressional investigation, even a Supreme Court case. In a way, this was the end of Reconstruction and the beginning of what we got now."

"I took Louisiana history at Tulane," I said. "How come I never heard of this?"

"Doesn't surprise me, but the colored men around here never forgot. After Lee Street, some of them started plotting revenge. They've been stockpiling arms, from what I hear. Meeting regularly, holding target practice with their hunting rifles."

"Reverend, you mean they're forming their own militia?" I asked. "Good God, that could lead to more bloodshed."

What kind of mission had I been asked to undertake? Europe and Asia were in flames, but now here I was in the crosshairs of a potential bloodbath in my home state. Fellow citizens who pledged loyalty to the same cause of freedom were willing and able to kill each other over an ancient sin so deep no one could name it, much less admit it.

"These men have had it. First, Lee Street, and now the McCollam murder has added fuel to the fire and members to their cause. I tell you, if they harm one police officer or one Klansman, Samtown could lie in ashes. Same with my church and every business on the strip. We could be Tulsa all over again. Axis Sally would have a field day with it. So, you see, you need to learn that history you were never taught. It can bite you on the ass." We sat in silence as we drove past the old shotgun houses of Samtown.

"So, after all the troops went home in 1877, what was the South left with?" Reverend White asked.

Roger lunged forward again, next to Reverend White's ear. "My people told me that everything in the South was burned or destroyed. I know there was a lot of hunger."

"I hope you don't take *Gone with the Wind* as a serious history lesson. It's a movie, Mr. Steadman, a good yarn. Think about it. The South was left alone to create a system to replace slavery. The planters had access to a cowered Negro population, with no legal protections or voting rights. They got to have their cake, virtually free labor. They got to eat it too. The big farmers no longer had to care for their workers. They didn't have to feed them, house them or give them a doctor. They now have a legal regime of White supremacy and access to cheap Negro labor with no legal rights. On top of that, they now control Congress. That's what I mean when I say the South won."

The picture painted by the reverend would please my granddaddy to no end. Not only did they chase the Yankees and carpetbaggers out, but they also got their way of life back, better than ever.

Reverend White drove us back to the Bentley Hotel. Bannister and Lewis followed us in their unit. As Roger and I alighted from the reverend's black Buick, I noticed four sets of eyes trained on us from men playing cards next to the Alexandria City Hall and two White men in suits getting out of a car driven by a leader of the colored community. These stares didn't escape the notice of Agent Bannister, who said to me, "You two just got made as suspicious persons. Guess you saw the reception committee over there next to city hall?"

I nodded. We had just left the automobile of a leader in the Negro community. Our presence there did not add up in their world. We were a threat, maybe outsiders come to cause trouble. Roger and I, while White, were the worst type of threat, traitors to our own race.

"Police chief's office is just inside that side door," he said. "Just so you'll know. In case you need to call a city cop."

I broke a crooked smile. I wrapped my arm around Bannister's shoulder and pulled him near. "I don't need no city cop, not when I got you and your six-shooter there inside your coat." I released my hug. We both chuckled and entered the Bentley Hotel.

The next morning, the four of us drove an hour north to Winnfield, Louisiana to meet with employees of a Negro funeral home. One the way up, we went through Pollock, a small village dominated by a large Baptist church in the middle of town. There were signs at the city limits: *Nigger—stay out of Pollock*. In a pasture just outside the community, we saw a large burned cross. There was no mistaking the message: no Negroes allowed, period. I felt like a stranger. A French Catholic was an alien here. I was an alien who was here to ask questions. This was Klan country. I felt grateful to have Bannister, Lewis and their sidearms close.

After arriving at Winnfield Funeral Home, we were shown into the nicely decorated office of the owner, Ben Johnson, Sr. Our agents waited in the lobby while Roger and I met with Mr. Johnson, and one of his embalmers, Gerald Lacoste. A very slight scent of formaldehyde permeated the dark-paneled executive office. Behind Johnson's desk was a poster displaying the Double V Campaign, promoted by the Negro press and the NAACP. The two Vs were victory over the axis and victory over Jim Crow. It depicted a gallant colored soldier marching forward into the smoke of battle.

Neither man was willing to give formal sworn statements but consented to talk to us frankly about what they knew, with the understanding their names would not be released to the public.

A tall Negro man with white hair and piercing eyes, Mr. Johnson spoke first. "Gentlemen, I am the owner of this place. I started it a few years ago with an embalming license and $2.50 loaned to me by some friends. The colored community simply did not have a suitable, respectable place to embalm and bury their dead. God has blessed me. We've been going ten years now, and now we have places in Alexandria and Shreveport as well. This is our home place and our business office. We have a parlor in Alexandria, where Mr. Lacoste works. He's the one who was approached by General Davis' staff. I'll let him tell you about it, but only if you assure me our names and the name of my business is not made public. I've worked too hard to see it go up in flames. Our colored people need us to bury their dead in a proper Christian manner. We can't do it swinging from a rope. You understand?"

"You have my word, Mr. Johnson," I said. "This is a confidential report for Mrs. Roosevelt and the president. So, Mr. Lacoste, what can you tell us?"

Roger pulled out his pipe and his steno pad. "Just taking some notes. Okay if I smoke?"

Johnson nodded, and we began.

Lacoste was a well-dressed, stocky Negro man in his thirties. He spoke in a soft, clear voice. "I was working that Saturday night at our Alexandria parlor. I was sleeping overnight in the bedroom in the back, catching any calls that might come in overnight. We run an ambulance also. About 7:30 or 8:00 that evening, I heard gunfire coming from downtown. Went on for ten or fifteen minutes. We have a police scanner. Something about a riot. State police were called. I heard military MPs on the radio, calling for support and more guns. Called Mr. Johnson at his home. Told me to stay put."

"What happened next?" I asked.

"About one in the morning, a major and two soldiers come knocking. Two refrigerated trucks idled in our parking lot. He tells me that he is asking for embalming services on behalf of General Ben Davis, who was overseeing this situation. He tells me General Davis says this is of the utmost importance and that the leaking of any information could be a catastrophe for our nation. He said this information could fall into the hands of our enemies and damage our war efforts. I knew this was something I had to call Mr. Johnson about, so I called and put the major on the phone with my boss."

"What was he asking your firm to do?"

"After he and Mr. Johnson talked, I was told to help the major in any way possible and to maintain strict silence. I was shown to the refrigerated trucks. There were five stretchers with five corpses in each, all young Negro soldiers."

"Did anyone say what had happened?"

"They didn't say, and I damned sure didn't ask. I was trembling inside. Never saw anything like that before."

"How did you get the bodies embalmed?"

"We couldn't do a job like that in Alexandria since there was just me and a part-time helper. Mr. Johnson and I agreed that we'd bring them up here, where we have three embalmers counting myself, plus Mr. Johnson. I called my part-time man to handle the Sunday service. I got dressed and led the trucks up here to our Winnfield location. I think we arrived here around 2:30 that morning. The four of us worked straight through into the next day, preparing those men for burial. Luckily, there was nothing scheduled here the next day, so no one came around while we were working."

"So, y'all prepared the ten bodies that night?"

"Yes, sir. Bodies stacked everywhere. Having to cut off those bloody uniforms. Blood all over the place. Those fine young men. I don't know how I made it. I kept thinking about the war, about men dying fighting the Japs, but these young coloreds had been cut down right here."

"Mr. Johnson, I take it you saw all this as well?

"I embalmed at least two myself and helped out on some others. Gunshot wounds, every one of them, from all angles. Front entry, rear entry. Some single-shot, some torn up. Another truck arrived that next morning with ten pine caskets. We were told just to embalm them. No makeup, no cosmetic work. We wrapped them in sheets, placed them in the pine boxes, then labeled each. The caskets were placed back into the refrigerated trucks. The three trucks drove off about noon the next day, and that is the last I saw of the bodies."

"Any further contact with the Army?"

"I received a personal note of thanks from General Davis after they paid the bill. I will show it to you but want it back." He pulled a letter from his desk drawer and showed me the thank you note from Davis. It also contained an admonition not to discuss any of this with anyone since it would harm US national security.

"Mr. Johnson, I know that someone had to sign for death certificates. How was that handled?'

"That was part of it. I was told this was urgent and that the Army needed this done. I believe Mr. Lacoste signed all the certification papers."

I looked at Mr. Lacoste.

Lacoste shifted in his chair, his eyes staring at the floor. "The major wrote in they died in training accidents," he mumbled. "I signed where I was told to sign, had to."

"We've read that as many as eighteen died that night. You fellas embalmed ten. Any ideas about the rest?"

"I heard through the grapevine that Hixson's did the others," Mr. Johnson said. "They the White funeral home. Don't know how many, heard six, heard it was eight. But I wouldn't advise going over there and asking. Just lead to trouble. Only reason I agreed to talk was you working for Mrs. Roosevelt. The Whites around here don't feel kindly toward her."

I thanked the undertakers. Roger and I were leaving their office when Mr. Johnson stopped me. "There's one more stop you need to make before you leave town. I spoke to Governor Earl Long yesterday when I knew you was coming up here. He wants to talk to you. His farm's just up the road. Don't be fooled—it's just a shack. He'll meet you there. I'll call him as you leave and tell him you're coming."

"Why would Earl Long want to talk to me?"

"Said he wants to thank you proper for something. That's all he said."

I thanked them for their time. We drove to Long's farm on the edge of town and stopped before a locked gate. A tall man in overalls stood behind the gate talking with two Negro farmhands. I exited the car. The smell of cow manure was heavy in the spring air. Earl Long extended his hand, grabbed mine firmly and flashed a huge smile. "Welcome to my Pea Patch Farm. You must be that Broussard boy."

"I am, sir. Jimmy Broussard from New Orleans. Glad to meet you. Mr. Johnson told me you wanted to thank me."

"Oh, I know you, Jimmy, even though we never met. You and Mr. Rogge helped make me governor of Louisiana!"

"Governor, we were just doing our jobs as prosecutors."

"I was hanging around as lieutenant governor, doing nothing until y'all got after Leche. We ain't met, but I owe you boys a big debt for getting rid of Leche and his gang. That ain't easy, taking down a sitting governor. Y'all did a great service for the people of this state. I found out all about y'all while the trial was going on. Rogge, that's a fighting yard dog if I ever seen one. Hell of a prosecutor. I know your people too, Jimmy. They good people, I hear. They ain't partial to me and my late brother, but that don't mean I ain't grateful for what you feds did for this state, and helping me of course."

"Glad to be of service, sir."

Uncle Earl had a reputation as a tough and crafty operator who loved to play the loveable fool. I was grasping for the real reason he wanted to talk to me, certainly not to express his gratitude.

"Governor," I said, "we are up here on more government business, so we need to be running back to Alexandria now."

"Don't run off just yet. You boys, come on in and let's drink some coffee and talk a bit. I may be able to help you with your new government business."

I introduced my three companions, and we walked down a long driveway to an old tin-roofed farmhouse. Earl pulled up some rocking chairs, and we all sat down together on his front porch while coffee was served by the two Negroes.

"So, Ben Johnson tells me you boys looking into that mess in Alex with the Negro soldiers?"

"Yes, we're here at the request of the president and his wife."

"First, and I'll say this until the day I die—Uncle Earl is the best friend the Negro ever had in the governor's office. I appointed more

Negroes to state jobs than anyone in history, and we were planning major voting reforms until I got derailed by that little worm from Lake Charles. Sam Jones claims he's a paragon of virtue and purity, but he's just another water boy for Texaco and Humble. People think they want clean, but I know where the gold is buried, and you got to know how to dig in the dirt to get to it. Jimmy, they trying to indict me right now, but they don't know what Uncle Earl has in store for 'em, like that Lee Street mess."

"What are you saying, governor? Do you have some information for us?"

"Know someone who might," he said. "Some of those high-minded sons of bitches from Alex got blood all over their hands. Sheriff, chief of police, state troopers—they all got soldiers' blood all over their hands. They trying to cover it up, but it can't be washed away. That's a horrible shame what they did to those troops, and when you boys take them down, the whole nation will applaud."

"Governor, I can't promise you that will happen. I'm not here as a federal prosecutor, but we are trying to get the real facts to the White House. Anything you can give us would be very helpful, but this is not a criminal investigation. What can you tell us?"

"My people down there tell me that it was a goddamned turkey shoot that night. The chief and sheriff don't like me, so sure as hell don't mention me to them. But I got a man on the Alexandria police force, and he was there that night. He can tell you what really happened from their side. He says it wasn't just police doing the shooting. Local men came out with their guns and joined in. You got to talk to him. Call him. Here's his home number, and tell him I sent you."

Governor Long handed me a slip of paper bearing the name and number of O.L. Tullos. Finally, someone from the inside of the department, someone who was on the other side of the blazing guns at the turkey shoot described by Long.

———————◆–◆–◆———————

I called Officer Tullos later that afternoon from my hotel room. After assuring him of secrecy and confidentiality, we agreed he could come to our room in the Bentley Hotel the next morning after completing his regular night shift.

At a little past 7:00 a.m., I answered my hotel room door. Standing before me wearing his police uniform and sidearm was a slender White man, who stepped quickly through the door, his eyes rapidly shifting between Roger and me. We exchanged handshakes with him. I felt sweat on his palm. He accepted a glass of water. We sat together at a table. After explaining our respective roles to him, I began my questions and Roger his shorthand. Mr. Tullos took a long swallow from the glass, breathed deeply and looked me straight in the eyes.

Q: Please state your name and age.

A: O.L. Tullos, twenty-eight.

Q: And the "O" is for?

A: Otis.

Q: Is it true that you are employed by the Alexandria City Police?

A; Yes sir, patrol officer. Mr. Broussard, I am speaking to you at the risk of my job, and maybe more. Do I have your word that you will protect me? I can't come to court or anything. I got a wife and two kids. You understand that, right?

Q: Mr. Tullos, everyone we've spoken to has the same assurance, straight from the president and first lady, and from me as a lawyer for your government—I give you my word. There's been enough blood spilled already.

A: *Well, I will hold y'all to it. Governor Long told me I can trust you and asked me to tell you what I saw and heard. So, go ahead—ask away.*

Q: *How long have you been on the force, and what are your duties?*

A: *I'm a patrol officer. Up for a move to corporal, soon, I hope. I guess you'd say as patrol officers we do it all from car wrecks, petty crime, security for public gatherings. Sometimes, we make a little money after hours working for nightclubs. I've been on a motorcycle detail here lately.*

Q: *Were you a witness to the events on Lee Street in January of last year?*

A: *Yes, sir. I was coming on duty for a night shift at 8:00 p.m., just as things were getting started. The main station is just two blocks away. Just after I walked in, somebody yelled that niggers was rioting over on the strip. Everyone was grabbing shotguns out of the gun case, and I started smelling tear gas, so we all grabbed our gas masks and ran toward Lee along Ninth Street.*

Q: *What made everyone so trigger happy that night?*

A: *Mr. Broussard, this didn't just happen out of the blue on January 10, 1942. This goes back at least a couple of years. Really started with the Louisiana Maneuvers here in 1940. I joined the force in 1939. Came here from Monroe. Alex was a sleepy farm town, a place for farmers and lumbermen to buy supplies and bring their families in to see a movie once a year. Crop prices were in the can. Depression hit hard here. CCC helped a little. Niggers worked on the cotton and sugar cane farms. Most of the White boys was cutting lumber. You got your Jewish merchants here and a few lumber families with money. But mostly everything was like it was fifty years ago. People knew their roles. Things were quiet.*

Q: *What changed here? How does Alexandria become a city where a massacre takes place?*

A: *In 1940, the Army comes to town with two-hundred thousand troops, trucks everywhere hauling men around, tanks running through the forests and fields. They started throwing up all these training camps around here. Brought in some jobs, so people liked that.*

But on the weekends, men of every color and from every part of the country were piling into town. They was chasing all the local girls, White and colored, some of whom didn't run too hard in the other direction. Next thing you know, we got the strip over here on Lee Street and clubs on the other end of town for the White boys. A few whorehouses opened. Fights all the time, we was constantly locking up these soldiers for fighting, drunk and disorderly. The MPs tried to help, but it was like a flood. We couldn't handle it.

Meanwhile, the local boys was getting pretty pissed about the whole scene. I started hearing about Yankee niggers stirring up things over in Samtown. We had a couple of burned crosses down on lower Third Street. Pressure was building up, but the money was flowing, so times was good.

Q: *So how do you get ninety police officers emptying their guns into a crowd of Negro soldiers?*

A: *Did you know that this wasn't the first disturbance on the strip? Back in September 1941, there was a huge fight outside a bar where a nigger soldier had been ejected. We had to use tear gas. Probably arrested twenty or so. MPs took them off and threw them in the stockade at Camp Claiborne. One soldier shot by a civilian. No one died that night.*

But this time, things seemed different. First, there was so many more soldiers in the street that night, and the tear gas didn't seem to phase them. Bottles and bricks kept flying toward the police line across Ninth Street. I heard a gunshot. Can't be sure where it came from. Just as I came up to the line, the shots started. I saw men on the top of buildings with hunting rifles firing down into the strip. These were civilians, I'm sure. How they got there, I have no idea. State police, sheriff's deputies, city police—every man with a sidearm or shotgun—all of them firing into the crowd. That's when the colored soldiers ran for their lives.

Q: What were you doing when the shooting started?

A: I just stood there holding a shotgun. I felt it was wrong. Men in uniform being shot like animals, fish in a barrel. I couldn't see what prompted the shooting, nothing except hating Northern niggers. That was it plain and simple, but that was enough. Shooting went on maybe ten minutes. Then, we converged from all sides on the strip. We drug the bodies up along Lee, and ambulances arrived to take the wounded back to the bases. I know a few civilians were hurt coming out the Ritz when it started, but I think all the dead were nigger soldiers. Military trucks got there quick and hauled them away, dead and wounded.

Q: How many dead Negro soldiers did you see?

A: Got to have been at least fifteen. Can't say I counted every one. A couple of wounded got away, and they found them dead down in Samtown, under some houses. I was sent out to secure a body down there. A military truck came and picked that one up.

Q: What was said among you police officers afterwards?

A: About two days later, they got us officers together at city hall—all of us who were there that night. Reporters from all over the state were swarming the city, asking questions. The mayor was there, Chief Gray, and a General Davis, who was the only nigger general in the Army. They explained that the Japs and Nazis would love to get ahold of something like this, so mum was the word. We didn't have to guess what would happen to us if we talked to a reporter. Some of the guys were saying they thought the nigger instigators that night were working for the Japs, just to hurt the war effort. I knew that was bullshit. But I also knew to keep my mouth shut and my head down.

Q: Otis, do you know what happened to the bodies?

A: I heard they was shipped out at night by train. KC Southern has a yard here. Maybe you can find out where, but those boys at the train yard gonna be scared too.

Q: Understood. Many thanks, and I assure you this will be held in confidence.

I thanked Tullos. Once again, I acknowledged the risk he took. After he left the room, I turned to Roger. "I can't help but think about the stories my grandfather told about the White League in New Orleans. Them running the carpetbaggers out of town with guns, even cannons. This kind of shit never stops, does it?"

"Can't say much has changed in Macon. While I'm sad, I ain't surprised."

"You think our report will help any? Tell me the truth."

"Hard to say, with the war going on," Roger said. "But if anyone can change things, Roosevelt can. Look at the New Deal. No one would've believed he could have pulled that off."

———◆◆◆———

Later that day, I received a call from Reverend White asking me to come by his office. The four of us drove there, but I was asked to meet with him alone. We eyed each other in silence. The air was heavy and stubbornly moved by the electric fan. His voice was barely above a whisper, a slight sheen on his brow. "I need to discuss that note, Mr. Broussard. It's about the Easter Avengers. Things are getting close to a flashpoint, sir."

"Why are you telling me, Reverend? I'm here to investigate the past."

"The group has obtained a case of rifles from an inside contact out at Camp Claiborne. No ammo yet, but this could unleash the hounds of hell on all the colored folks around here. I have two of my churchmen inside the group. They are older, wiser men, leaders here. They've been trying to talk sense to some of the younger ones. Now this."

"What can I do about this, Reverend?" I asked. "Why are you talking to me?"

"I want you to meet with my two men. Talk to them. Tell them about the president's desire to see justice done. Maybe they can use what you say to calm this situation down before it's too late. We must put this off long enough that this insanity passes. Their blood must be allowed to cool. Killing McCollam or anyone else won't solve anything. Vengeance is mine saith the Lord. I got these two men here to talk to you. Will you speak to them? And swear to me that this stays between us."

I nodded my agreement, and Reverend White escorted me past my waiting colleagues and into the church sanctuary. He locked the doors behind us and asked me to sit on the front pew. Then, he walked into an anteroom behind the stage on which his pulpit was located. After disappearing briefly, he emerged with two gray-haired Negro men who sat beside me on the pew. Reverend White walked up the aisle and out the doors of the sanctuary, which he locked behind him. I was alone with the two men in the quiet of the sanctuary.

We looked into each other's eyes for several seconds until the taller one said, "We need to hear from you. Who sent you, and what they gonna do about all this? We're trying to calm these young men down, but we got to see that some justice is coming."

"Sir, it is true that I've been sent by Mrs. Roosevelt. She and the president want the truth. She put the FBI on the investigation." I showed them my badge and papers. "There are two FBI men sitting in the church office. The first Negro federal judge, Judge Hastie, has assisted me. The eyes of the nation are now on this town and what has happened here. But I can't tell you what the future will bring. What can I say to help prevent violence?"

"Mr. Broussard, some knuckleheads stole a case of Army rifles from the base. They haven't got ahold of the ammunition, but God help us if they do. Me and my friend here are deacons here. We're serving Reverend White, trying to defuse things. We don't want another Tulsa, Mr. Broussard. Those White devils up there killed over three hundred souls, burned houses, churches, businesses. Can we tell those young men the president is behind them, that he wants the killers brought in?" He looked intently at me for something he needed.

"Sir, tell them that the president is moving ahead. Ask them to hold off until this thing is over. That's the best I can do right now. Will that help?"

"Thank you, Mr. Broussard. We tryin' to stall them. We tryin' to get a couple of their leaders drafted into the service. Talked to a friend on the draft board. That would help a lot. We'll see. We tryin' to do what Reverend White wants us to do, head off a bloodbath."

The other Negro went to the window of the sanctuary and looked back at us with fear. "Who those men on the street?"

"No problem. They're FBI, protecting me and my colleague."

"FBI? You won't tell them about the guns, will you, sir?"

"I'm not down here for the Army or to see about stolen guns. What you told me and what I told you stays here." We walked back up the aisle and left the sanctuary.

Next, we needed to trace the rail shipment of the coffins. With the intercession of the White House through the regional office of the Interstate Commerce Commission, a meeting was scheduled for us to talk to the local agent of the Kansas City Southern Railway and to review whatever records might document a shipment that had taken place on or around January 11, 1942, according to the witnesses. To spare him the fear and concern expressed by other witnesses, we showed him our FBI badges and told him we were investigating possible contractor fraud against the War Department. The agent met us in an empty office next to the KCS Alexandria railyard. He gave us two boxes of shipping papers covering January 1942. Roger and I went through the boxes.

Within minutes, he handed me a folder with a bill of lading attached to the folder. "Here she is,' he said. "Eighteen wooden boxes containing truck parts bound for Camp Van Dorn, Woodville, Mississippi. Train to depart Alexandria January 12, 2:00 a.m. I think that's our coffins."

I read through the shipping documents. "This says they were picked up by the Army on the thirteenth. Roger, I guess we're heading to Mississippi."

I thanked the railway agent. Upon return to our hotel, I called Mrs. Roosevelt's office for assistance with Camp Van Dorn. No one there would open the door for us. We would have to force it open with the help of a higher power.

Our group left for Centreville the next morning. The trip to southwest Mississippi would take the better part of a day. We crossed the river at Natchez and drove down US Highway 61. We were scheduled to meet the base commander of Camp Van Dorn later that afternoon. As we drove down the spine of America through the sandy hills and kudzu, the events of Saturday night, January 10, 1942, were playing out clearly in my head. I knew I could tell the truth to Mrs. Roosevelt. Eighteen soldiers lost their lives on Lee Street that night. Their only offense was letting off steam in a violent race-crazed town in the Deep South. I was hopeful that somewhere on the forty-thousand-acre tract of Camp Van Dorn, we would find their bodies and maybe succeed in returning them to their families.

After stopping at the main gate at Camp Van Dorn, I presented our FBI documents and stood by the guard shack while a call was placed to verify my appointment. Lewis and Bannister showed their badges as well. I stood in the guard shack waiting on a call from the base commander, allowing us entry.

An Army bus pulled up behind us and stopped to discharge its passengers. A group of Negro troops filed off the bus. Suddenly, a local police car pulled beside the bus. A heavyset, White officer exited the passenger side while a slim, White officer exited the driver's side. They immediately started yelling at the colored troops, who argued with the officers rather than backing down. I could not hear the subject matter of the argument. The slim officer took out his nightstick and whaled away at the troops. The shouting increased. I ran outside the guard shack to intervene and help stop the fighting. The heavyset officer unholstered his revolver and fired one shot into the air. I froze. More MPs ran toward the gate, but they were more than a hundred yards away from the ruckus at that point.

Another shot exploded from the revolver of the heavyset officer. A Negro soldier fell to the pavement, his blood running out from a head wound. The slender officer drew his sidearm and pointed it at the head of a colored soldier he had clubbed lying on the ground before him. I drew my wallet from my coat and darted toward them, holding out my FBI badge. Bannister and Lewis drew their guns and ran with me toward the melee.

"Stop! FBI!" yelled Bannister. "Holster your sidearm officer! You're on federal property. What the fuck are you two doing?"

Both local police officers stopped, shocked to see three White men in suits pointing guns and waiving FBI badges. The Negro soldier on the ground scurried to the safety of the base gate. Army MPs swarmed over the area and separated the belligerents.

Medics burst through the gate with a gurney, but anyone could see the colored soldier lying on the ground was dead. The colored troops were put back on the bus, which took them into the camp. The MPs took the two police officers into a nearby building. The gates were lowered, and the base was placed on lockdown. Our meeting with the base commander was canceled. We drove back to Alexandria largely in silence.

——————◆◆◆——————

After calling the office of the first lady, we were instructed to return to Washington, D.C. and submit the statements and documents that we had gathered along with this report. I was called into Mrs. Roosevelt's office a few weeks later to discuss my investigation.

"Mr. Broussard, I've read your statements, the shipping documents and your excellent report. Job well done, sir. Terrible about the trouble you saw at Camp Van Dorn, but it just proves the need for your work. Did you know that the officer you saw shoot the soldier was the local sheriff?"

"It was murder, ma'am, plain and simple."

"Yes, all too common down there. I'm afraid there will be no prosecution." She opened a lower drawer on her desk, pulled out an

165

envelope and handed it to me. "Open it, Jimmy. More news from the Alexandria *Daily Town Talk*. More lynchings."

I read the headline aloud. "Two Negroes Found Hung in Rural Grant Parish—Dead Men A Part of Army Gun Theft Ring."

I never knew their names until I read them that morning in her office, but given the ages of the men, I knew the two men were the deacons who were trying to head off a race war in Central Louisiana—the ones who pleaded with me to seek justice for the Lee Street dead. Chief Gray of the Alexandria Police told the newspaper that the two had been under investigation for stealing guns from Camp Claiborne, but that his office received an anonymous call informing them of the lynching and the location of the bodies. The sheriff found empty gun cases from the US Army in a barn near the pecan tree where the two men were found hanging. The lynching had all the earmarks of a Klan murder. Only I knew of the deacons' involvement in the Easter Avengers. Nothing would be gained by telling Mrs. Roosevelt.

"Ma'am, we know there are eighteen bodies, probably buried somewhere at Camp Van Dorn. That's about all I accomplished. Any chance of bringing them home to their people?"

The first lady turned in her chair and looked out the window. Then, she turned back and faced me. With a sorrowful countenance, she said, "Five days before you saw Private Williams shot down at Camp Van Dorn, White workers at Alabama Dry Dock in Mobile rioted over having to work with Negroes. We had to send troops to stop it. They hung a Negro private at Fort Benning. A mob murdered a Negro soldier in Missouri. The McCollam murder is still festering. Do you know what happened after that murder you witnessed? The Negro troops were so angered, they tried to besiege the armory and grab rifles to start shooting. I'm afraid now is not the time to start digging up bodies at Camp Van Dorn. The South is a bomb waiting to explode, and we just can't afford a lit match. Not now, maybe after the war. Your report is on the president's desk. You have the president's deepest thanks, and mine as well."

I thanked her and left the White House. My gut was churning. Shame for my homeland burned inside. I wondered how many Lee Streets littered my land. Maybe every city in America had one. Once again, I thought of war, not the war raging overseas, but the war that had been ongoing in my land since 1861. I would join in that war. I would leave the peaceful precincts of Capitol Hill and become a prosecutor of the criminals waging a long bitter war against the America I loved, the one of Lincoln's better angels. There would be no medals, no glory. But I had no choice.

Hobby Shop

I f it had been up to him, the father would have never taken the boy there in the first place. But that boy—he'd wear you down. The kid could talk. He could whine. He could argue. There was a logic to it all; even the father would admit that. He had to give the kid his due. For a nine-year-old, this boy knew how to get his way. Rather than taking his son to a hobby shop to buy a model airplane, the father would have much preferred to take his boy to a gun shop to buy him a .22, something to learn on. But it was Christmas in America, and the kid had seen some model airplane in the back of a comic book. All he talked about was getting one of those for Christmas. It was the kind of model that flew around in a circle at the end of some strings, wires, something like that. The father, he didn't know anything about a plane that flew around on the end of a string.

The boy loved, loved anything, anything about World War II. He bugged his father until the father gave him all the ribbons and medals he earned during the war. The boy kept them in a cigar box with his most precious baseball cards. The son watched TV shows about the war, *Combat!* and *Twelve O'Clock High*. The war was all over the movies. He and his buddies played army in the woods behind their house. His grandmother gave him a picture book on the war written by Winston Churchill. He read it constantly.

The father didn't need to read books or watch TV shows about the war. He had lived it—close up. He knew what war was. He knew all about the Germans. He had killed Germans, young ones, like himself. He came home after it ended and tried to forget. He married and built a home, went to college. Then the children came, his two daughters and then the boy. They would be raised in a world without war. This was his hope. No need to talk about the war. He left the girls to their mother. He would take a keen interest in the boy, show him the ways of men. He'd teach him about guns, about hunting, how to track an animal. He bought a boat to take the boy fishing.

The boy didn't care to kill animals. He thought waiting for a fish to bite his hook was a bore. He wanted to stay home on weekends and play war with his buddies. They built forts in the woods, divided up into opposing forces. They'd ambush each other. They threw small rocks. Most of the time, no one was harmed, but not always. They used sharpened sticks or scrap lumber as swords. The boy won almost all his duels. He was quick with his hands.

The father pursued the boy like a spurned lover. The more the boy said no, the harder the father tried to win him over. The father secured a duck lease and built a blind. He shot ducks while the boy shivered in the dark, asking over and over when they were going home. He bought a retriever, a black lab named Blue. But he, and not the boy, was the one who ended up feeding the dog each night. One day, he saw the boy wearing his garrison cap, the one with the blue parachute patch sewn on the side. The boy ran past him and the dog into the woods.

The boy was drawn to pretty things. He saw a photo in his picture book of goose-stepping Nazis reviewed by Hitler and his gang. So well dressed and sharp, especially Himmler in his black dress uniform. In the photo, the sun was shining, and everything was in perfect order. The boy knew that these sharp-looking men had been the enemy his father had fought. But that was all he knew.

The boy knew nothing about National Socialism or the rest of that sorry lot. He just knew he liked how they looked on that sunny day in 1939. Another thing—he loved their tanks and planes. The Nazis built great-looking machines.

The father never planned not to tell his boy what he had done in the war. But the boy was just nine. He would wait a couple of years, maybe after they started the boy in history classes at his school. He'd tell him about jumping out of planes, about the Battle of the Bulge, about entering a nation destroyed by a war whose people had brought upon themselves. Maybe when the boy was a bit older, then he'd tell him about taking another man's life, maybe even tell him about the camps. But not now, no way. The boy should love hunting and fishing now. God, he would have loved hunting with his dad when he was nine. He'd just have to be patient, wait on the boy to get a little older.

The picture book had plenty of photos of German planes waging war across Europe. Junkers bombers over London, Messerschmitts taking on the Eighth Air Force, even jet planes years ahead of their time. The boy studied each plane with great care. The plane that captured his imagination was the Stuka dive bomber, its screaming siren sowing fear into panicked foes below. He saw himself in command of such a sleek and deadly machine, standing out from all other aircraft. Its inverted gull wings and screaming Jericho trumpet screeching out of a cloud bank to wipe out its enemies. He never thought about the why, just the what, the look, the outside. He imagined himself in a smart black uniform flying a Stuka. Boy, would that be great.

The father was sitting in his recliner reading *Field and Stream*. The boy brought him a comic book and pointed to an advertisement for a gas-powered model airplane. The boy had gone with a neighbor's family to an airpark where people flew such model airplanes. He had seen his friend down the street fly one, and now he wanted one for Christmas. The boy told the father that his friend's dad had helped get the model ready and had shown his friend how to fly the model in a circle. His neighbor's dad let the boy take a turn at flying a few circles. Maybe they could get one and fly it together. The father put the boy in the car and drove to the field where the models were flown. The city had converted a softball field into a field for flying these model airplanes on a string. A circular strip of asphalt had been poured for the models to take off and land. The father realized that flying models was something he had missed out on. Apparently, flying these gas-powered models on a string was sweeping the country. Otherwise, the city wouldn't have given up a softball field for an airpark.

The boy and his father went to the hobby shop in town, which sold flying model airplanes. His father talked to the man behind the counter while the boy stood next to the three models for sale. Each was made of plastic and was a faithful reproduction of the most famous fighting planes of the European theater—the British Spitfire, the American P-51 Mustang, and the German Stuka. The boy held each model in his hands and admired the small details captured in plastic. Behind the faux glass on each cockpit, a small pilot was in control of their killing machine. The boy tried to imagine himself in such a cockpit, flying into the sky to do battle. He grabbed the Stuka and went to his father. This was the model he wanted to fly.

The father looked nervously at the man behind the counter. He told the boy that maybe he should pick the Mustang. He told him that Mustangs had saved his life in a great battle with the Germans during Christmas of 1944. Wouldn't he rather fly one of those? But no, the kid knew what he wanted. He wanted the Stuka. The man behind the counter said the Stuka was wicked, but a real beauty.

It was Christmas. After all, it was just a model, and the kid was just nine. Okay, but we'll have to wait until Christmas to fly the plane. Maybe after Mother finishes serving dinner, then we can go to the airpark.

The son finished Christmas dinner and ran back into his room to retrieve his precious new gift. The fuselage and gull wings were painted forest green. The underside was a gray-blue to deceive antiaircraft guns firing below. Under the cockpit, a small plastic man wearing a plastic aviator's cap. This was a tiny version of himself, in command of a beautiful flying machine, free to go anywhere, open to new discoveries. He ran back to the dining room, where his father was rising from his chair. It was time for the maiden voyage. The father and the boy would take this voyage together. The boy ran to the garage with the Stuka under his arm. The father fetched his car keys and brought the small can of fuel along with the strings and hand control. They drove straight to the airpark.

The father read the instructions. Simple enough. You fill the tiny tank with fuel. One person stands in the center of the field and holds the hand control at the end of the strings, while the other person starts the engine and holds the plane in place on the ground. When the controller is ready, the plane is released. The controller allows the plane to become airborne and gently circles around with the hand controls, allowing the plane to fly until it runs out of fuel. Then, the controller gently guides the plane to lower levels as it slows and lands on the circular asphalt landing strip. No problem. The father showed the boy how to start the engine, and the father flew the plane on its maiden flight, circling around and around until it slowed and glided back to the landing strip.

The boy then marched to the center of the field. He picked up the hand control. He would do what his father had told him.

He would do just what his father had done, the same thing he had seen his friend's father do, the same thing he had done a few weeks ago at the airpark. His father started the Stuka's motor. The high-pitched whine struck his ears. The boy smiled ear to ear. He nodded for his father to release this beautiful machine. The Stuka soared into the air. The boy circled around in an arc. He felt a tug on the control and thought he should bring the Stuka a bit lower. He pointed the control just a bit toward the ground, but the Stuka suddenly pitched forward and dove sharply, crashing into the asphalt strip. It smashed into pieces. It was no more. The boy was breathless. He was shocked. He was stunned. His dream of the Stuka was shattered.

He was the pilot and had only himself to blame. There were no more words between the father and the boy that day.

J'Accuse!

I was driving my brother home from rehab when this whole mess started.

Tad slept for the first hour of our drive to his home, back to the life he almost lost. My brother's marriage had looked perfect on the outside. He had a thriving law practice. She was a stay-at-home mom with two bright, happy kids. So, it floored me when Amy asked me to be a part of an intervention team to get Tad to treatment. She wanted me to sit through the intense sessions of his family week near the end of his month-long stay. I said yes. A lot of dirty laundry and a few skeletons, but nothing I wouldn't expect from a young husband who leaned a little too heavily on the bottle. I volunteered to drive him home when he was discharged.

We sped through the thick hardwood forests toward our hometown. Tad awoke but stayed silent for several minutes as the orange leaves swirled around and back of us in the wake of moving air created by my car. He took a long drink from his water bottle, then looked at me and smiled.

"So, what's the biggest single thing you learned in there?" I asked.

"I learned that when I drink, I black out. That was huge. Every single time in the last five years or so, I blacked out. Automatic. My body can't handle it. If I keep it up, the next step is wet brain. I'm clear on that."

"I had no idea," I said. "Not until Amy called. Hell, I've had a few blackouts myself. By blackouts, how did that hit you? You lose the entire night or just part?"

"Depends. Toward the end, it was the entire night. But there are things I do recall, even in the middle of a binge, like it was yesterday. Like a lucid dream. Vivid. It's like my memory has been opened up. Things in the past that I haven't had access to. Now that my mind is clean, I see them clear as a bell."

"Pleasant, I hope?"

"Some. I won't deny having some good times. But other times are dark, like seeing a slaughtered animal or a murder. Shit like that. Can't get it out of my mind. Can't unsee it."

"Things you did? Or things you imagine?"

"Oh no, this shit's real."

"Such as?"

"You don't want to know, believe me."

He was right about that. I had signed up to help, but that job went so far. I was looking to end it at Tad's doorstep when I dropped him off in another hour. God knows I had had my own stuff to deal with—I didn't have much headspace left for serious baggage. But what could I say? I was here, and he was my kid brother. "It's up to you," I said. "Only if you want to share something. I'm here to listen."

"There are a couple of things I didn't bring up in family week. Amy didn't need to hear all this. For starters, I was raped by Father Riley at the rectory after church when I was thirteen."

Just like that—he said it like he was telling me about getting lost at camp or his dog dying. It crept up on me, the import of what had just spilled out of Tad's mouth. Just a sliver of doubt settled into my gut. "Come on, Tad! No shit?"

"It was Good Friday. I was the altar boy that day at the noon service. I started drinking about two weeks later. Remember when you and Dennis McCarthy stole his old man's beer? That was my first drink, and it felt so fucking good going down. Don't you remember getting me drunk that night? I puked all over the place."

"Sure, I remember the beer. Mom raised four kinds of hell with us. Never said a word to Dad. Thank God. But you never mentioned anything to me about Father Riley."

"What'd you expect me to say? Hey, Father Riley pulled my pants down and blew me? I was ashamed of what happened. Don't you remember a few years back when all the stuff came out about him in the papers? Riley was named along with three others. He died a couple of years before. I tried telling Mom right after it happened, but she thought I was crazy. You know her and the church. Had me thinking I made it up. Honestly, I shut it out until maybe two weeks ago. I was working with my therapist. She had me do a psychodrama about the traumas in my life. It just came out, that and more."

"Let's drop by the lake," I said. "We need to talk. We can sit down by the water. I want to hear what you have to say. Amy will wait. Go ahead; call and let her know."

The family lake house had always been a place of respite for the two of us. Our family spent most summers there. We opened it to youth groups from the church and the Boy Scouts on occasion. Our bond as brothers was forged in large part during long canoe rides and forest hikes around the lake. As college students, we brought our girlfriends out there. After I entered seminary for a year, I spent time there, alone in contemplation, wondering about my path. The place was like a living museum. Every painting, stick of furniture, and family photo spoke of good times spent together.

"No need to call her," he said. "We'll talk whenever I get back. Sure, Chuck, let's go to the lake house. Perfect." Tad slouched back and shut his eyes.

It was late October. The last of the red and yellow leaves were still hanging on up in the hardwoods. There was a north breeze blowing across the lake, so we stayed inside and drug out some kindling and firewood. Tad got a fire going. I popped a couple of Keurig cups in the machine. We sat before the fire and sipped our coffee.

"Tell me what happened with Riley. Did he set you up? Groom you?"

"Oh yeah. He'd take me fishing, camping," he said. "Don't you remember? He ran the CYO and trained the acolytes. There was another kid, Timmy Fisher. I think he was after him too. Timmy was an altar boy with me. We never talked about it. After that thing on Good Friday, I started pulling away. It scared me, not of him. I was scared of me. I kind of liked it. What would I do? What was I capable of? Then, the crap with Mom."

"Tad, I'm so sorry. How did this affect your faith? Don't you have to have a relationship with God to work the AA program?"

"For some reason, I never held Riley's actions against God. I've always believed, and talked to God, even when I was a blackout drunk. But the church; fuck the church. After all the shit they hid, not just around here, everywhere."

I rose and stirred the fire with a poker. "To think at one time, I wanted to join them," I said. "What a mistake that would've been. I gave a year of my life to them in seminary and all the years leading up to that. The summers as a camp counselor, the mission trips in college. If I had known what happened to you back then, I could never have conceived of such a thing. Riley never came on to me."

"So, tell me, why did you really leave seminary?" he asked. "What happened to change your mind?"

"Nothing specific. I started wondering about my life as a parish priest, trying to imagine growing old in some parish, alone. Law school started percolating in my brain. After a while, I knew I wasn't cut out for it."

"So, nothing happened to make you change your mind?" Tad rose and stood at the picture window overlooking the lake. Then, he shot a stare back at me. "You sure about that?"

"Yeah, I'm sure," I said. "Why do you ask?"

"Remember when Amy and I spent a long weekend up here with you? We all drank and played cards. You remember?"

"We were all on spring break. My last semester in seminary. I swear I didn't cheat in that game. I won fair and—"

"No, after that, after I blacked out on the couch. Remember screwing my wife?"

"What the hell are you saying? That Amy and I had sex? Are you out of your mind? I'm your brother, Tad. I could no more sleep with your wife than fly to the moon." How could this be happening? He was passed out cold that night. "Is this something your therapist helped you remember?"

"She didn't help me remember anything. It's clear as day in my mind now that I'm sober. I was lying on the couch and woke up. I looked over the top of the couch straight into that first bedroom. I saw the two of you. I must have slipped back into sleep or whatever it was, but I now see it clear as day. A couple of weeks later, you told the family you were leaving seminary for law school."

"Have you confronted Amy about this?" I paced around the living room, trying to keep from screaming.

"Not yet. I may or may not bring it up with her later. I wanted you to hear it first."

"Good lord, Tad. Amy'll flip out. How about your therapist? What did she say? Surely, she must have told you how to handle this."

"She was guiding me when this memory came out. We discussed not even bringing it up. The ninth step tells us not to dredge things up if, by doing so, we'll hurt others. This is a close one. It's not about me. It's about what the two of you did."

"Look," I said, "you're a prosecutor. You know about false memories. Remember the McMartin Pre-school fiasco out in California?"

"But those were children," he said. "I'm a grown man, and I know what I saw."

"Tad, you just got out of a month in a rehab unit. You told me an hour ago that you had problems with blackouts, memory loss. Now, after your psychodrama therapy, you not only recall being raped but witnessing your wife and brother committing adultery."

"Blackouts? You just admitted to me you had blackouts, too. I could ask you the same question. Maybe it's wiped from your memory. All three of us were smashed that night. What, maybe three, four bottles of wine? On top of a couple of joints."

"So, what if Amy backs me up?" I asked.

"I'd expect her to deny it," he said. "That's why I might not even get her involved. I don't want to wreck my marriage, not after all I put her through already."

I wheeled around and stood eye to eye with my brother. "So, what do you propose? To just dump this on me, and we just pretend all this never came up?"

"We've been doing it for what—fifteen years already?"

I marched over to an etagere loaded with family photos and grabbed one from the christening of Tad's oldest child. Amy was still wearing her pregnancy dress; smiles beamed from proud parents and grandparents. I walked back to Tad and handed him the framed picture.

"Tell me, look at those people and tell me if you see moral

monsters who can commit mortal sins and cover up that kind of betrayal? Seriously, Tad. Are Amy and I monsters to you?"

"No, you're both humans who got really drunk one night and did what humans do when they're drunk."

"Tad, you've built a box here. It's like one of those escape rooms, but no way out. If you won't tell Amy, then we're just caught here with nowhere to go."

"Look, this family has plenty of secrets we'll never face." Holding the photo in front of his chest, Tad pointed to it. "Look here at these nice people in the picture. Here's a lady who convinced her young son that he was crazy. Rather than protecting him, standing up for him, she gaslighted him, threw him under the bus. Then, here's Dad, smiling but checked out, he and his scotch, his valium. Shucks, I meant high blood pressure medicine. Oh, and here is the big brother. The good one. The chosen one, almost a priest. He gets his little brother drinking at thirteen. Knocks up his college sweetheart. Has everyone thinking he's perfect. But no, turns out he's human after all."

"You know I never claimed to be perfect. But I damned sure didn't have sex with Amy, sober or drunk. No way."

"Sorry. I know what I saw."

I pulled out my cell phone. "If you won't call her," I said, "I will. Come over here and just listen. Don't say a word. I won't tell her you're here. I'll put her on speaker. Listen to what she says, and maybe you'll see I'm right." I called Amy's cell.

"Amy, this is Chuck. We're at the lake. Tad's down by the water. Look, you and me, we need to talk."

"Why are you calling? Is Tad okay?"

"This isn't about Tad. It's about us, well, kind of. Tad's therapist had him do some psychodramas in the hospital, and now he claims to remember the two of us having sex one night when we were all

180

drunk. Remember that weekend we spent spring break at the lake house?"

"I remember the weekend, but I assure you that nothing like that took place. Are you kidding me? Who does he think I am? Who does he think you are? You two are like clones. You're inseparable. Where is he? Get him on the phone."

"Look, we were talking about blackouts and how memories can be distorted. We both have had them when we drink. I can't recall anything like that ever happening, but I may have blacked out. All three of us were wasted that night."

"Chuck, you two may black out, but I damned sure do not. God! You sound like your mother. That woman lives to convince people that they're going crazy, that they are seeing and hearing things that don't exist, or that they didn't see something that does exist. Get him on the phone. Please. His children are waiting to see him." I shot a look at Tad, who turned away toward the fire.

"He's down at the water. Let me try to sort this thing out, Amy. We won't be too long. But Amy, there's something else."

"Good grief, let me hear it."

"He also remembered that he was molested by Father Riley when he was an acolyte."

"Good God! What next? Why didn't we hear all this in family week? I've got him an appointment next week with a therapist we both know. Just get him home, Chuck. We need him home tonight. Please."

I walked down to the water and stood by Tad, looking at the sun going down over the lake. "Let's grab some paddles and go down to the boathouse," I said. "Maybe take a short spin." Tad nodded, and we walked down together.

We slipped the canoe into the cove and rowed toward the dam and weir at the other end of the lake. We worked our paddles in synchrony—not a word between us. We neared the dam and scared up a huge blue heron. Heavy rain filled the lake the day before. Water was pouring over the weir. Our canoe coasted silently to a stop, only the sound of falling water.

"You remember that Caprice station wagon Mom drove?" I asked. "The one with the rear-facing backseat."

"Sure. You'd get me back there alone on those trips home from the lake and whup up on me. Dad would be driving, sipping his scotch."

"Mom would yell like crazy for us to stop, but we were too far away," I said. "And remember, there was an up and down switch for the rear window. We'd drive 'em crazy just sending the back glass up and down."

Tad laughed and reached out to touch my shoulder. "How about the sock puppet shows we'd put on for cars behind us?" he asked. "Used our dirty socks. Think how freaked out drivers following us must've been? We laughed until we hurt."

He swirled his paddle gently in the dark water, lifting it like a dipper. The drops made tiny circular waves on the still surface. He locked eyes with me. "I love you, Chuck. I love Amy, but I saw what I saw."

I said nothing.

A large fish broke water a few feet behind me. Tad pointed to the ripples left in its wake. He twisted around and glanced back at me, his face beaming. "Look there, a big one. You see him?"

I dug my paddle deep into the lake water and pulled. "I learned a few things in seminary from a wise professor. He told me forgiveness was simply choosing to act as if the other person didn't owe you anything. Like cancelling a past debt someone owes you because collecting it will probably kill you. That made sense to me."

"Yea, that makes sense. I can do that," he said. And after a pause, "But I can't unsee what I saw."

"So, you can forgive my debt? Wipe the account clean?"

"Yea, I suppose I can."

"And Amy, can you forgive hers, too?"

He nodded and looked toward the setting sun.

I dipped my paddle into the dark water, got a good purchase, and turned us back toward the lake house.

Minor Miracles

r. Jimmy Barton sat waiting, bathed in the filtered sunlight. Before him lay a sea of life. Scores of happy parents held their babies aloft, beaming with pride and joy. They held balloons, flower bouquets and poster boards bearing their child's birth photo. New mothers beamed; smiling fathers were tan and athletic. The female babies sported colorful bows. A spirit of celebration and satisfaction filled the air. But Jimmy's attention was elsewhere. All he could think of was getting on his jet and flying with his voluptuous and witty public relations director to his condo in Aspen for some late-spring skiing.

This happy scene was one he viewed annually as a regular part of his public relations program. His clinic, the South Texas Fertility Institute, sponsored the event annually for all the new parents who had come to experience the joy of parenthood through his treatments. In addition to thanking his patients, Jimmy gave a talk on the latest developments in the field of reproductive medicine. It was held in the atrium of his office building located in Houston's sprawling Texas Medical Center, where he held the unchallenged distinction of being the top man in high-risk fertility treatment.

Dr. Barton was the fertility doctor of last resort—and had the highest fee. If Jimmy couldn't make it happen for you, nobody could. That's how he saw it, and that's the message his lover and PR director, Jackie Travis, constantly and persuasively reiterated.

After the crowd settled down, Jackie stepped to the microphone to introduce Jimmy.

"Welcome, everyone, to our annual baby shower we call Minor Miracles. We here at the South Texas Fertility Institute know that every one of your precious babies is indeed a miracle and a gift from God. We also believe that God must work through people, and in this case, the Lord has chosen to work through the man I am here to introduce.

"To you who are family to us, our patients, you know and love Jimmy Barton. But for those who may be first-time visitors today, let me give you a brief introduction to this extraordinary man, my boss. Dr. Barton is a Texas native, hailing from Port Arthur, who attended Lamar University in Beaumont as an undergraduate. He graduated with highest honors from UT Medical School at Galveston in 1978 and went on to complete his residency in obstetrics and gynecology at the Cedars-Sinai Hospital at UCLA Medical School in 1982, where he began to develop a passion for the treatment of those wishing to parent children. Dr. Barton completed his fellowship at the prestigious University of Cincinnati in reproductive endocrinology and came back to the Texas Medical Center to establish his fertility practice, which draws patients from the world over. He is a fellow of the American Society of Reproductive Medicine.

"In recent years, he helped pioneer the latest technology for pre-implantation genetic diagnosis of potential birth defects in fertilized embryos and holds numerous patents in this field. In addition to his constant work in medicine and technology, Dr. Barton is active in shaping the evolving medical ethics in this field. Just last month, he appeared on PBS with noted television host Bill Moyers to discuss the challenging moral and ethical questions we face every day in our practice. This is the topic he will speak about today. Friends, Dr. Jimmy Barton!"

Jimmy rose and walked to the podium, soaking in the loud applause. He smiled at the beaming Jackie Travis and thought about getting her alone in his hot tub after a day on the slopes. He brushed back his shock of white hair, looked slowly over the crowd of smiling parents and said softly, "Thank you, everyone, and thank you, Jackie. What a scene today—all these smiling faces—especially the tiny ones—I never get tired of seeing all this life in one place. It's what makes me want to get up in the morning. Thank you. You're so kind. Thank you."

The applause died down, and the guests took their seats in the folding chairs set out for the event. Dr. Barton began his prepared talk.

"Just yesterday, a friend and colleague from the American Society of Reproductive Medicine sent me an email containing a link to a YouTube posting from a reality program starring (and I use that word loosely) Nadya Suleman, whom we have all come to know as Octomom. Despite my revulsion at this sad spectacle that has played out in the media, which had done untold damage to the reputation of reproductive medicine in general, I chose to click on the link, mainly because a highly respected colleague suggested I watch it.

"The show involves filming daily slices of life for this young woman, who not only must attempt to parent the eight babies recently born to her as a result of in vitro fertilization, but she must also care for the six children she bore previously, all IVF babies. The YouTube clip featured a sequence where Octomom brought her brood to a park for an outing with the film crew. During this chaos, her IVF four-year-old can be seen and heard pitching a fit, as four-year-olds are wont to do. But this young child can distinctly be heard calling her mother a 'bitch.' I sat there stunned. This disgusting episode summed up what is so terribly wrong with

Octomom and the medical professionals who knowingly caused this ethical train wreck. What this clip summed up for me was what we who help create life must continually hold up as the crucible of all our ethical decisions in this field, this question: What will be the ultimate outcome for the child who is born? Where will the child live? Who will care for the child? Will the child be loved and cared for properly? These are critical questions. I suspect that the doctors who brought fourteen IVF children into the world for Octomom failed to ask any of these important questions.

"In these past months since Octomom surfaced, I have fielded more ethical questions about reproductive medicine than at any time in the last thirty years. I am afraid that Octomom is doing to reproductive medicine what O. J. Simpson did to the legal system. Our field has always been one filled with ethical dilemmas. At first, there were huge religious and moral concerns voiced over the basic notion of aiding the reproductive process. We had to overcome accusations of playing God. Questions abound concerning stem cell research and the cold storage of embryos for long periods. The use of surrogates in child birthing has led to thorny ethical and legal disputes. The issues of economic class and availability of treatment are hotly debated. As a result of these questions, the American Society of Reproductive Medicine and the American College of Obstetrics and Gynecology have promulgated numerous guidelines to assist fertility practitioners in operating a thoroughly ethical clinic for the best interests of the patients and the babies they will eventually parent. I am proud to have served on the committees that developed these guidelines. The South Texas Fertility Institute has strictly adhered to these rules from day one of our practice.

"All of you who have been through our program know the rigorous history we take, and some of you were determined enough to be parents that you went through psychological evaluations and counseling as required by the guidelines. My message to you today concerning the questions raised by Octomom is this: There are ethical rules in our field, and there are fertility doctors who strictly adhere to those rules. You can rest assured that here at South Texas Fertility Institute, we will continue to do so. We will continue to ask that most important question: What about the child? Thank you for your trust. I will never betray it."

Jimmy soaked up the enthusiastic applause and waved to the adoring parents. He shook hands with his office staff and some parents sitting near the stage. He took time to pose for photos with beaming parents and babies.

"I'm leaving for Hobby," Jackie said. "Your pilot has a three o'clock slot for takeoff. If you leave the office in thirty minutes, traffic down I-45 should be fine."

"I need to run upstairs," he said. "No more than thirty minutes. Shake some martinis for takeoff."

She smiled and squeezed his forearm lightly, then moved away. They exchanged a furtive, but knowing glance; their affection remained hidden from the gleeful parents.

Jimmy headed for the elevator to drop by his office one last time before leaving for a week. As he stood waiting for the doors to open, he heard a voice from behind, a woman calling him by another name.

"James. James. Can I talk to you a minute?" she asked softly. The name was out of place. He had been called James in another life, a very long time ago.

Jimmy Barton turned around. He stood transfixed as he locked eyes with Bonnie Adams, his former fiancée from his college days in Beaumont. She presented her hand in friendship. "James, how are you? Do you recognize me? Can I call you James? That's what you are to me, you know. I can't call you Jimmy."

"Bonnie. Wow. Of course, I recognize you! You look lovely."

This was not a lie. She wore her graying red hair very long, pulled together down her back, and she still had a shapely if not slightly matronly body. She wore a linen sundress on this bright spring day and held a straw sun hat in her hand.

"What are you doing here in Houston?" he asked. "How long has it been? I think we talked a few years ago, right?"

"It's been a few years. I think we talked last when you were leaving your second wife, Sandy? I was going through a lot of stuff with Frank in Austin. Maybe the early nineties?" She stepped closer to him. "I came here to see you. I saw this event on your website. I figured you might have a few minutes after your talk, so I drove down from Fredericksburg. I left a friend running the gallery. I need to speak to you in private." She put her hand on his forearm and stared straight into his eyes. She meant business.

"Sure. We can go up to my office. We'll have the place to ourselves. Everyone else is down here. I was just stopping by the office myself. I'm leaving later this afternoon for a vacation, so I can spare a few minutes. I wish we had more time. Maybe we could have lunch sometime?" The elevator doors parted, and they ascended to his office.

In the space of four floors, Jimmy's other life, the one he kept stashed in a small, dark room in the attic of his memory, played out. Bonnie and James had lived in a small, rundown duplex in the barrios of Beaumont, Texas. The year was 1973, and James was a pre-med student at Lamar University with a tremendous determination to make the grades that would send him to medical school. It would be his ticket out of the life he had been born into in Port Arthur. His daddy worked in a local chemical plant, and his mom was a server at the city's best steakhouse. The place was revolting. There was a good reason why Janis Joplin ran as far and as hard as she could from Port Arthur. He wanted to do the same.

When he was a sophomore, he met Bonnie. She was a freshman from Huntsville, with wild red hair and a stunning figure. She studied art history and had a job in the art department modeling nude for art students. With her modeling earnings and some money from her folks, they had enough cash to afford their little duplex. He studied and she worked, both striving toward his future in medicine, somewhere way beyond the barrios. They were young and on their own. Everything was great until Bonnie turned up pregnant. This was prior to *Roe v. Wade*. Abortion was illegal in Texas and all the surrounding states. James talked to a friend who had taken his girlfriend to Houston, where a doctor performed abortions. His buddy said it was no big deal, there and back the same day, like nothing ever happened. The cost was $300. Steep but not impossible. James revealed this to Bonnie, who agreed it was for the best.

Jimmy would never forget sitting in a bar around the corner from the abortion clinic. As he sipped his beer that hot Houston afternoon, he sat there among real men, men who had real lives—wives, children, mortgages; men who went to work, who didn't run away; men who were stand-up guys. He wondered what they would think of him if they knew why he was there, sitting in that bar. For just a second, he flashed on a picture of Bonnie on that table, her feet in stirrups, but he shut that thinking down quickly.

When he picked her up after about an hour, she seemed fine. They made small talk on the way back to Beaumont. She went to bed early and slept late the next morning. He recalled she had some minor bleeding but no major complications. The complications began in their relationship. He started cheating on her a few weeks later with another pre-med student. Bonnie caught them together at the duplex. Her nude modeling session had been canceled, so she came home earlier than expected. She went home to Huntsville and transferred to UT in Austin the next semester. Surprisingly, they remained distant friends and confidantes over the years. Jimmy prided himself on maintaining old friendships. He couldn't bear the idea of being hated by anyone. He tried hard to be liked by his two ex-wives.

The elevator doors opened on his well-appointed reception area. They walked down the hall and entered his wood-paneled office. He walked over to two leather armchairs that sat before his mahogany desk and asked her to sit down next to him. Photos of his four adult children adorned the wall behind his desk. The absence of any mothers in the photos was a necessary omission, owing to his two divorces.

She took it all in after sitting down in the leather chair. Then she looked directly into his eyes. "James, I've come to ask you for a favor. It's not for me, of course; it's for my daughter, Hailey, and her partner."

"Bonnie, of course I'll help her. Just tell her to call my staff. What are their names? I'll get them in right away. No problem."

"That's it. You've already seen them. They've been tested. They're ready to go through with it, but you refused to treat them. That's why I came today."

"What do you mean? We refused them? Who are they? Why did I refuse?"

"My daughter is Hailey Walker, and the father will be Troy Calhoun. You saw them about three or four months ago. You had them go for a psych eval, and you told them afterward you couldn't help them and refunded their twenty-thousand-dollar deposit. I need you to help them, and I'm pleading with you." Her voice cracked slightly.

Jimmy Barton arose and walked around his desk to his computer terminal. "Let me look at it. I can't keep all the names straight. You said 'Walker.' What's her date of birth? I'll bring it up on my computer—we're paperless around here. I'll look up her chart."

As he typed in the date, his cell phone rang. "Hey there. Yes, I'm through with downstairs, but I'm up here in the office with a patient. Yes, it's important. But I'll be leaving shortly. Tell Dave to try to move our takeoff slot back. We can make the time up once we're in the air. I'll call you when I grab a cab. Well, if I catch the rush hour, we'll just get up there late. I'll call you when I get out of here." He hung up and turned the cell phone off. He read Hailey Walker's file, including the report of the clinical psychologist who evaluated her and the prospective father.

He walked back and sat in the leather armchair across from his former fiancée. "Your daughter apparently lied to me about her intentions for the child. She admitted to the psychologist that she is in a long-term relationship with another woman and that Mr. Calhoun is really nothing more than a sperm donor. That's a problem, Bonnie. It's not only the lesbian relationship but the lying. Whenever I find deception, I make it a policy to end the doctor-patient relationship at that point. I'm sorry, believe me," he said.

"James Barton, are you telling me that you insist on total integrity from all your patients, no exceptions? You, of all people? Hailey and Jane have been together for eight years. They both have advanced degrees and own a home together in Austin. They'll make wonderful parents. But does that really matter to you?"

"Listen, I'm sure she's a fine person, but when we have deception in a crucial area like this, we don't know what else there may be out there. It's for the protection of the child, Bonnie." He sighed heavily.

"James, they've tried everything, doctor after doctor. You're their last chance, and I'm asking you, pleading with you. Please, James, if you won't do it for her, do it because you goddamned well owe it to me. Remember, James, I bent my ethics for you. I fucking climbed on that table for you and your career. Now, I'm asking you to do this for my daughter."

Jimmy got up and walked behind his desk. He looked out his window at the downtown skyline. How he wanted to be flying off to Aspen at this moment, sipping a martini with his integrity intact with Jackie squeezing the inside of his thigh.

"James, look at me. I want to ask you a question. Have you ever performed an abortion? You know, in your training?"

He turned and looked upon the angry woman he once had planned to marry.

"Bonnie...look. I don't know what to say. I'm sorry about what happened between us. I'm sorry we never talked about it. Haven't I told you that I'm sorry? I felt terrible, but I thought it was the best thing to do at the time for both of us."

"For both of us? Or for your career? I don't recall having much say in it at the time. Look at me. I want to know. Have you performed an abortion?"

"Of course, I have. We're required to learn all therapeutic techniques during residency. I performed several during my residency. What's your point?"

"Have you ever done one on a scared young girl? What did her face look like? Did you look at her face when you inserted that cold suction device?" Bonnie trained her angry eyes upon the man she once loved. "James, you owe me. Now please, do what I ask."

Dr. Barton walked over to his mahogany desk and picked up his handheld recorder. "Mary, please call patient Hailey Walker. She lives in Austin. Schedule her for an IVF workup. She'll need new labs. We'll need to contact the father also. Look in the chart for his contact info." He put the recorder down and looked at Bonnie. He nodded slightly and said, "Consider it done."

Jimmy fidgeted and looked at his watch. His crew was going over the pre-flight check on the tarmac at Hobby. His beeper was on vibrate mode and was going off for the third time in the last five minutes since the cell call. "Okay, Grandma. I guess you'll have your grandchild." He smiled as she pressed his hands into hers, squeezed them hard, and gently kissed them.

Bonnie teared up. "Thank you, Dr. Jimmy Barton. I swear to you that you're doing something so right. Please know it. I give you my word." They rose and walked out of the office, shaking hands once more on the ground floor. Bonnie disappeared into the crowd of happy parents.

On the cab ride to the airport, Dr. Jimmy Barton pondered his promise to Bonnie. This had been an unpleasant shakedown, emotional extortion. He could simply sabotage the entire IVF procedure. After all, results are never guaranteed. He began to resent being shamed by Bonnie into doing something he didn't want to do. He had come to believe that God was working through him in his practice. God doesn't like a shakedown.

A Town Named Out of Spite

"It all started with a hanging," said the old man wearing a Cat hat. "Two niggers from up North tried to stir up our niggers by starting a school after the Civil War. The Klan hung 'em and burned their school. The carpetbaggers and niggers running this state back then didn't appreciate that. So, instead of being named Red River Parish, we got named Grant Parish. Instead of Calhoun's Landing, we got renamed Colfax for Grant's vice president. Rubbed it in our faces. After all the maps were made and such, there was nothing to be done but to live with it. But here in *this* parish, we've always made sure those bastards who named us knew we weren't changing one damned bit. They teach you that down in Baton Rouge?"

"Thanks for the history lesson," I said. "No, can't say I've heard that one." I returned to reading my paper. I just wanted to eat my breakfast in peace, but it was impossible that morning. Too many angry men spouting off after reading the latest news from the Colfax Chronicle. It was the summer of 1959, and Hooker Rhodes' Café was packed every morning by small groups of farmers and working men holding forth on the latest outrage. This had been going on since the Brown decision a few years earlier. The outbursts were fueled by a venom toward negroes and the federal government, which I had not seen in my short life. It seemed to me the whole state was going crazy. In the governor's race, one of the leading candidates was making the case that the federal government was flanged up with the commies to mongrelize the citizenry and destroy our way of life. One of his posters was prominently displayed by Hooker behind the lunch counter, where I couldn't avoid looking at it. The poster depicted a large negro man lurking menacingly over a little white girl. The only text read, "Vote Rainach Governor."

Between the hate-filled grumbling and the stomach-turning art, for me, a peaceful breakfast wasn't in the cards. But I kept my mouth shut. First, I wanted to keep my summer job at the courthouse. Second, there was no other eating place in town. So, I sat on my stool at the counter, kept my face in my paper and ate my breakfast.

At the table behind me were four men I had known all my life—Elmer Cook, Floyd Smith, "Tiny" La Croix and Mitchell Thompson, all muscle for our local Klan. Elmer ran a used car lot and loan company, which catered to mostly poor white sharecroppers and occasionally a negro family, who had scraped together a down payment. The others were his posse. The talk was Elmer made his real money in shady card games held in the back room of his car lot office.

"God damn that Uncle Earl," shouted Elmer. "First, the bastard signs up all them niggers to vote, then he starts whoring in the French Quarter every night of the week and now the governor of the great State of Louisiana is locked up in a looney bin. We got the feds trying to put niggers in the New Orleans schools, another Little Rock. Mark my words; they'll try here before long.

"Only one looking out for us is Rainach. You see where Willie is going from parish to parish, striking those coons off the rolls? Hell, it was all a fraud from the start. None of them qualified to vote. Ain't no way in hell.

"Floyd, I got a hundred Rainach posters in my truck. Put them up around town this morning. Tiny, you and Mitch go put some over in Dry Prong and Pollock. Wille's speaking at the courthouse at noon tomorrow. Spread the word. Tell the boys over there to round up all their people. We want a big crowd."

I was on summer break from LSU and had been home only a few weeks. My father had arranged for me to work in the office of the Grant Parish Clerk of Court. It kept me out of our fields that summer. My father thought working in the clerk's office would be a good introduction to the local legal system. I was set to enter law school in the fall.

While I was grateful for the job, a lot about my hometown was starting to grate on my conscience. I learned in Dr. T. Harry Williams' class on the Civil War and Reconstruction that everything I had been taught in school had been a lie. The war wasn't about economic domination by the North, but about slavery, plain and simple. The slaves weren't happy and content. The Klansmen weren't honorable gentlemen fighting for their rights, but white supremacists spreading terror and death. Reconstruction had been a brief candle, extinguished by violent white power. I had been raised in a carefully constructed bubble where everything made sense, but that bubble had been cracked open for me during my time in Baton Rouge. It took all I had to come back home that summer, try to keep my head down and my mouth shut.

I finished breakfast and walked around the corner to the courthouse where I was assigned to Mrs. Funderburk, keeper of the conveyance and mortgage records. I spent my workdays as a scribe, checking those records for liens, judgments or other items that could be a cloud on a title for a prospective buyer. My day was spent pouring over dusty record books, looking for clouds as sweat gradually worked its way through my undershirt to the pressed white cotton shirt my mother laid out for me each morning.

By closing time at four-thirty, I was seeing double and had sweat rings under each arm and around my collar.

I stood over the index of vendors. Working next to me was the only unmarried woman in the office, Julie Van Horn. We were the only employees under the age of thirty and had been classmates at Colfax High School. "The natives are restless over at the café," I said. "They're ready to burn a cross, just to let off steam. All this crap about communism and the feds. Senator Rainach has really got their backs up. I could hardly eat breakfast this morning. Now they're plastering those ridiculous posters all over the parish."

"I hear he's coming tomorrow. His opening campaign rally for governor," she replied.

"Yeah, at noon. I think I'll pass. Too many white sheets in one place for me." A secret smile passed between us. We returned to our reading and note-taking.

The morning of the rally was a true Louisiana dog day, ninety degrees by ten o'clock. By eleven, my shirt was soaked. Through the courthouse windows, I caught an occasional glance of Rainach's men nailing posters to the oak trees and erecting a temporary podium for their white savior. Trucks equipped with loudspeakers prowled the city streets, announcing the rally. Around eleven, they began repeatedly playing Dixie, which blared right outside our office. As the busy work outside continued toward noon, my shirt got wetter. A lump formed in my stomach. I wanted to gag. Julie and I exchanged smirks, head shakes and rolled our eyes at each other.

I did not intend to go to the rally that morning. I had seen and heard enough of Rainach on TV. His voter purge was all over the papers. I planned to go out the back door and walk over to Hooker Rhodes' Café for lunch. I'd have no problem getting served since everyone else in town would be at the rally. I can't say what made me turn right and go out the front door to the rally. When I walked outside, the whole courthouse lawn was filled with Rainach supporters. Willie was standing on the wooden podium with several local politicians and town fathers. As Dixie finished playing, Hooker Rhodes, also Mayor of Colfax, introduced him. The crowd roared with vigorous clapping, hoots and whistles. The loudspeakers blasted "Dixie" once again, while Willie took in the adulation and waved to the friendly crowd. I was standing about thirty feet away from the podium, just a few feet away from a historical marker about the Colfax Riot, which reads:

Colfax Riot

On this site occurred the Colfax Riot in which three white men and 150 negroes were slain. This event on April 13, 1873 marked the end of carpetbag misrule in the South.

Willie let the crowd settle, then stood erect and looked at them for a few seconds in dead earnest. "Ladies and gentlemen," he began, "I am so happy and proud to be here in Colfax today and to be a warrior in the great struggle for the soul of our state and our nation. This place, your fine city, holds a very special place in this struggle, and a very special place in my heart. It should hold a special place in the heart of every citizen of Louisiana and the United States of America. In this city, on this very spot, the good people of Louisiana said 'Enough! Enough to outside control! Enough to rule by central government! Enough to forced mixing of the races!' It was on this very spot, in April of 1873, that the common people rose up, and threw out the Yankee carpetbaggers! As this marker shows, this brave act marked the end of tyranny here in the South! That's what I'm trying to do for you again, but I want to do it this time without bloodshed! I want to do it through the ballot box!" The place exploded with applause and cheers. The loudspeakers fired up "Dixie" once more while the crowd sang along and clapped.

I was standing by the marker, which I had seen unveiled nine years earlier when I was just a schoolboy. In the following years, the marker had gone unnoticed by me and most of the town. No one ever mentioned the Colfax Riot in my history classes, even at LSU. I read the words of the marker again, maybe for the first time. Something clicked inside my brain. It had to do with the numbers—150 negroes versus three whites. 150-3. Something wasn't right. Just what the hell kind of "riot" was this? 150-3? When the music stopped, Willie was about to hold forth again.

I wanted to yell out, say exactly what I was thinking. Before anything came out of my mouth, I heard someone yell, "Senator Rainach! Excuse me, sir. I have a question. How can you have a riot where the numbers are 150 to 3? That ain't a riot, sir. That's a massacre." The questioner was Benny Lee, a young negro about my age. I knew him from my childhood. He was the son of the lady who made drapes for us at our farmhouse. His dad worked with my father on our farm during hay bailing. Benny and I had tossed bails together, ate lunch in our fields together.

Benny was standing apart from the crowd on the other side of the marker from where I stood. His timing was perfect. The crowd was briefly flummoxed. Even Rainach stood speechless for a few seconds. Then, deep grumbling began among his supporters.

"Shut up, nigger!" Someone in the crowd yelled,

"Boy, our Louisiana Commerce Department put it up on this official marker," Willie said. "So, it's accurate, rest assured." The crowd began to surge toward Benny. I saw two sheriff's deputies converge around Benny and grab both of his arms as they hustled

200

him around the corner of the courthouse and away from Willie's speech. I stayed and listened to the rest of what Willie had to say. After his speech, I walked toward the café. Glancing down the side of the courthouse, I saw the two deputies drag Benny out of the side entrance and shove him into the back seat of a waiting Buick. Elmer Cook was driving. Two of his posse sat on either side of Benny. The back of Benny's head grew smaller in my sight as the car sped south out of town.

A knot formed in my stomach. Cold fear spread down my spine. Where was that car taking him? What was I witnessing? Exactly what should I do? What was my duty? A man had spoken his mind. I see him manhandled by deputies and rushed away by Klan members. No use going to the sheriff. I stood for minutes just staring blankly in the direction of the Buick. I was a twenty-one-year-old white man, a college student, still a mere youth in the eyes of the adults who ran my town. I did what a youth would do. I drove back to our farm to speak to my father.

Father was working on a tract of land over the levee near the riverbank. He and two negro hands were clearing debris left over from the spring flood of the Red River. I parked my car and walked across the cleared red earth to where they were eating lunch under a pecan tree. I told him about the rally, and what I had seen.

"You tell anyone what you saw?" he asked.

"No way I could go to the sheriff and say anything. Didn't know what to do. I came straight out here. Momma told me where you were working."

Father wiped his face with his kerchief. "Last I heard of Benny, he had joined the service. Must be home on leave. First thing son, we've got to go let Earl Lee and his momma know. Let's drive to Bagdad. They live near the colored Baptist church." We left the hands eating lunch and drove to the small community of Bagdad a few miles away.

As we turned off the blacktop and down a dirt road to the Lee home, Earl was bent over the open engine of his truck, and Helen Lee was hanging clothes on the line. They both welcomed us warmly with handshakes. We sat in wooden chairs on their porch. Small children played with a dog under a shade tree. Father looked at me and nodded for me to begin.

I took a deep breath and said, "I attended a campaign rally at noon at the courthouse. Willie Rainach was speaking. Benny was there, kind of in the back. After Rainach said some stuff about the Colfax Riot, you know, that marker, Benny challenged him on it. Next thing, the crowd got angry, and some deputies hustled Benny away. I thought they were just trying to get him away; keep him from bothering Rainach while he spoke. A few minutes later, I saw the two sheriff deputies push him into a Buick. Elmer Cook was driving, and two of his boys were with him. They drove south down Highway 8."

Mrs. Lee dropped her head into her hands and started sobbing. "I told him not to go into town, but if he did to wear his uniform," said Earl Lee. "Thought it might protect him." He then walked to his sobbing wife and embraced her.

Father said, "It's two-thirty now. Maybe we can head something off before it gets out of hand. Let's all go down to the sheriff's office and file a report. Maybe that will let them know that someone is watching."

Earl, Father and I jumped in my car, and drove straight to Colfax. We entered the sheriff's office in the first floor of the courthouse and Father asked to see the sheriff. We were kept waiting a few minutes, and then shown into a small conference room. The sheriff was already seated, smoking his customary cigar. "What can I do to help you fellas?" he asked.

Father began. "My son thinks he might have seen a kidnapping, or something close to it. Tells me he saw Benny Lee pushed into a car driven by Elmer Cook and his gang about one o'clock. They drove away with Benny, and his parents haven't seen him since."

The sheriff asked, "Is that right, Earl?"

"Benny's home on leave. Just finished basic at Fort Benning. Here for two weeks. He went to town around nine. Haven't seen or heard from him since," said Benny's father.

"Earl, I was there listening to the speech," said the sheriff. "Heard the whole thing. In fact, I sent two of my men to get your boy out of trouble. Told them to put him inside our office until the rally was over. I didn't want no trouble. There were people there who'd be happy to split his head open after Benny called the senator a liar. I hadn't seen him since they whisked him out of there. They told me that Mr. Elmer was going take him back home. Let me go in my office and call Elmer and find out what happened." He left the room but returned a few minutes later.

"Elmer tells me that he volunteered to take your boy back to Bagdad. Tiny and Floyd were all with him. Says they drove him out there and let him off where the blacktop and your dirt road meet. Says Benny told them he'd walk from there. They drove back to Elmer's car lot, been there ever since playing cards in the back room. Don't know nothing else."

Earl stood up and put both his hands on the wooden table and looked the sheriff straight in the eyes. "That dirt road ain't but a half mile to my house. Sheriff, you tell me how a grown man, twenty years old, a soldier, tell me how he gets lost walking down that road going home. Tell me that."

"Wait Earl. I ain't saying what happened to him or where he is right now. We don't know. He could have gone fishing or walking in the woods. Like you say, Earl, he's home on leave. Maybe he's blowing off steam somewhere, got a girl or something. From what I heard at the rally, sounds like he has some steam to blow. That's why I got him away from there," explained the sheriff.

I blurted out, "If y'all were so concerned about Benny, why give him to four Klansmen?"

The sheriff looked at me and said in a low tone, "Son, you're home from school. Maybe you think you learned some new things down in Baton Rouge, but *please* keep your mouth shut about things you really don't know nothing about. We got enough problems here already." After a pause, he told us, "Sounds like what we have is a missing person, missing for about three hours so far. If he ain't home by tomorrow at noon, come in and fill out a missing person report." He got up from his chair and left us alone in the conference room. We left and drove back to Bagdad in silence, a progressively dark shadow growing among us.

I tried to sleep that night, to little avail. Thunderheads were racing across the Red River Valley with bursts of thunder and spikes of lightning throughout the night. Despite our attic fan, my room was stifling. My bedsheets were soaked in sweat. I walked to my window several times that night to stare at the darkened cotton fields surrounding our farmhouse. Images of Benny being pushed into the Buick were flooding my brain. In my fitful dreams, I saw Elmer and his boys taunting Benny, beating him. Sometime in the black night, I found myself walking under an oak tree, standing next to the marker outside the courthouse. Benny was on the other side of the marker. Blood and torn bits of scalp flowed from the back of his head, but his eyes were bright and locked upon me.

"Come with me to meet these men," he said as he beckoned me. "Those who died that Easter morning, the one hundred fifty, they shall never grow old, and they shall never leave this town. They are the soldiers who fought the Battle of Colfax."

I was mute before him, like a sheep before his shearer. I had to go where he led me. We ascended the nearby levee and came to a place across the along known as batture. It is a place reclaimed every year in the spring by the flooding of the Red when the blood-colored mixture of water and soil pushes against the levee. The batture is owned by no man, and cannot be truly owned, except by the river. There were many square stones arranged in a crooked row, some partially sunk into the red dirt. Nothing was written on the stones. Like the trees and bushes of the batture, the standing stones were coated by a sheen of red-brown mud left over from the flood.

Standing before us were lines of negroes, as if waiting to march in a military parade. They appeared at the ready, awaiting only the word of their commander. Each one bore a bleeding wound in the back of the head, identical to that suffered by Benny.

"Who are these we see?' I asked.

"These are the prisoners, taken by Colonel Nash and his gang after the battle," replied Benny.

"Their wounds, all the same. Why?"

"Bullets in the brain, all of them. Just like me."

"Why are they waiting? Are they standing in formation?" I asked.

"They await their commander, Levin Allen. But he can't come to them. He burned up in the courthouse on that Easter morning, along with sixty of his men. Those you see were captured after they surrendered. Each was shot in the back of the head. They were buried in this mass grave over the levee. These grinding stones came from the old sugar mill. They were placed here by the families to mark the spot. We call this the Devil's Backbone. It's a holy place."

We walked back over the levee, and I found we were entering another burial ground, one that bore the bones of some of my ancestors. It was the town cemetery where all the white families of Colfax buried their dead. I had been to the graves of my grandparents after their funerals but found no cause to dwell there, so I knew it well. I stared at the bleeding wound in Benny's head as he led me deeper into the graveyard. I noticed the familiar family names of Colfax on the gravestones as I passed. It was a steamy night, water vapor like a cloud hung in the summer night air. I looked ahead, and saw a white obelisk appear out of the mist. Benny and I stood before the shaft of white marble, which rose above our heads.

"Now for the three white soldiers. Here is their stone. The other side of the battle," Benny said. He pulled a candle from his pocket, and struck a match to illuminate the inscription carved into the white rock:

In Loving Remembrance
Erected to the Memory of the Heroes
Stephen Decatur Parish
James West Hadnot
Sidney Harris
Who fell in the Colfax Riot fighting
For White Supremacy
April 13, 1873

Our rooster crowed around six. I awoke in a panic. I recalled every detail of my journey during the night. Hadnot. This was a name from my mother's family. I knew nothing more. At breakfast, I asked Momma, "Who is James West Hadnot?"

"James Hadnot was my great-grandfather on my mother's side. He died in the Colfax Riot. When I was a little girl, they erected a monument to him and the others in the cemetery across from First Baptist."

"So, there *is* a monument down there? A white marble one?"

"Why sure. Haven't you seen it?"

I was quiet for a moment. Then I muttered, "Can't recall it. Yeah, I must have seen it at grandmother's funeral."

"What else do you know about him?"

"He was a decorated Confederate officer. My sister has his medals. She'd be glad to show them to you."

"Momma, did he help kill all those negroes? The hundred and fifty they talk about? Was he in the Klan?"

Father interrupted, "Son, you must understand that the Klan was different back then from what it is today. Those men were fighting for their freedom. It wasn't about the negroes; it was about the carpetbaggers. You go back and ask your professors about that. They'll confirm it."

"Son," said Momma, "we considered all those men back then to be Civil War heroes, fighting for our state. You've learned what the Yankees did when they came up the Red River? The towns burned, crops destroyed, lots of people starved."

"Sorry," I said. "I didn't mean to refight the Civil War. I just know for sure I saw four Klansmen kidnap a young negro who was just speaking his mind. And we got a sheriff who doesn't lift a damned finger. Hell, his deputies threw him in their car. What kind of place is this? That's what I really want to know."

I put on my fresh cotton shirt and drove bleary-eyed to work. I was beginning my day's work as a scribe, very confused and fighting a severe headache. Julie approached me and asked, "What happened to you yesterday? Everyone in the office is talking about it. Did you and your daddy talk to the sheriff? No one's heard from Benny yet. That's what I hear."

"Julie, I think they killed him. He's not coming home. I just feel it in my bones," I said.

"How can you say that now? Did you see something else?"

"No, I only saw them take him. That's all I saw with my eyes. But he's not coming home. This whole town is crazy. Let's tell Mrs. Funderburk we're going to the café for a cup of coffee. I need to show you something."

We walked instead to the town cemetery, where I made my way once again to the white marble obelisk honoring the Colfax Riot. Julie and I stood before it, she for the first time. "I've never really read anything about this riot," she said. "Never read the marker. Never seen this monument."

"See that name—Hadnot. That's my great-great-grandfather. Momma's kin. He helped fight this battle. I got his blood. And he's got the blood of one hundred fifty men on him. Couldn't be anything but a massacre. Just read the numbers. That's what Benny yelled at Rainach yesterday. I wanted to yell that, but I couldn't. That's what got him killed." Tears welled up in me and spilled down my face; rage began to build. Julie hugged me while I wept.

We walked toward the café, and across the street, I saw Elmer's car lot. I asked Julie to wait for me in the café. I walked across the street, not knowing exactly why. Elmer was seated behind his desk, alone in his office. His thick neck and shoulders supported a box-like head sporting a fresh crewcut with just a touch of Butch Wax was on the front. His eyes blazed with hate and contempt as I came through the door.

"Well, here is the college boy turned Dick Tracy. I hear you reported me and the boys to the sheriff. You think we was kidnapping that smart-mouthed young nigger buck?"

"I didn't know then, Elmer, But I know now. You killed him. You put a bullet in his brain. I saw the whole thing."

"Boy, you crazy. Get outta my office before I decide to really put a bullet in someone's brain."

"Elmer, you're going to burn in hell. Count on it. And when you do, there's a whole company of negroes going to escort you down there. Remember, I saw the whole thing. Bullet to the back of his head. Sleep easy tonight." As he rose from his desk, I turned, walked out of his office and across the street to meet Julie.

We sat at a booth to drink our coffee. I wrote a short note to the clerk of court and Mrs. Funderburk. "Julie, give this to Mrs. Funderburk. I'm going to Baton Rouge for the rest of the summer. There may be a posse coming for me."

"What did you say to him?"

"I told him I know what he did."

"But how? How do you know for sure? How can you know if you didn't see it?"

"Call it a hunch, but I know it as sure as we sit here. I can't stay in this town a day longer. It's not the kind and gentle place we thought it was when we were kids."

I left Colfax that afternoon and never returned. Benny Lee never returned to Bagdad. His body was never found. About a year later, during my second year in law school, Momma sent me an article from the Colfax Chronicle. During an argument over a card game in the back room, one of Elmer's marks pulled out a gun and blew off the back of his head. So it goes.

Harold and Harold

I had no training in psychiatric medicine. This was my first job, a night nurse at East Louisiana State Hospital in Jackson, Louisiana. My instructions were simple enough. First, give the medicine as prescribed. Second, make sure the patients don't kill one another. We were always shorthanded. If I got into trouble, there was a phone to call security. I mostly stayed locked in a glass-enclosed office with a view of the common area on the ward. I figured with four catatonics and two middle-aged manic depressives; I could manage just fine. But it was Friday, movie night. Trouble was brewing among the two patients who could talk.

The men were standing face to face near the TV and VCR in an alcove filled with worn leatherette chairs and huge ceramic pots holding long-dead house plants. I could hear raised voices as an argument broke out. Both were wearing their light green hospital togs and state-issued slippers. Both veteran patients on the ward, the two normally were quite chummy, playing cards and watching TV together without incident. One of them, Tom McGinnis, was holding the remote control high in the air, while the other, Harold Chaisson, tried to grab it away.

"If I hear Cat Stevens sing one more time, I swear I'll throw that VCR in the trash!" McGinnis said and stepped away from the grasping hands of his antagonist. "You can't be wanting to see that movie again, Harold. You watched it last week. You watch it every time it's your turn. Come on, man. We got *Star Wars*, *China Syndrome*, *Coming Home*. Good movies, not some crap about a suicidal queer screwing an eighty-year-old woman."

"McGinnis, have you actually watched this movie?"

"Thanks to you, I seen all the parts of it at various times. If you mean, have I sat down with you through the whole sick thing? No, can't say I have."

"There you go," Harold said. "The single thing guaranteed to keep a man in ignorance is contempt before examination. As for Cat Stevens, his music is joyous. You might want to try joy sometime. You might like it. Besides, it's Friday night, and it's my turn to choose the movie."

McGinnis slapped the remote into Harold's outstretched hand and huffed over to the glass barrier surrounding the nursing station. He gently tapped it and moved his face to the opening. "Miss Arnold, I wonder if you might help us head off a dispute here. So, see, Harold wants to watch the same movie we watched last week, and I thought—"

"Tom, I heard the whole thing," I said. "He's right. It's his turn to choose. Being there are only six of you on the ward, and the other four are catatonic, you two need to learn to cooperate. You know, agree rather than disagree. If you don't want to watch *Harold and Maude*, then go read a book, take a walk in the courtyard, listen to your radio. There's lots of stuff here to pass the time. Maybe you could work on your feeling diary."

McGinnis threw up his hands and sulked down the hall to the room that he shared with Harold. I finished preparing the tray of medications that I administered to the ward patients at night. Each patient was represented by a small paper cup containing the chemistry that helped them stay connected with the world the staff knew as reality.

"Medication, Mr. Chaisson," I said and extended the paper cup with Harold's nightly meds. "What's this movie about?" I asked.

Harold merely extended his arm to grab his paper cup off the tray, not averting his eyes from the TV screen. "Are you asking just to make conversation, or do you really want to know?" He pressed pause and turned his huge green eyes toward me for my response.

"Maybe a little of both," I said. "It looks like it's from the sixties or maybe seventies."

Harold rubbed his chin as if he was stroking a beard that once graced his face. "How old are you, Miss Arnold?"

"Twenty—but I got my LPN."

"Mmm. I see. But I was only asking your age." He tapped his pointer finger on his cheek. His green-eyed stare continued. I looked down at my chest to make sure my uniform hadn't popped a button.

"You were five," he said.

"Pardon? I was what?"

"This movie was released in 1971. You were five. It's the only thing keeping me from tying my bedsheets together and hanging myself, so I guess you can say I adore it. It's about life, Miss Arnold, and the reasons we carry on rather than giving up. It's a classic. Want to watch it with me?"

"I'd like to, but I have the meds to hand out. I think Jenkins in Room 122 needs a sponge bath. I have some charting to do."

"You're here until seven tomorrow morning Miss Arnold. Give yourself a little gift. I promise you won't regret it."

"Oh sure. But you'll have to pause it in a few minutes so I can finish the meds. Not that much going on tonight."

"No problem. I'll rewind it so you can see it from the beginning. Just promise me we won't be caught by lights out."

"That's a promise. We'll finish the movie before lights out."

The movie began with the camera following a well-dressed young man, maybe a teenager, walking deliberately down a spiral staircase and through a richly appointed room lit only by filtered sunlight. A joyful Cat Stevens tune kept pace with the young man's actions of writing his name on a small notecard and pinning it to his coat, then lighting a candelabra. I expected the scene to unfold to a similar joyful conclusion, but suddenly the young man stepped onto a chair and into thin air. The camera focused on his twitching feet as he hung by his neck from a rope. I had witnessed a suicide. What kind of movie had I agreed to watch with this patient? Maybe I was being manipulated. Maybe Harold Chaisson wasn't just a harmless depressive. I felt confused. First, a joyful song and setting, followed by a senseless death. I locked eyes with Harold, who was smiling wryly.

Harold paused the movie. "It's a comedy, Miss Arnold. Relax."

On the TV screen, I saw a formally attired woman enter the room, unphased by the body swinging from her ceiling. She sat near a telephone and dialed the number of her hairdresser. She turned, then addressed the swinging corpse, "I suppose you think this is very funny, Harold." It then dawned on me that the entire opening scene was a prank played by the teenager, the onscreen Harold, on his self-possessed mother. The audience had been pranked, but not Harold's mother. She had dealt with his antics before. She scheduled her hair appointment and told her swinging son to appear for dinner at eight. But the prank had worked on me. Now, I wanted to know what made both Harolds tick. Yes, the movie had me, but more important was what my Harold saw in this movie.

"Now, watch this, Miss Arnold," my Harold said. "It's Harold's shrink. Listen to this crap."

Onscreen Harold is sitting in a stuffed leather chair next to his psychiatrist. He stares blankly into space, so the good doctor gives his patient an optimistic verbal nudge. My Harold was mouthing the precise words of the psychiatrist in perfect time with the movie. "That's very interesting, Harold, and I think very illuminating. There seems to be a definite pattern emerging, and of course, this pattern, once isolated, can be coped with. Recognize the problem, and you're halfway on the road to its solution."

My Harold hit pause once again. Leaning over the arm of the worn faux leather armchair, he looked intently into my eyes once again. "Do you believe that? Do you think simply recognizing a problem is half its solution?"

McGinnis returned to the patient's lounge. He yelled across the room, "Don't let him hook you, Miss Arnold. There's no end to this rabbit hole. Trust me." McGinnis walked back toward his room and shut the door.

I rose, holding the medication tray to serve the other patients. "Harold, pause it a minute while I give out the meds."

My Harold waved dismissively at his roommate, who disappeared down the hall. "He's full of crap. So, what do you say? Do you think that self-knowledge is the key?"

"Maybe yes. Maybe no," I said. "I guess it depends on the problem. Don't you have to realize you have a problem to begin with?"

"An excellent response from a worker bee in the giant mental health hive. I see they have taught you well." Harold pulled a bright yellow tennis ball from his front pockets and bounced it repeatedly against a wall next to his chair. After a few bounces, he turned to me and said, "Catch?" He offered to toss the ball to me.

I placed the tray on a nearby side table and opened my hands. "Toss it." After a few rounds, I tossed it back and picked up my tray. Harold slouched back in his chair, rolling the tennis ball in one hand.

"Harold, I have no mental health training. I'm here to give y'all your meds. I'm just an LPN, that's all. But I'm anxious to learn, maybe become a psyche nurse someday. Get my RN. Maybe run the group meetings on the day shift."

"Aha, you haven't been contaminated yet. Excellent. So, let me tell you about self-knowledge, Miss Arnold. Those four catatonics down the hall, do you think that at any point that self-knowledge could have helped those men?"

"I have no idea. Are you saying they were born like that?"

"Perhaps, but here's the truth. The human mind is fragile, Miss Arnold. Bigger forces out there are working against us. Our petty brains are helpless. One of those forces is our own memory, another is the hive. It makes no difference what we think we know about those forces. They win every time, like trying to go one on one with Mohammed Ali. You lose every time. You see what I'm saying?"

"But at some point," I said, "we all have some choice in how we respond to life, don't we? Before we respond, we have to know something about ourselves."

"I've been in this vast system of hives for sixteen years. First, the VA, then down in De Paul, now here. Every shrink pushes this crap about self-awareness. Then, they bring out the Thorazine. It's all bullshit. But hey, this movie is a comedy."

I left to serve the medications to the other ward patients. Returning, I took my seat next to Harold, who hit the play button. Onscreen Harold purchases a used hearse and attends the first of several funerals depicted in the movie. Standing among total strangers by the grave of a corpse he never knew in life, he first sees Maude, the elderly woman who will become his guide and muse.

She is sitting among the graves, apart from the mourners, eating a green apple.

Later, after being chastised by his mother for purchasing the hearse, he's sent to talk to his Uncle Victor, described by his mother as "General McArthur's right-hand man."

Onscreen Harold sits mute on a leather couch in the office of his uncle, a military commander. Uncle Victor pitches the many benefits of joining the Army and fighting in Vietnam. He promises "action, adventure, and plenty of slant-eyed girls." Walking past posters of Richard Nixon and Nathan Hale on his office walls, Victor tells his nephew, "It'll make a man out of you, Harold. You'll walk with a glint in your eye and a spring in your step, and the knowledge in your heart that you are working for peace and serving your country."

My Harold hit pause and sprang to his feet. "I had an Uncle Victor. He was my father. He attended the Ole War School in Baton Rouge as a cadet before Pearl Harbor. He fought at Iwo Jima. Purple Heart and Bronze Star. I adored him, so I joined ROTC at LSU. Graduated. Second Lieutenant US Army, Republic of Vietnam. One month into my first tour, I was fragged by a couple of my men for busting up their drug ring. A grenade in my tent." He pulled up the right leg of his trousers, baring a prosthesis.

"Your fellow soldiers did this?"

"Fairly common over there."

"I've never heard of such a thing," I said. "How could someone do this to their fellow soldier?"

"Bless your young heart. You don't have any concept about war, do you, Miss Arnold?"

I reached over and lifted his pants leg again, exposing the plastic and metal device attached to his stump. "Maybe not. I grew up sheltered." I ran my fingers along the hard skin-colored plastic that served as a pitiful substitute for flesh and bone.

"Yes," he said, "but don't you see? What happened there started decades before, on the other side of the world. Those two were just worker bees in the great hive. The workers have no way of knowing what the queen bee is up to. She was alive long before we were born, and her ways are not our ways. I can't hate those worker bees. Hell, I was one myself until I lost my mind. Now, I can't pick up her signals. So, I try to figure my mission out by myself, but it's tricky. This movie helps. Come on. You'll see."

We settled into the comic core of the film. Scenes of Harold and Maude's budding friendship attending funerals together were interwoven with Harold's continued prank suicides. The delicate hilarity of Harold's antics brought a warm light into the gathering darkness that surrounded the movie's characters and the culture they inhabited. While vaguely referring to her approaching departure, Maude continued to teach the sullen young Harold lessons on the wonder and allure of life.

"I like to watch things grow," Maude said. "They grow and bloom and fade and die and change into something else. Life!"

This was what I had been hoping to see in the film. After all the horrors endured by my Harold, Maude's life-affirming message was sustaining him when nothing else would work. I settled in to watch more deeply, maybe learn more about my tortured patient.

A door slammed down the hall. McGinnis slowly trudged toward the patient's lounge wearing his bathrobe and slippers. "Isn't it time for lights out?" he yelled.

I rose quietly, wanting to preserve my Harold's reverie. I placed my finger on my lips and approached McGinnis. "I'm allowing him to finish it. Come on, give him a break. Besides, I'm watching it with him. I like it. So please, just go back to your room, and you can go to sleep now if you like. We'll go lights out when the movie is over."

"Okay, but I warn you. He's going to get weird." McGinnis shuffled back to his room and shut the door.

Onscreen Harold and Maude are having a quiet dinner at the redecorated railcar, which serves as her residence. Harold tells her how he overheard his self-centered mother swoon with a dramatic flourish after she was mistakenly told by police that Harold had been killed in an accident at his boarding school.

"I decided then I liked being dead," onscreen Harold said.

"I understand," Maude said. "A lot of people enjoy being dead. But they're not dead, really. They're just backing away from life. Reach out and take a chance, get hurt even. But play as well as you can. Go team, go! Gimme an L. Gimme an I. Gimme a V. Gimme an E. L-I-V-E. Live! Otherwise, you got nothing to talk about in the locker room."

My Harold hit pause again. He sat in silence, staring at the dirty shag carpet and the dead plants by the window. Then, he turned his green eyes to me. "Did you notice his last name, Miss Arnold? Back at the funeral scene in the church when they introduced themselves. Did you notice his last name?"

"No, I missed it."

"Don't feel bad. I didn't catch it the first time I saw the movie. His name is Harold Chasen. C-h-a-s-e-n. My name is Harold Chaisson. French, you know. Chasen, Chaisson. Harold, Harold. This movie was made just as I lost my mind and entered the hive of mental health hospitals. Is that clear enough for you? At first, I also liked being dead. Much easier that way. God knows I tried." He pulled up his shirt sleeve to show me thick razor scars on his wrist and forearm. "But when I saw this movie, I knew this film was made for me. Now, I need to listen to what Maude has to say."

I leaned across my chair and touched the reddish scars running vertically and horizontally along Harold's arm. I slowly ran my fingers along each slash, all the time my eyes locked with the green lanterns in Harold's face. There was a connection between us, but a single stroke of the skin couldn't tell a story decades in the making.

"So, Harold Chaisson, do you now believe life is worth living? It is, you know."

"Maybe, yes. Maybe, no. As you said yourself. Sometimes, I like being dead and just take my Thorazine. Sometimes, this movie gets me through another week. Those big forces, those memories; they keep coming. I thought that they might burn them out with the electric shock treatments a few years back, but no. Now that's taboo. Let's finish the movie. It's getting late, and McGinnis will be more pissed at me than usual. He can't sleep unless I'm tucked in. He won't admit that, but it's true."

Maude, as muse, began to transform the shy and sometimes suicidal Harold. He took up playing a banjo she gifted him. He helped her save a withered tree strangled by smog in the city, transplanting it in a primeval forest, hilariously frustrating an uptight motorcycle policeman in the process. After a long day of innocent fun and life-affirming play, Harold confesses his deep love for Maude, and she confirms her love for the young man. Their day culminates in a discreet but profound night of dancing and lovemaking, depicted only by a scene of Harold awakening in her bed blowing bubbles as the morning light flooded into her bedroom. I was pulled deeper into the sweetness and innocence of their budding relationship. I saw exactly why my Harold needed this movie. Given onscreen Harold's fake suicides, not to mention my Harold's suicide attempts, I should have known better.

Unbeknownst to Maude, Harold decides they should be married. Onscreen Harold stages a lovely and romantic dinner for his beloved. When he presents an engagement ring to Maude, she declares, "I couldn't imagine a lovelier farewell." She explains, "It's my eightieth birthday. I took the tablets an hour ago. I'll be gone by midnight." This is followed by scenes of Harold riding with Maude to an emergency room and Harold being given the news of Maude's death by her attending doctor. A black chasm of defeat and remorse opens as Harold drives his Jaguar turned hearse over rain-soaked country roads and eventually off a high cliff next to the Pacific. It crashes down with a deadly thud among the sand and rocks. After soaking the viewer in this toxic brew for several pregnant seconds, the camera pans back to the top of the cliff where onscreen Harold holds his banjo and begins crudely fingerpicking a joyful tune the two sang earlier in the movie. Another prank, perhaps the ultimate; light and hope are redeemed.

My Harold didn't see it that way. "That damned bitch killed herself. It's all a lie! All the shit she said about loving life, it was all bullshit. That stupid kid couldn't know, but he was in love with a liar, a hypocrite! Fuck her. Fuck Mary, fuck Jesus, fuck Ronnie, fuck Nancy. Fuck the church. Fuck the joint chiefs. Fuck all the shrinks. Fuck Thorazine. Fuck the queen bee. Fuck Charley. Fuck Uncle Victor!" My Harold ran down the hall and slammed the door to his room. I stood with the VCR remote in my hand, my mouth agog.

McGinnis came out of their room with a bundle of cotton sheets and a wool blanket in his arms. He approached me and handed me the bundle. "Look in the closet inside your nurses' station," he said. "There's a set of rubber sheets and a special blanket. I'll turn down his bed for him. Oh yeah, you may want to call Dr. LeBlanc for a shot of Haldol. I think he'll take a double dose tonight. He'll wake up tomorrow and be fine. Now you've seen what I'm talking about, can you please try to get that movie off the ward?"

I opened the locked door to my glass cage, gave McGinnis the rubber sheets and then called for the Haldol. As I sat in my chair and stared down the hall, I realized I knew nothing about the human mind or the dark forces that controlled it. I had no training in psychiatric medicine. I knew nothing about war, or pain, or a lot of things in the world out there beyond the walls of our hospital.

Tuesday

"*I* get kidnapped all the time. That's the problem."

"Is that why you're here? You say someone kidnapped you?"

"Happens all the time. They just keep running me down, snatching me up and throwing me in places like this joint."

"Mr. Collins, you say someone, some group, is kidnapping you. Who? Who are they?"

"It all started a long time ago out in California. Well, that's not true. That thing in California wasn't the first kidnapping. It really started back in a nuthouse for juveniles out on Long Island in about 1955. Parents threw me in there. That's where I met Tuesday, and that's where all my troubles started."

"Who's Tuesday?"

"Who's Tuesday? You kidding me? Young buck like you don't know who Tuesday is? Tuesday Weld—you know, the hottest chick in Hollywood. Least she was at one time. Come on, tell me you know her. What the hell year is this anyway? How old are you, son?"

"The year is 1976, and yes, I've heard of Tuesday Weld, the actress. Haven't seen her movies. She peaked a little before my time. As I told you the last time we met, I'm John Galloway. I'm 23 years old, and I'm studying for my master's in psychology. I'm a part of the Tulane intern program here at Jackson Acute Adult Unit."

"You say we met before? I don't think so."

"I'm your monitor in our clinical trial of Thorazine as compared to a newer medication being tested by McNeil. It's a double-blind study. You remember, you volunteered for it. We talked last week. What's all this about Tuesday? You didn't say anything about her. Did you know her?"

"Oh, yeah. Wish I hadn't. But yeah, I knew her. We both grew up in New York. I was an upper-middle-class juvenile delinquent out in Westchester County, and she was a teen model in the city. Tried to kill herself. We both got thrown in a fancy lockup for troubled teens way the hell out on Long Island. They told us we were already alcoholics, but you can't hear such a thing when you're fifteen. We laughed at 'em. That was my first stay in a joint like this."

"How many places like this have you been in?"

"Like this dump? Not many as dirty as this one. You seen the bugs crawlin' around on the ward? And the food here, sick. But you never forget your first time—when I met Tuesday."

"First of what? Tell me what you mean."

"First of a lot of things—first kiss. First time I fell in love. Only time I fell in love. Couldn't help it. You had to have seen her then, son. God Almighty! She was a young goddess. Aphrodite, I used to call her. She was only thirteen or so. The first time I heard her talk in group therapy, I was a goner. Chased her all over this country, much to my regret."

"You said you loved her. Was she your girlfriend?"

"Not really, but I kissed her once. We'd been making eye contact in group and later in the cafeteria. After supper one night, I ran into the girls' bathroom after her and kissed her. Kissed her and ran out. Made her promise not to tell. She didn't scream, so I assumed she liked me. I went to bed high as a kite and not a drug in my body. She was gone a few days later, went out to the West Coast, they said. That kiss was enough to light a burning fire inside me. I couldn't think of anything else. Couldn't sleep. Drinking my old man's booze was the only thing that gave me any relief. He was up my ass all the time. I didn't know where she was or how to reach her. Then, I saw her on Dobie Gillis, so I took off for California. Just left in the middle of the night. Stuck my thumb out and headed west."

"Are you telling me you left your parents' home, a kid in high school, and hitchhiked across the United States?"

"Tried to. Didn't make it. They picked me up for vagrancy in Dallas. They put me in a psych unit for a couple of weeks, and then my parents came and fetched me back to New York. Spent the next few years in a mental hospital upstate, near Syracuse. They juiced my brain quite a few times with the high voltage, then just kept me chilled with meds—that Thorazine? I tried it when it was brand new. But that place was clean, and the orderlies didn't beat the shit out of you like they do in this dung heap here. I was twenty when they released me. Still couldn't get her out of my mind. Stuck my thumb out again and made it to L.A. Saw in a movie magazine that Tuesday was shooting a movie with Elvis up in Napa Valley, so I went there to see her."

"Did you ever meet up with her?"

"Just for a minute or so, but I had me a run-in with Elvis and his goon squad. They were shooting scenes around Calistoga. I hung around the edges of the set, and they ran me off a couple of times. Late one afternoon, I saw a couple of real nice cars leave the set and followed them in a beater I stole off a used car lot in Oakland. They drove to the hot springs outside town. I parked down the road and circled back of the springs, hoping to see her swimming. I hid in the bushes but couldn't see nothin'. So, I climbed a tree like ole' Zacchaeus—you know, that midget who was tryin' to see Jesus?"

"I know Zacchaeus. I was raised Baptist, Sunday school every week. He got to talk to Jesus for his efforts, even though he was small. Jesus told him he needed to be born again."

"Well, my climbing didn't work. I shimmied up that tree to get a better look, and I saw her. Sure did. I saw Tuesday swimming in a yellow bikini with Elvis and his wife, The most beautiful dark hair—down to her waist. I yelled to Tuesday, then called out my name. She musta not heard me. She was splashin', playin' splash with Elvis. Never turned around. Right after that, Elvis' goons ran up and drug me down from the tree. They gave me a good workin' over and then called the cops. Ended up in another nuthouse down near Bakersfield, I think. Stayed there most the rest of the sixties, full of Thorazine and other shit."

"Did you ever see her again?"

"No, but I did save her life."

"How's that?"

"First thing I did when I got out was hitch straight to Hollywood. She was in big-time films by then. I kept up with her in the movie magazines. Wouldn't you know—got kidnapped again."

"Where did they throw you in that time?"

"It wasn't the same. I hitched a ride in a van with some wild hippie chicks and a couple of longhairs outside Los Angeles. They said I could stay with them at their ranch out in the desert. I figured I could chill out there and at least stay out of trouble for a while. Maybe I wouldn't get thrown in the nuthouse and pumped full of drugs. I was actually looking forward to some peace and quiet."

"Did you find it—peace and quiet?"

"Hell no. The ranch they brought me to—that was Charlie Manson's place. All those chicks wanted to do out there was take LSD, drink wine, play music, fuck Charlie and lie around all day. Most of the longhairs were hardcore criminals. Place was filthy, very little to eat and drink. Girls were bat shit crazy, and Charlie started to scare the hell out of me. Claimed he knew the Beach Boys and damned if we didn't go to one of them's home one night. Like a dream man, like a dream."

"So where did the kidnapping come in?"

"I kept asking this dude, Tex, if he'd bring me to town so I could go find a job. He told me to shut up about that and that if asked again, he'd break my arm. The guy was the real deal—cold. Eyes were dead, nothin' back there. I took him seriously. Then, they had me going around with one of the longhairs, casing joints we might rob for money to keep the tribe going. Charlie had been preachin' to us all along about a race war. Crazy shit about the end of the world. He wanted to kill someone big, and I had run my mouth about Tuesday when I first got out there. Charlie kept talkin' about her—killin' her—that they could blame the niggers for killing the perfect American girl, and that'd do it—the war would be on. Him and Tex rousted me hard to find out what I knew about her, but I fed them a line of bullshit. Told them she had moved back to New York, that I had got a letter from her in the hospital, that she had to take care of her dyin' momma. She hated her momma. Did you know that? Her momma, she forced Tuesday to go out and sell herself to the highest bidder—older men, producers, directors, men with money for momma. She had no childhood, forced to work from the start. Her daddy abandoned them when she was little. I guess I must have convinced them she was back East. So, I guess you could say I saved her life. That little motherfucker was a determined SOB when he set his mind on doin' something. After that, they started lookin' elsewhere. You know the rest."

"How did you get out? Were you there when all the killings went down?"

"The night they left to go to Sharon Tate's home, Charlie sent me with another guy to rob an all-night grocery store. We started talkin' on the way there, and both of us were scared to shit of what was about to come down. Those gals were crazy, man, and Tex—he'd do it just for the hell of it. We knew they was coming back with blood on their hands, so we just kept driving east. Only had enough gas to make it to Needles, but at least we were out of the fire. The car we was driving was stolen, so we ditched it and hitched into Vegas. We went into a Salvation Army shelter there and saw all the shit the next night on the TV. I bought a movie magazine and wrote a letter to Tuesday's agency telling her about Charlie and to be extra careful. Never heard anything. I think they nabbed Charlie and the girls a few weeks later."

"You ever call the cops?"

"Hell no. I've been drunk for the last seven years. Stopped trying to find her and just kept tryin' to forget it all. Kept thinking about Sharon and that little baby they ripped out. Drank everything I could get my hands on and took every pill I could swallow. All that got me kidnapped quite a few times—drunk tanks, jails, psych wards."

"Says here you've been in Jackson about six months. They picked you up in Faubourg Marigny. You were sleeping in a doorway and catatonic. In fact, until earlier this week, you were very uncommunicative. All this is a big change from when we met last week. You mumbled a few things. Our last meeting took up two minutes, and most of that was me talking."

"Must be the new pills. But yeah, I do feel like talkin' today."

"Do you feel like you're being kidnapped right now? You described this unit as a dung heap. Was living on the streets of New Orleans better?"

"One place is about the same as another. I'm just tryin' to climb up that tree again, bust this whole joint called earth. Maybe

Zacchaeus came down too early. Maybe he shoulda just kept climbing. Maybe he woulda found something better. That's what I been trying to find, but they won't let me. They keep draggin' me back. You, those orderlies, the cops, the men in white coats, doctors, the nurses, the Salvation Army soldiers—they just keep draggin' me down from my tree, kidnapping me. My ransom is a piece of my heart, and when I finally give that up to 'em, they throw me back in the desert. Out there, with Charlie and his like."

"Thanks for the time, Doug. Try to remember how you feel during the week, and we'll chart it again next time we meet. Take care."

"Hello, Dr. Heller? John Galloway here. I've just had a very interesting session with one of the patients in the study, Doug Collins. He's a Haldol patient, and I've seen a marked increase in his communication skills after only a week on the drug. Total turnaround."

"He hasn't said three words since he's been here. What did you two discuss?"

"Sorry to tell you he's still psychotic. He talked a bunch of gibberish about being a friend of Tuesday Weld and Charlie Manson, but at least he's talking."

"Tuesday Weld and Charlie Manson—now that's a pair. From what I recall of Collins' history, between the Orleans Parish drunk tank and the Depaul Alcohol Unit, that poor man hasn't had much time in recent years to meet such luminaries, but I guess it's better than fighting off Russian secret agents or green men from outer space. Keep me posted after you visit him next week. Good news about the Haldol."

Another World

The sheer joy he had come to know in loving her was intoxicating. His feelings were so strong and unrelenting he had to write them down each night in a diary. On page after page during the months of January through May, he poured out the passion and confusion of one who was new to the dance between a man and a woman. All of this was unknown to him. He was fourteen when he met her on New Year's Day 1967. His home had been a peaceful and nurturing place, but his only lessons of passion between a man and a woman came from the black and white television his family watched every night after supper. Finding a girl who wanted him enough to French kiss him for hours on end was not something for which he was prepared. She would shut the door to the living room at her parents' home, put Johnny Mathis on the stereo and come to him on the couch with her huge mass of strawberry blonde hair and the scent of Estee Lauder. They would hold each other tight and kiss for what seemed like forever. He was a goner, and he knew it. He said as much each night in his diary, going on about how much he loved her and how God had brought them together. They talked for hours on the phone—hours. For him, there was no holding back, and as far as he knew, no reason to hold back.

They lived in a small Louisiana town. Her parents ran a Rexall pharmacy on the town square, which her daddy purchased from an old family in town. They had moved from Oklahoma, and she enrolled in the town's high school as a freshman. This made her somewhat of an outsider to all her classmates whose families had lived there for generations, some going back before the Civil War. She became a joiner of clubs—the Future Nurses of America, the Glee Club, the school newspaper. In her spare time, she volunteered at the hospital as a candy striper—helping the ward nurses and clerks on the weekends. She wore a red and white striped smock and a starched white nurse's cap. It was there she met him when he came to visit a friend injured in a hunting accident. They rode the elevator to the fourth floor. By the time the doors opened, something special had passed between them—a smile, a second look, a lost breath. He stopped and talked to her at the nurse's station on the way out. It had unfolded from there like one of those spring storms in Oklahoma, which she knew and feared as a child. It was exciting, dangerous, thrilling and unsettling. It was her first taste of passion. But after five months, she had a real boyfriend, and he was all hers. She no longer felt like an outsider.

His rite of passage to manhood occurred on May 30, 1967—his fifteenth birthday. He marched into the DMV to take his driver's test and came out with a small piece of paper that allowed him to drive the '65 Mustang his father purchased for him. She was to be his first passenger. The stated destination that evening—the one given to her watchful father, the pharmacist—was the Twin Drive-In, where a steamy movie based on a Tennessee Williams play was showing. This was the official plan, but where he hoped to end up was parked on the banks of Lake Belle Isle, joining dozens of other young couples in the ritual of teenage summer love. As he drove toward the new subdivision where her parents lived, he admired the oak-lined streets of the older part of his town. Each home represented something separate and distinct. He knew each family and something about their story—the Broussards, the Wells, the Nelsons, the LeBlancs. It all made sense to him—this life he saw them living. All of them were very much like his parents—sober, reliable and content. His life was on track to do the same. Someday, she and he would make a home for themselves on a tree-lined street, maybe in one of these houses. This was his first trip as a man behind the wheel of a car, driving to pick up his girl. This was the beginning of his journey to his tree-lined street. He felt he was well on his way.

As she waited for his car to pull down their long gravel driveway, she looked out her kitchen window, occasionally fending off questions and admonitions from her father. It was only the third time she had gone out with a boy in a car and her first trip to a drive-in theater. She had orders to be home at eleven, fifteen minutes after the movie ended. She was reminded that she had earned the trust of her father. He warned her not to do anything to lose it. It was not made clear to her exactly what might be done to lose his trust, but he told her that he hated a liar. She was reminded of the huge fight between him and her older brother over a lie her brother told to cover drinking and wrecking their car. Her father told her that he liked and trusted her present boyfriend, knew his parents to be good church-going folks and would never have allowed her to go with just any boy to a drive-in movie. Her mother told her she looked pretty and whispered in her ear that it was only because her daddy loved her so much that he droned on about such things. She just wanted to get out of the house and get away, especially from the man sitting at the kitchen table talking in the most oblique manner to her about what was really on the mind of the nice young man about to pick her up. She didn't know what was on her own mind; how could he possibly know what he was talking about? When she heard the first crunch of gravel on the driveway, she darted out the front door but then walked back into the kitchen, kissing her father's forehead and hugging her mother before leaving with the young man.

She opened the car door and sat down in the bucket seat beside him. "Thank God you're here! I was beginning to think I was going to be picked up by Jack the Ripper to listen to Daddy." She smiled and leaned over for a quick kiss. "So where is it? Let me see it. Daddy won't teach me to drive yet, so I haven't seen a new one."

He pulled out the paper given to him by the grim woman who took his money at the DMV. "It's just this piece of paper. They say I'll get one with my picture in a few weeks."

"Did you smile real big? You got such a nice smile."

He chuckled. "How could I frown? This is the best day of my life. A driver's license, driving damned near a new car, and now, goin' to a movie by ourselves. Are you kiddin'? You can't wipe this smile off my face. I don't think even your daddy could get me to stop smilin' right now." She reached over the space between them, took his right hand and held it with both of hers. She brought it to her mouth and kissed it, and then laid it in her lap, still encased by both of her hands. How large her hands were, and how warm. She released it after kissing his hand once more, and he took full control of the wheel. They left her house for the drive-in.

"Hey, you missed the turn! What about the movie?" she said and looked back at the neon sign of the Twin Drive-In receding behind them.

"I told Dennis we'd come out to the lake. He's going there with Beth to go parking. Look, we got three hours. This is our first real date. I thought we'd make it special." He reached and grabbed her hand again.

"Well, I kind of wanted to see that movie. Natalie Wood, I saw her in *Splendor in the Grass*. She's so good. And Robert Redford, he's so good looking."

"Look, you're better looking than Natalie Wood, and you got me to look at. Let's make our own movie. We'll call it Splendor in the Backseat." He smiled and squeezed her hand.

"You are Jack the Ripper! And I...I am a liar, which my daddy hates. Oh my goodness..." She smiled and held his hand tight. "What if he asks about the movie? What'll I say?"

He smiled and told her, "Say it was very sad. It's called *This Property is Condemned*. It's got to be sad, and it's got to end badly. Just say that, and tell your momma how good-looking Robert Redford was and how he broke her heart."

"Okay, anything you say, Mr. Ripper, but we'd better be home by eleven." She smiled, wrapped both of her large warm hands around his right hand and brought it to her lips once more. She kissed and released it. He drove out into the country along the dark bayou that flowed from Lake Belle Isle. They left the lights of their small town and entered a darker canopy of sky where billions of stars witnessed the comings and goings of the humans below. As they went on through the night, he was conscious only of the sounds of the wind through his window and the sweet smell of Estee Lauder.

"Hey, what's that over there?" she asked and pointed to a side road off in the distance.

"Looks like a fire, and a big one. I think it's a building on fire!" He strained to see details through the groves of live oaks along the bayou. He drove closer, and said, "I think that's Mount Triumph Baptist Church. Looks like a Roman candle! God, that's some big flames!" As they came to the side road, he looked at her and said, "I think we need to go down there and check on it. Someone might need our help."

She was uncertain. "Can't the firemen help? We're not supposed to even be out here."

"Firemen, out here? When something burns out here, there's no help around. Out here, you have to be your own help. Let's just go and check it. We got plenty of time."

He steered the car down the tree-covered lane to a large clearing in the woods where the church and its parsonage were nestled among a grove of pecan trees. His attention was drawn to the front of the old wooden church with doors flung open and the steeple and roof engulfed in bright orange flames, illuminating the pecan grove like footlights on a stage. Two gasoline cans lay at the front entrance. On the side of the church, a large man in blue overalls held a revolver against the back of the head of another man who was on his knees. The kneeling man was bleeding from a wound on the side of his head, and the large man standing over him was screaming something. The young man opened the car door and ran to the side of the church.

Her attention was drawn to the front of the parsonage, where a woman in a white cotton dress tried to keep two crying children from leaving the front porch. She squatted between them, wrapped her arms around them and held on fast as they struggled to break free. In front of the parsonage, she saw another young woman about her age standing next to a pickup truck. She was screaming at the large man with the gun, "Daddy, please don't shoot him! Don't do it, Daddy. Please!" The daughter's eyes were blackened, and blood dripped down her chin from her lower lip. The young woman got out of the car and ran toward the two women.

The young man approached the man with the gun, who looked back and asked, "Who the hell are you? Why you here? This ain't none of your business."

The young man said, "Came to see about the fire, mister. Hey, don't use that gun. He's a preacher, you know. Please, sir!"

"Do I know? Do I know he's a preacher? Hell, he was my

preacher, and my family's preacher and my daughter's preacher. That girl over there—you see her? He done screwed her, and she's gonna have his baby. She ain't eighteen yet. Hell yes, he's a preacher. But this preacher, he's gonna meet the devil right shortly, so he can speak with some authority about hellfire and so on. You like that preacher man? You wanna go straight to hell?" The kneeling preacher said nothing he could understand, but he repeated something low and guttural. He never looked up, but the sounds kept coming. "Talkin' in tongues now? You son of a bitch! Talk all you want. That steeple's the only tongue of fire you gonna see today."

The young man stared across the clearing to the parsonage and saw his girlfriend comforting the wounded daughter. He felt the cold steel of fear down his spine and in his gut. The heat from the fire singed his hair. He thought he might vomit. "Look, you kill him, and you go to jail for a long time. Angola ain't no place to be. Or maybe the chair, maybe they'll give you the chair. Come on, mister. Please...don't to do this to your daughter." The man with the gun said nothing and stared at the back of the preacher's head. Time was frozen.

The young woman sat with the wounded daughter in the pickup truck. She took her lace-trimmed handkerchief and wiped blood and tears off the girl's bruised face. "Thanks so much. I'm so sorry. Oh my God, what if he kills him! I shouldn't have told him the truth. I should've lied. I could've told him that I slept with that soldier I seen from Fort Polk, and that I couldn't find him, that he lied about his name. I shouldn't have told him the truth. Daddy's always been a hothead. He slapped me once for coming back late. I didn't know what else to do. I'm gonna' start showing soon. I had to do something." She turned her swollen face to look out the back glass toward the burning church and the kneeling preacher.

The woman in the white cotton dress managed to open the screen door and push her children inside. She leaned hard against it as the children stared through the rusty metal screen and cried for their father.

The young woman left the truck and stepped up onto the front porch. The woman in the white cotton dress said to her, "He thinks my husband slept with his daughter. He's crazy! I called the police. God, I hope they get here in time!" The young woman jumped off the porch and ran across the clearing to the kneeling preacher. She grabbed the young man's arm. "Let's get out of here! The police are coming. His wife called them. The firetruck will be coming. You can't do anything here! We can't be here, and we can't do anything to help. Let's go!"

"You hear that? The cops are coming. Please, mister!" the young man yelled. The man with the gun turned and fled to his pickup, which he drove back down the lane to the main road, speeding into the night with his wounded daughter. The young man and young woman ran to his car and sped down the lane to the main road. In the distance, they saw the flashing lights of approaching police cars. They drove toward Lake Belle Isle and away from the mayhem that had drawn them in only minutes before. Neither said a word until they reached the levee along the lake where they were to meet their friends. Approaching the gate through which they would drive to reach the levee, he stopped the car and took a long deep breath, then looked at her and asked, "What was that back there? What did we see? I've never seen anything like that. Hey, I'm sorry. It wasn't supposed to be like this."

"You beautiful, sweet boy. You really don't know anything, do you? You just know what you want, and that's not always what you get."

"What do you mean?" he asked. "That stuff back there, that

kind of stuff don't happen to good people. The man was a preacher. He has a wife and kids. That little gal probably made up the whole thing, and look what her mouth caused. Hell, the cops'll probably come look us up. We're witnesses to arson, that and a helluva' beating."

"I don't know who was telling the truth and who was lyin'. But that girl back there—the one that was beaten up—I have a daddy like that. He slapped me last year when he got mad. I'm frightened to death of him. He beat up my brother once when he came home drunk and wrecked the car. He's probably sitting at our table, looking at his watch and drinking his bourbon. What time is it?" she asked.

He looked at his wristwatch. "Nine thirty. Wait. Are you tellin' me your daddy hit you?" he said.

"Slapped me, not hit me. He got mad and slapped me. He's got a temper. I saw him slap momma a couple of times, but he never hit her, you know, with his fist. They yell a lot. Now, Butch, Daddy hit him when he came home drink after running our car in a ditch. Oh yeah, they both hit each other. Fists were flying."

He stared blankly out the windshield, trying to envision her father, who he had often seen behind the counter wearing his starched white pharmacist's coat, rolling around with his eighteen-year-old son trading blows to each other's faces. "I guess he's always been good to me. I've never seen him that way. You want to go up and see Dennis and Beth? We got time."

"Sorry baby, I just can't go up there. Let's drive back. I'll tell Daddy that the movie was too racy, and you insisted we leave. He'll love you for it. We can go into the living room and put "Chances Are" on the stereo. I'll freshen up my perfume. You'll see. I'll make you think you had been out here the whole time, with me in your backseat. Daddy'll never know anything happened, and he'll love you for getting me back early. We can kiss all we want in the living room, as long as I'm under his roof and he knows where I am. Come on. Let's go back to town."

She looked in the rearview mirror at her hair and make-up. "Look in there," she told him. He looked in the mirror at his face. "See, you look just fine, and I do too. Nothing's happened. Just a bad movie. Oh, you take this," she said and handed him her bloody handkerchief. "If Momma asks, I'll tell her I lost it at gym class, in the locker room. Throw it away for me, where no one will find it." He silently took the bloody cloth and stuffed it in his pants pocket.

"Guess we should've stayed in town and gone to the movie," he said. "Next weekend will be different. Skip's having a swim party at the Aquatic Club. You can show off your bikini, and we can dive off the high board together."

She pulled his hand to her face and held it there, kissing it briefly three times. "It's fine, baby. Nobody died, and we haven't got caught doing anything wrong. You saved that man's life. See, birthday wish came true. Now drive. We have two hours together. Momma can make us some hot chocolate." He started the car and drove back toward the lights and tree-lined streets of their small town, along the dark bayou that flowed from the lake.

Poachers

*P*a told me to stay inside and keep quiet. If anyone came up outside the camp, hide the meat, get in the space between the walls, and don't say nothing. If they found me, play like I was deaf and dumb, that I couldn't hear or speak. God knows how a nine-year-old was supposed to pull that off, but that is exactly what he told me to do. We was living at an old deer camp way out in the woods. I don't think anyone had used it in years. Me and Pa was on the run ever since he snatched me away from Momma on account of her drinking and such. I never saw a police car, but Pa made it clear. We were to avoid police at all costs.

This place we were staying, it was a hunting camp. The first floor was cinder blocks. We slept on a wood frame second story with two bedrooms and a kitchen. The first floor had two spaces for trucks and a small room in the middle for skinning and butchering deer. There was an old water well, but it had stopped running long ago. We hauled our water from a nearby creek and boiled it every night. That was my job. Each morning, Pa would go out in search of deer meat, and during the few weeks we stayed there, we ate good. There was a farmhouse a couple miles through the woods. Pa slipped around and stole us enough eggs for breakfast. About once each week, he'd drive to a country store and buy some cereal, candy bars and canned beans. I mainly played around the camp and tried my hand at catching fish in the creek. During the day, I'd gather firewood. I didn't see no one that entire time—until I saw the game warden that bright spring day.

I heard his truck before I laid eyes on him. His motor was straining to get through the mudholes that dotted the path from the county road to the camp. I could hear his tires spin and then hear him shift into four-wheel drive. I ran from the creek bank where I was fishing, trying to make it to the camp to hide. Before I could make it to the stairs, his big green truck pulled up between me and the camp. Out lumbered a man who looked like a grizzly bear. He was wearing one of those flat-brimmed hats like the highway patrol. He wore a shiny badge on his chest but no gun on his hip. Mirrored sunglasses covered his eyes. God, was I scared. First thing— hide the meat. I bolted for the door to the skinning room and slammed the screen door, locked it with the metal clasp. I grabbed the old ice chest where Pa kept the meat cooling with ice he brought back from the store. I was trapped; even at nine, I knew that. I grabbed a mangy old Indian blanket and threw it over the ice chest. Then, I sat down on top. That was as good as I could manage.

The grizzly bear man stood smiling at the screen door. I suppose he saw the whole thing. "Son, what you running from? Hope you're not scared of me. I ain't here to harm you, boy."

I was told to play deaf and dumb, so I did my best. I finally walked over to the door and pointed to my mouth and ears, showing him I could not hear or speak. He chuckled.

He gently poked a huge bear hand through the old rotten screen and unlatched the clasp to open the door. He stepped forward and pulled out a flashlight, making note of everything in the dusty skinning room. In the corner were two of Pa's hunting rifles. Three deer skins were hanging from hooks. He then flipped the blanket off the ice chest and looked inside.

"Looks like someone has been bagging a few deer here lately. Ya'll been eating good?"

Like an idiot, I just stared at the ground. He put his hand on my shoulder and gently walked me through the door. We sat on a wooden bench just outside the skinning room. "Son, you need to stop the play-acting. I ain't here to hurt you. My job is to protect wildlife, fish and birds. I work for the department of wildlife and fisheries. They call me a game warden. I need to find out why you are here and who you belong to. Go ahead, talk to me, son."

"My name is Earl Quinn, and right now, I belong with my pa. He's Dwayne Quinn. He and Momma had a big fight on account of her drinking and having men stay the night. So, he picked me up after I got off the school bus and brought me out here. He's out hunting more deer meat. He keeps it in the ice chest."

"Are those his guns in the corner?"

"Yes, sir. He's using his thirty ought six today. Those there are for rabbits and squirrels."

"Deer season closed about three months back. Did your pa say anything about that?"

I just shook my head, knowing nothing about deer season or any other season for that matter.

"How long since you been in school?"

"Since we been out here. Three weeks or so."

"How long since you had milk?"

"Same."

"Where do you get your water?"

"In the creek over there. I bring it up in buckets while Pa is gone each day. Then, I get a fire started to boil it by the time he comes back each afternoon. I caught me a couple of brook trout under an old stump. Caught 'em on worms. Fried 'em myself."

"Ain't you something! Why don't you show me where you caught 'em? You got a pole for me?"

I gave the friendly bear man one of our poles. We dug some worms under a rotten log and took up our positions by the old stump on the creek bank. I figured more fish was hanging around the shady spot, under the old roots.

"Earl, tell me a little about your pa. Did he and your momma come to blows?"

"Oh, no, sir. They yelled and cursed a lot, though. They was fighting over me. Where I should live. After their fight started, I ran into the woods."

"Do you know if your pa is wanted by the police?"

"I don't know if the police is after him, but I know he wants us to stay away from them. He told me to hide if anyone comes up. I guess I didn't do a good job. Are you a police? I see your badge."

"Not a police, but I do help enforce hunting and fishing laws. Sometimes, if I find someone breaking those laws, I gotta' arrest them. I gotta protect all the animals that live out here. Tell me about those guns. Is your pa good with them?"

"Sure is. He's teaching me. I want to be a good shot like him. He learned how to shoot in the war. Got a marksmanship medal and a Purple Heart. I started on a twenty-two, but he ain't let me shoot the big one yet. I gotta get bigger. Kicks too much, he says."

We watched our corks for a while but just got a couple of nibbles. The bear man lumbered back to his truck and told me he hoped he'd see me soon. I smiled and waved goodbye as his green truck disappeared back down the dirt trail toward the county road.

The rest of the day I spent doing my chores of building a fire and boiling water, I hauled up from the creek. I heard Pa's truck coming down the trail near dusk. I ran to meet him and got a hug.

"Didn't do no good today," he said. "Spotted a doe and a

couple of her young ones but didn't get a clear shot. I see you got the fire going."

"Yes, sir. Second bucket's boiling now."

"That's good. We'll fry up a couple of shanks, and I'll open a can of peas to heat up."

"Pa, a man came by this morning. He had a badge on, but he wasn't a police. He said he took care of animals and fish. I couldn't pretend long, so I talked to him."

"God dammit! I told you to hide."

"Pa, I was down at the creek. When he drove up, I tried to hide the meat like you told me but wasn't no use. He found it all. Asked about your guns."

"Jesus Christ, Earl! We'll have to leave first thing in the morning. He'll be coming back, and he won't be alone this time. Boy, you don't understand. They're be looking to charge me with kidnapping. You got that? The law is after us. Momma wants me in jail. You want to wind up in an orphan's home? No talking to police. If they wearing a badge, you run and hide. If you gotta' run into the woods, hide there. I gotta' pack. We leave at dawn."

I laid in my bedroll all night. Hardly slept. Kept hearing Momma tell me what a pain it was to watch after me. Kept hearing Pa scream at her for drinking all his whiskey. Now, I had talked to the grizzly man. We both would get locked up. I could see Pa tossing as well. Every sound made him jump. He was up and at the window with his flashlight many times that night. I felt lower than a snail's belly. Seemed like all of this was on me.

Pa was up well before me the next morning. He got up and got the fire going. Made me drink a cup of his drip coffee. Fed me a bowl of cereal. Then, Pa cleaned out the guns and ice chest from the skinning room. He was running back up the stairs when I heard the big green truck spinning its way through the mudholes on the trail. Pa stopped what he was doing and just stood listening. There was no way out. He put the guns into the truck and then sat on an old log by the fire to await our pre-dawn visitor.

A grizzly man stepped out and yelled out of the shadows to my father, "Mr. Quinn, I'm Dan Beard, wildlife and fisheries. Can we talk? I mean y'all no harm."

"Sure. Come on over and have a seat by the fire. Want some coffee?"

The big man walked slowly over and stood by the fire, rubbing his hands. Pa handed him a steaming cup. "Fine boy you got there. Damned good fire, son. You catch any after I left?"

"No, sir. I started carrying the water to boil and got the fire going. No time left for fishing."

A pine branch popped in the fire. No words were said as we all settled into the crisp dawn air, enjoying the leaping flames of orange and blue and the gentle crackling of the burning wood. This had been our entertainment for the past few weeks. I favored fire gazing over reruns of Star Trek.

"I guess you gonna take me in for poaching," Pa finally said. "You saw the meat, the deer hides. I got no excuse, 'cept that's what we had to eat."

"Mr. Quinn, I could write you up, even take you in. But after talking to Earl here, I'm more concerned about the two of you. What y'all doing out here? This ain't no place to try raising a boy, even one who can hunt, fish and make a decent fire."

"I snatched him from my ex-wife. She's turned our double-wide into a whore house. Some of those characters she's banging are meth dealers. She smokes the stuff. I don't want my boy with a bullet through his head. Tried talking to a lady at the courthouse but got nothing. I guess they got a warrant out for all that, so I guess you'll take me in for kidnapping. We was trying to lay low until it cooled down. After that, I was gonna make a run for California. Got a sister out there."

"Hmm, well, I guess you had a plan, but it ain't no way to live. Looking over your shoulder all the time. Look, I called the sheriff back in your county. She filed charges against you, but the sheriff knows all about your wife and her buddies. They're watching her place. He knows you served overseas, knows your record. He just wants to be sure the boy is safe."

"You saying the police ain't after me?"

"Let's say they ain't looking too hard. It'd be wise for you to stay away from that county for a while. Let everything settle down. Your ex may be in jail soon, from what I heard. First thing, we need to get your son situated. He needs to get back in school. How old is he?"

"Nine. Fourth grade."

"My wife is a teacher in town. We can get him in school tomorrow."

"Mr. Beard, we got no money, and I had to leave my job back home."

"Dwayne, let me show you what I brought with me."

Grizzly man walked back to his truck and lifted an ice chest. He opened it before the fire: two bottles of milk, eggs, sandwich meats, a loaf of bread, and a jar of mayonnaise, along with two bags of ice.

"That should help y'all for the next couple of days. Keep that deer meat cold, don't want to lose it. I know a fella in town that can make you some fine sausage with all that meat. You bring Earl to my office in town tomorrow morning, and I'll take y'all by the school. You can stay out here a couple of days. Old man Carter hasn't been out here in years. Wife had a stroke. We may be able to find you a place in town. I hear they need men on the big job down at the reservoir, rebuilding the dam."

Mr. Beard sat down beside me on the log. He pulled a small plastic box from his shirt pocket. He gave it to me. "Ever fished with artificial bait? This is supposed to be the hottest thing now. It's called a rattletrap. Go ahead, open it. Shake it."

I opened the box to see a small silver fish. It rattled when I shook it. I smiled and thanked him. He and Pa shook hands, and his big green truck lumbered back through all the mudholes.

"Looks like you made the right call, Earl," Pa said. "I can see why you decided to talk with Mr. Beard. Damned glad you did." He took the lure in his hand to inspect it. "That's a mighty fine lure, son. Go ahead over to your fishing hole and see if it works."

Prank

*A*s a paperboy, I was supposed to be the one doing the throwing, not the other way around. Something was out of joint.

The time was six-thirty in the morning, the first day of summer 1964. The sun was just beginning to poke through the live oak canopy, which ran from the French Quarter all the way to the park. The air was heavy but not quite suffocating yet. I was pedaling along Esplanade Avenue toward City Park, tossing my paper route for the *Times-Picayune*. I had a few homes left to throw, all along Bayou St. John.

Maybe three blocks from the park, the paper bag hit the pavement in front of me. The bag came flying out of an old school bus painted all kinds of crazy colors, also headed for the park. A woman wearing nothing but a red t-shirt stood on a little platform on the back of the bus. Her flowing blonde hair blew in the wake of the bus. She smiled and yelled something to me as the bag flew out of her hand. I stopped quickly, no traffic around. Inside the bag were twenty-five white tablets of some sort. The bus passed me and stopped ahead at the intersection of Esplanade and Carrolton Avenue, in front of the entrance to the park. I took off after it, thinking this was a mistake. That lady lost her medicine.

The light turned green. The brightly colored bus drove on toward the museum, with me pedaling hard to beat the light and hopefully catch it in City Park. The lady needed her medicine.

I made it to the intersection, but the light was yellow, then red. I bore down and raced after the bus. Drivers cursed and honked their horns at me, but I made it to the other side. The bus circled the New Orleans Museum of Art. I chased it around the museum and followed it through another left turn under the oak canopy until it came to a stop in front of Storyland, a children's playground of huge painted concrete statues of fairytale characters.

I stopped a few feet behind the bus and pushed my kickstand down, grasping the brown paper bag with the lost medicine tightly in my hand. Jazz music blared from loudspeakers on the top of the bus where there was some type of opening, like a turret. A man poked his head through the turret. He wore the floppy hat of a court jester and smiled down at me. On the side of the wildly colored bus was written in spray paint, *A vote for Barry is a vote for fun!* The bus door opened. Men and women in the bus piled out. They were all smiling, even gleeful. Dressed in mostly crazy varieties of red, white and blue clothing, they made a beeline for Storyland, no words, just hooting and wild laughter.

I searched the crowd for the woman who had lost the bag. As the bus riders rushed by me, I was unable to identify her. I was left holding the bag, standing by the open school bus door.

A shirtless driver remained, tapping his hands on the steering wheel to the jazz music still blaring out into the park.

"Hey sonny, what's in the bag?" he asked me.

"Not sure. A lady on the back of the bus lost it over on Esplanade. I picked it up and rode after y'all. Do you know who lost it?"

"Step up here. Let me see inside."

I climbed the stairs and stood by him as he grabbed the bag and looked inside. "What's your name, son?"

"Ronnie LeBlanc. What's yours?"

"Neal. Pleased to meet you." We shook hands. "Hey, do you know this place? Storyland? I'm digging the huge statues."

"Sure, my sister and I played here all the time. All the fairytales have huge painted statues. They're all here. Little Bo Peep, Rapunzel, all of them."

"Ronnie, that bag isn't lost. That lady threw it to you. It's her gift to you, and just you. You see these tablets? You take one, and you'll be inside a living fairy tale. How's that sound? Come on, daddy-o. Put one under your tongue, and let's go play in Storyland."

Neal bolted out the door, yelling joyously to his friends who were awestruck by Little Bo Peep and her sheep. Some walked reverently around the base of the statue, and others stroked her face. Two men pawed and stroked Humpty Dumpty as he sat on his wall at the entrance. They were smiling and laughing, encouraging Humpty not to fall. Two women tried to climb a huge live oak, to no avail.

Maybe it was their earnest search for beauty, maybe the playfulness in Neal's voice, but I did as he suggested. I put a tablet under my tongue. A bitter blast filled my mouth and ran down my throat. I followed Neal to join in the fun. I sensed these happy people were out-of-towners, and given my familiarity with City Park, I would be their guide through the fairytale world that they were now entering. I sensed this pack was led by the man wearing the jester's hat. He was waving at the others and urging them to come with him.

"Sir, I'm Ronnie," I said to the jester. "I know this place. I can walk you through if you like."

"I'm Ken. This is my band of seekers. We're called the Merry Pranksters. They seem to be hung up with the entrance, so lead the way. Let's see more. This way, gang! We've got a guide, a real New Orleanian. Follow Ronnie." Down the path, we walked under the vividly green live oak umbrella toward more beauty. I led them, followed by the court jester and his fellow fun-seekers. They pranced, skipped, twirled each other in circles. Hooting and singing, the women's hair swirled in the thick summer air. I noticed my feet were heavy, like walking in mud. The reds, whites and blues of their clothing ran behind me like a gentle stream.

The first stop along our journey was the Old Woman Who Lived in a Shoe. She was cast in concrete, crying out for her children from a window in a huge pink boot. She called them to return to dinner and pronto. But they were nowhere to be found. I became very concerned about these missing kids and ran into the huge azalea hedges to look for them. "Help me find her children!" I yelled to the Pranksters. "I think someone took them. Help me find them."

By that point, I felt something stirring inside my body, a force beyond me and yet the essence of me. I suspected this force had something to do with the tablet I placed under my tongue. I welcomed this new energy. I noticed my hands moving through the summer air, beckoning the Pranksters to walk with me to the giant pink boot straddling the path. Yes, my hands obeyed my brain's commands, but their images seemed to remain and float in the thick summer air. Unusual, but enchanting. Concern was rising inside me. I needed to find her children.

The woman in the red shirt ran to my side. "You're the boy on the bike, the paperboy." She put her arm around me and walked me back toward the path. "I'm the one who threw you the bag. I'll take care of you. My name is Trust. Relax, come with me."

She became a mother to me in my new and shifting universe. Her bare arm wrapped around my shoulders. She comforted me. Her embrace invited me to calm down and go deeper into the new realm of brighter colors and living stories appearing before me. She would be my guide and my safe place. I followed her back to the pink boot and the calling concrete mother.

"That bag belonged to a friend," she said. "We called her Stark Naked because she'd stand naked on the back of the bus and wave at truckers. She ate too many of those tablets and had to drop out of our trip. So be careful, one at a time."

Trust and I walked slowly toward Rapunzel's tower. Several Pranksters pranced ahead and started pleading, "Let down your hair, Rapunzel! Let down your hair!"

Neal, the bus driver, ran to the base of the tower. "Let down your hair. I want to take you away from your tower. I want to kiss you and break the spell!" At this, all the Pranksters gathered around him and hoisted him onto their shoulders to boost him to the top of the tower.

"Let it down. Let it down. Let it down," they chanted in unison. As if on cue, they all collapsed in a happy pile, Neal in the middle. They all cackled and rolled on their backs upon the glowing, emerald carpet. Like everything else around, its color and even existence were magnified beyond words. Every blade of grass was beautiful and had a story. Time and space slowed so that I could see the true beauty of everything that had been there all along

Trust stayed close to me throughout. When the force inside me became too much for my young mind and body to bear, I would go to her. She stretched her loving arms around me, laying my head on her chest and patting me on the back. "You're a good boy, a very good boy. Ronnie, you are a sweet, kind boy. All is well with you."

I would take a deep breath and return to delivering my lines in whatever psychodrama was playing out both inside and outside me involving the Pranksters. I played my roles well, until the play ended.

The sleeping figure of Snow White under the shade of a giant oak greeted us along our path. She was exquisitely dressed, and her sweet face lay in peaceful repose, sleeping the sleep of the dead. She sprawled on a deep purple bed prepared by the dwarves. I ran to her side.

"She's caught between heaven and hell," I said. I laid my hands on the warm concrete contours of her face. "She's not dead! I felt the blood still pumping in her. Wake up, sweet girl."

Several of the Pranksters circled and shook her, trying to rouse her from her slumber. My pathos was too much, the agony inside too great. I ran back to Mother, who calmed my fears.

Our stroll through Storyland ended on a lighter note. We encountered the Three Little Pigs, the hairy fang-toothed wolf, and their house. The pigs were all happy, admiring their house made of brick. The unfortunate wolf was trying to climb down through the chimney to eat his prey, unaware of the clever trap just below. Three female Pranksters danced around the three pigs, blowing them kisses and wrapping brightly colored scarves around their necks.

Ken played the wolf. "Let me in, or I'll blow your house down!"

Neal came back with his best Porky Pig. "Not by the hair of my chinny, chin, chin." This sent us all into a spasm of laughter, so deep it hurt my side.

We all made our way out of Storyland and back to the magic bus. On the front of the old school bus, just over the front windshield, normally naming the final terminus of the bus trip, appeared painted letters reading *Further*. I was ushered up the steps. My bike was placed on the back platform. Trust suggested I lie down on one of the many bunk beds in the back of the bus. "Take a rest," she said. "Come with us out to the lake. We're going for a swim to cool off."

I lay down and stared at the ceiling, which was heavily painted.

Near the rear of the bus appeared a long green serpent, winding around a tree, which for me became the Tree of the Knowledge of Good and Evil. This tempter wound its way toward the apple, which would condemn me to a journey into hell. I tried to ask for help from Trust, but suddenly, I saw her as the Evil Witch in Snow White, who had tricked me into eating the poison apple. Like beautiful Snow White, I was paralyzed and unable to move from my bed. I and I alone had placed that tablet in my mouth, but I was tricked! Now, I was caught somewhere between heaven and hell, not dead, but not alive. I was a prisoner of the Witch.

I screamed and ran to the front of the bus. I had to escape from the Evil Witch and from the King of Lies represented by the crawling snake on the ceiling. I was caught and gently embraced by several Pranksters. They tried to soothe me and assure me everything was well. The bus was moving. I had no idea where "Further" was; I just wanted off. Eventually, I calmed down. The woman I knew as Trust laid me down upon a bed once again, but this time she lay beside me and lovingly held me, repeatedly whispering to me that I was fine, that this was just like any dream. It would pass. Time and space had ceased to matter. I became a young child being held by his loving mother. My wild fears departed. I snuggled against her while we sped along through the Crescent City toward Lake Pontchartrain.

We came to a stop, and all the Pranksters, save my new mother and I, quickly disembarked, wearing shorts and a few swimsuits. Trust gingerly raised me from my bed. "Ronnie, we're here. Let's join the others for a swim. Come on. It'll refresh you."

I followed her out of the bus into the bright of the afternoon summer sun. We walked through an entrance to a park and down a small midway. The roller coaster was tiny and filled with Negro children screaming gleefully. Beyond the end of the midway, past a small beach, the Pranksters played in the blue-green water of Lake Pontchartrain. Mother and I waded up to our chests and began playing with our fellows in spraying water at each other. I was not conscious of others in the water, not until I had wandered out among my new friends.

I noticed that we were surrounded by Negro men, and they were moving closer, encircling us. This I had never seen, Whites and Negros swimming together. In fact, it was forbidden in my city. At first, I felt merely curious at this new type of encounter, but as the men grew nearer, I saw the hostility on their faces. I sensed the Pranksters were still caught up in their watery bliss, oblivious to their surroundings. They were out-of-towners.

From my vantage point out in the lake, I looked back at the beach—all Negros. The picnic tables beyond were occupied exclusively by Negro families. One of the young Negro men approaching our gang said loudly to his companion, "Lot's of trash floating in the water today."

Neal said to them, "Hey there, daddy cats, you guys staying cool out here? Love this place. We're just taking a dip, headed east out of town, making the scene in Florida tonight."

"Better be real soon," the Negro man said. "Like right now. You people are in the wrong place. This is *our* beach, Lincoln Beach, man. No Whites allowed here. Can't you read? They got signs."

Ken whispered something in Neal's ear. Then, the two began to walk toward the shore, beckoning the other Pranksters to follow. Trust and I went with them. The young Black swimmers walked us to the beach and waved goodbye. I was still under the spell of whatever was in the white tablet, but the water and the confrontation had taken me a few steps back toward my old reality.

I knew I was in a different world, for me a new part of New

Orleans. This place was separated from my White world by a thick invisible barrier. All my life, I had seen Negros in my city but had never had a real conversation. Now, a Negro man had spoken directly to us. He wanted us to leave. We were the ones out of place.

The Pranksters moved out of the water and quickly boarded the bus. Mother and I were standing outside the bus door. Neal walked up pushing my bike, my tightly rolled newspapers still in the basket. He gave me the handlebars. "Daddy-o, this is adios. We're bound for New

York City via Pensacola. Wild ride, eh?" He bounded up the steps into the driver's seat, and the engine roared to life. On came the jazz. I stared blankly at Trust.

"Remember Ronnie," she said. "It's all just a beautiful dream. That's what these tablets do. They induce dreams out of the wonderful reality we live in. You'll be fine. A few hours and you'll be back to where you were this morning." She hugged me and boarded the bus. Away drove the Pranksters. I stood at the curb of the Lincoln Beach Park, a skinny White boy from Mid-City, soaked to the bone. I was a sad fish, out of the water, with a strong dose of LSD still coursing through my blood.

I moved toward the sound of laughter, pushing my bike. I reentered the park. Gone was the thick green live oak canopy of City Park. I looked up and down the shoreline from this point. The lake was dotted with fishing camps and wharves extending out into the water, far removed from the busy city I knew. In the distance, I could see marshes. I wondered where this strange new world was located, how or if I could return to the one I left just hours before. The laughter and squeals drew me farther into the park.

I stood holding my bicycle near the edge of a huge swimming pool filled with Negro kids of all ages. Everyone was splashing or diving into the crystal-clear waters. My contemplation of the scene was broken by several Negro teenagers who approached and circled me. One grabbed my arms behind me. Another grabbed my bike, mounted it and pedaled off. "White boy, you need to beat it. This ain't your place," one said. The one holding my arms pushed me to the cement, and they all ran off after the newly stolen bike. I sat on the wet sidewalk, stunned, not quite comprehending what had transpired.

"Boy, what on earth are you doing here?" A tall Negro woman wearing short pants stood over me. I was speechless, like a sheep before his shearer. Gray-haired and commanding, she wore a whistle around her neck and a shirt with the words *New Orleans Recreation Department* sewed on her front pocket. "Come on, young man, let me get you out of here. Dry you off. You pitiful, boy."

I stammered something. Feeling grateful for her concern. I did what she told me to do.

"Come on. Come to my office. I'll get you a towel." I followed her into a nearby building containing offices, a café, and changing rooms for bathers. She had me sit in a simple wooden chair in front of her desk. She handed me a clean white towel and left the office. While I dried my hair and patted my wet clothes, a small bulletin board on the wall of her little office attracted my attention. I rose and was pulled into a study of each of the pictures tacked to the board.

In the middle, a picture of a Black Madonna and a Negro Baby Jesus. As a faithful Catholic and former altar boy, I knew of Negro priests and Negro parishes in the city. Like everything else about this parallel world, it existed on the other side of an invisible bubble that kept the races apart. This image of my beloved Mother Mary and Jesus made me smile and drew me into another way of viewing the Holy mysteries. So, we all saw Her through our own eyes. Of course!

To the left, a poster promoting a concert at Lincoln Beach Park starring one of my favorite performers, Fats Domino. His hits, Walking to New Orleans and Blueberry Hill, were local legends. I listened to his music constantly on the radio. Next to the poster was a photo of Nat King Cole crowning a Miss Lincoln Beach in a beauty contest. Nat King Cole was known and loved the world over. He had a television show. I realized for the first time that Lincoln Beach was huge in the music world. Why had I not known of these invisible Negros? We had been living next to each other my entire life.

To the right was a small postcard tacked to the board. It bore a grisly image of the lifeless bodies of five young Negro men hanging from a single small tree. The caption explained the scene was from Sabine County Texas in 1908. Beneath the caption was a poem. It read:

> The Dogwood Tree
> This is only the branch of the dogwood tree;
> An emblem of WHITE SUPREMACY.
> A lesson once taught in the Pioneer's school,
> That this is a land of WHITE MAN'S RULE.
> The Red Man once in an early day,
> Was told by the Whites to mend his way.
> The Negro, now, by eternal grace,
> Must learn to stay in the Negro's place.
> In the Sunny South, the Land of the Free,
> Let the WHITE SUPREME forever be.
> Let this a warning to all Negroes be,
> Or they'll suffer the fate of the DOGWOOD TREE.

I stared at this postcard, watching the young men sway in the gentle breeze. With the aid of the Pranksters, I was present in 1908

Sabine County, Texas. I was part of the white mob at this mass lynching. Revulsion gripped me. What kind of monsters could do such a thing? Was I a part of this mob? Why? The young men's legs and feet twitched as the life flowed slowly out of them. They were caught, as Snow White, as I, between heaven and hell, held by a rope and a beautiful tree. I could see the fear and desperation in their twisted faces. I could not look away.

"Oh, you're upright. What you doing over there?" asked the gray-haired lady.

Mute once again, I pointed to the postcard.

"Paperboy, you sit here." I did what she told me.

"Your bike and newspapers are outside. I saw those boys take it from you. They all in my church. I know all their mothers. They sorry. No need to call the police. Police just beat them senseless, maybe kill them. That's why I got it back for you. Come on; talk to me, young man."

"My name's Ronnie. That postcard, did that really happen?"

"Ronnie, I'm Mrs. Toussaint. I run this park, keep an eye on the kids at the beach and the pool. Sorry that card upset you, but yes, it happened." She walked to the bulletin board and placed her finger on the card. "That young man right there, that was my uncle. He died 'fore I was born. My momma's brother. That's why I got your bike. I didn't want no one to die for something stupid."

"How on earth did you end up way out here at Lincoln Beach? I guess by now you know it's for colored."

"I met some people who were crossing the country in a school bus. I rode out here with them. I must have taken a medicine that helps you dream in the middle of the day. Where are we, Gentilly?"

"Son, you way beyond Gentilly. You in Little Woods, way up on the lakeshore. You saw the lakefront? Those camps and wharves? This was a fishing village not too many years ago. Where you live, son?"

"Mid-City, near Bayou St. John," I said.

She pushed a telephone across her desk. "Call your momma, boy. Ain't no way you gonna ride that bike home. You still look a bit puny. What's that you say about some dreaming medicine?"

"Ma'am, it's too strange to explain. Let's say it just opened my eyes and took me to another world that was here along."

"I saw those people who brought you here in that colored bus. They grown, adults all of them. They crazy, son. Don't be hanging out with crazy people, you hear me?"

"Yes, ma'am. I hear you." I smiled and called my momma to come get me.

I have two postcards in my desk drawer at my office to this day. One is a photo of Kesey's bus, Further, and the other a copy of the postcard dogwood tree. Both are reminders of the hidden worlds of beauty and brutality I discovered on the first day of summer 1964.

Sub Rosa

On the fourth day of the silent retreat with the Jesuits at Grand Coteau, it finally dawned on me that I did not need to do anything in particular, but that the whole point was just to "be"—nothing more. After beginning with a mass and Eucharist, the group of eleven men and women had all gone our separate ways, to our cells. We met once a day with our spiritual advisors and were directed in contemplation of various parts of Ignatius Loyola's *Spiritual Exercises,* upon which the retreat was based. Although we ate in a dining room together, we were to have no conversations among ourselves. During the rest of the day, we prayed and contemplated the questions and scriptures given to us by the priests leading the retreat. We were free to roam the beautiful oak groves or gardens, pray in the chapel or to remain in our cells. I was a roamer.

On the first day, I was drawn to the graveyard of the many priests who served at the venerable seminary complex dating to 1835. I sat among their graves and calculated their ages, trying to imagine their lives and what formed the basis of their devotion. A nearby oak served as a canopy from the warm spring sun. As I lay on the soft St. Augustine grass, I stared into a deep-blue sky framed by huge boughs of newly sprouted oak leaves. Hours and days rolled by under that oak, near the resting places of the dead brothers. From time to time, I would glimpse another of my fellow retreatants wandering the grounds. We carefully avoided direct eye contact and maintained our distance from one another. As the days passed, I began to wonder about the others. I knew none of them personally. No names were exchanged. We were from different cities. What were they experiencing? What were their struggles? The desire to converse began to work on me. Meals became maddening due to the proximity of the men and women comprising the group of eleven. I always viewed eating as a communal act, and the enforced silence was all the more difficult. I think I took refuge among the graves mostly out of the sense of community I felt among the white marble markers. The business of just "being" was indeed difficult stuff.

Another of my favorite haunts was a rose-covered grotto dedicated to St. Francis. I went there to pray each day at sunset. Late on the afternoon of the fourth day, after lighting a votive candle, I settled into reciting the *Prayer of Saint Francis*. The use of this prayer in the eleventh step of Alcoholics Anonymous had led me to this retreat, which my sponsor had strongly recommended. After five minutes of intoning the words of the famous saint, a woman belonging to the group of eleven walked into the grotto. Our eyes met. We did not avert them. She did not turn away. As we continued to look at each other's faces, she sat down on a bench opposite me. No words were said. She pulled a rosary from her pocket, looked at the ground and began her chant, "Hail Mary, full of grace. Blessed are You, and blessed is the Fruit of Your womb, Jesus..." I sat across from her and listened to the rounds of her prayers. The candle flickered in the deepening darkness. We were two wanderers—sitting around a campfire—covered by a dome of rose petals.

After a few minutes, she stopped her chanting, looked me straight in my eyes, and then waved her hand toward the rose dome. "These roses are here for a reason, are they not?" she said.

"What would that be?" I asked.

"Have you heard of the term *sub rosa*—under the roses? The tradition goes back to the Greeks. In their time, the ceilings of dining halls were painted with roses. Anything shared among friends under the roses had to be kept in confidence. It was a matter of honor; thus, the expression." I nodded to her. She looked at me and asked, "Can I tell you something—here, under the roses? I don't know you, but here we are. I need to share this with someone."

"Sure. It'll stay here."

"When I was twenty-three, I was engaged to a young man who I knew was my true soul mate—David. We were very poor and lived in a dingy apartment in a very large city on my salary as a legal secretary. Our plan was that I would work while he attended medical school. I thought he was so noble. Remember when we used to look at doctors as healers rather than entrepreneurs? Long time ago. So, I was in love with a holy man, a smart, holy man, who would someday become a doctor, a heart surgeon. I would be a doctor's wife, and we would share the perfect American life, far away from the small backward town where we both grew up. So I became, or tried to become, anything he wanted me to be. I gave him food when he was hungry, money when he was broke and sex whenever he asked. Every time our talk turned to details of our upcoming marriage, he grew more remote and talked of the pressures he faced in school. At the student parties, he began to leave me alone, and he huddled in corners with his buddies talking shop. His hours at the lab and in hospitals grew longer. After the second year started, we rarely saw each other during waking hours.

"One night, when he expected to be free, we made plans to meet at a romantic Italian place. It had been months since we had time for a date. I sat there at the café, staring at a candle melting

262

down the side of a Chianti bottle for over an hour before I finally accepted that he wasn't coming. I had been stood up, and I left the place feeling torn between concern and anger. As I opened the door to our apartment, I saw no sign of him. Hours passed, and anger triumphed over concern. I caught the bus down to the university and walked to the lab where he worked all those late hours. It was vacant. I sensed for the first time that I was being lied to. Then, I remembered the nearby apartment of one of his schoolmates. I thought he might be there, up to no good. I walked the few blocks and knocked on the door. I saw lights on inside; there were voices, or at least I thought I heard voices. It was the middle of the night by then. Despite my knocking, no one came to the door. I just knew there were people inside. So, I banged on the door—still no answer. Then, I started to call his name—banging on the door, and then I began yelling his name. Neighbors down the hall opened their doors and stared at the crazy woman. Still...nothing. I went home, feeling humiliated, guilty, confused, wondering if I was crazy or if I was living with a liar.

"I didn't see him again until I got home from work the following day. We sat at our kitchen table, and he looked me straight in the eyes and told me that he didn't know whether he loved me and that he wasn't prepared to marry me, or anyone, at that point in his life. He felt school had taken away his ability to have a relationship with all the demands upon his time. He didn't explain what had happened the night before but flatly denied being involved with another woman. It was so damned practical and so damned true. Maybe that's why I hated hearing it from him so much. I was ready for a fight, but this made sense, and it still hurt like hell. I couldn't get mad. I couldn't feel rage. I just whimpered and went quietly into our bedroom and shut the door. I felt crushed. I had nowhere to go. My well-laid plans had ended in failure. A couple of weeks later, I packed my stuff into my momma's station wagon and drove back to stay with my parents in our hometown. I felt like a dog going home with its tail between its legs. I didn't talk to my mother the entire way back.

"During the Christmas holidays, we saw each other a few times around town, and on a very frigid New Year's Eve, we ended up making love in the backseat of my parents' Oldsmobile. He went back to medical school, and I got a job at the local bank. There, I met a boy who was the polar opposite of my former fiancé. He was a country boy who drove a truck, voted for Nixon and worshiped the ground I walked on. I needed that. After a few weeks, I found an apartment, and we had some wild times. Nothing complicated. He just thought I was the greatest thing that ever happened to him. I was drunk with desire and dizzy with my newfound sexual prowess. I was so giddy, I forgot to use birth control one night and ended up pregnant. I was stunned—stunned and scared. Suddenly, I wanted nothing to do with my new plaything—too dangerous. In a fit of self-pity and confusion, I called David.

"I lied and told him that I was pregnant from our New Year's Eve encounter. I cried. I manipulated him. I had no clear plan, and I was shocked to hear him suggest that we visit a medical school friend of his who could perform a safe abortion. This was before the *Roe* case, and abortion was still illegal in most places, certainly in our home state. He offered to pick me up and bring me back to the medical school where we could take care of our "problem," as he called it. He sounded so rational, and once the lie had come out of my mouth, there was no turning back. There was absolutely no discussion of marriage. I agreed to his proposal, and after hanging up the phone, I knew I had made a terrible mistake, but I didn't know how to unring the bell.

"David came and picked me up at my apartment, which only

a couple of weeks before had been the scene of such fun with my country boyfriend. The ride back to the city was nothing but an awkward silence punctuated by small talk of family and our now separate lives. He escorted me straight to the obstetrics unit, where we met a second-year resident. It was a Saturday, and very little was going on in the teaching wing of the unit. They escorted me to an examining room, and David left me alone with the resident. The resident explained that he had done the procedure many times during the past two years during his training, and he felt very sure that it would go smoothly. He told me that he had done the same thing previously for two of the students' wives and that neither had experienced any problems. I got up in the stirrups and closed my eyes. There was the feel of the cold steel instrument entering me, and then the sound of an electric motor powering the vacuum. I felt very little in terms of pain. I felt no pain afterward, but a lot of bleeding. But I did feel guilt for what I had done by pulling David into my problem.

"We went home the next day, another ride in virtual silence. When we arrived back at my apartment, it was late in the afternoon, and I asked him to stay with me that night. He agreed and said he would go by to visit his parents the next morning. After I fixed us a meal, we sat down to watch TV. About seven that evening, my country boy showed up unexpectedly at the door. I had told him nothing about why I suddenly dropped out of his life and had simply avoided him since I had found out I was pregnant. He became very angry and vocal about David's presence. David tried to reason with him, but he became violent. He grabbed David around the neck with one arm and started pounding him in the face. I screamed and picked up a chair and hit him across the back. He kept pounding David's face and shrieking at him. I picked up the phone and called the police. At that, he stopped and ran to his car. David was lying in a pool of blood that streamed from his mouth, nose and eyes. An ambulance took him to the hospital. He had a badly broken nose, and the bones around his eye socket were crushed. The muscles around the right eye never worked properly again. He developed permanent double vision. I stood by him and helped him recover. We moved back in together and eventually married. With his vision problem, heart surgery was out, and he eventually became a psychiatrist. We have been married thirty-five years, and I have never told him the truth.

"I have asked God to forgive me for the abortion, but I can't face David with the real truth. So, now Father, at least you know. Can you give me absolution?" She looked into my eyes, waiting for a response.

I sat in stunned silence, and after a long pause, said, "I'm sorry, but I'm not a priest. I'm one of the retreat participants. I'm just here searching like you."

"But I saw you talking to one of the priests. I thought you were one of them."

"No, sorry. I'm from around here. I know Father L'Enfant. We were talking before the retreat started. I come out here to AA meetings each week. But, I can assure you that I know what confidentiality is. Your secret is safe." I could see tears dripping down her face. We sat for a while, staring at the flickering candle. I looked at the glow of candlelight on the newly blossoming roses overhead. I reached over and touched her hand and asked, "Can I share a story with you?" She nodded, and I sat back and took a deep breath.

"I grew up in a small town here in South Louisiana. I'm guessing we're about the same age. I was in college, early seventies. Down here, they started the war on drugs real early. Back then, you could get sent to Angola for possessing a joint. For whatever reason, that didn't seem to faze me. I thought I was invulnerable, and I was so much smarter than the cops or the narcs. Well, turns out I wasn't, and they busted me one night outside a local bar when I was home for summer vacation. One of my high school buddies set me up, but there I was, and I was plenty scared. The head narcotics agent told me I could either go to prison or start helping him the rest of the summer. I had no choice. So, I started my life as a snitch, and not a very good one. I fed them a lot of baloney and took them on a couple of wild goose chases to find marijuana patches that I had allegedly been told about. They weren't pleased and started making sounds about the prison option. One night, they told me they wanted me to attend a party at the home of a suspected dealer. I played football with the guy back in high school, and I was welcome at his place anytime. The thought of giving him up made me sick.

"My best friend from way back in elementary school was Trey Taylor. He was Donald K. Taylor III and was from an old and respected family in town. Trey had gone to Vanderbilt and had completed his second year in pre-med. He was engaged to his high school sweetheart, and I had helped him pick out her ring just before I got busted. We loved to drink beer together, but as far as drugs went, Trey was a straight arrow. He knew nothing of my drug use, and my drug bust remained a secret around town.

"The night of the party I was ordered to attend, Trey and I were drinking beer at a place called Happy Hollow. Coldest beer and great shuffleboard tables. I looked up and realized I had let the evening slip away. We were in Trey's car. If I didn't make it to the party and get some information for the narcs, I could be in Angola instead of college next semester. I asked Trey if he could give me a ride to my buddy's apartment, and he gladly did so. Though I told him to wait in the car and that I just needed to run in and pick something up, he insisted on coming in and seeing our old friend. We were welcomed in, and as we walked into the living room, I saw a sight that shocked me. Several guys were sitting on the couch, and before them on the coffee table was a wooden box chock full of hospital-quality hypodermic needles mounted on glass syringes, all laid neatly in rows. I had suspected there might be some weed being exchanged that night, but this sent a cold chill down my spine. They shut the box as soon as they saw us, and Trey never saw what was going on. We caught up on old times with my old teammate, drank a beer and left. I had the information I needed to get the narc off my back. Trey dropped me off, and I went in the next morning to meet with my handler. Actually, after seeing the needles, I had no qualms about telling them what I had seen. Grass was one thing; heroin was something entirely different. I felt it was a danger and a real crime. I told them what I had seen with my own eyes, but I said nothing about Trey being with me. The narcs used my testimony to get a search warrant, and they made several arrests the following night. All the guys in the apartment that night got busted, and they all eventually served time for heroin trafficking. Before the bust, the head narc told me to go back to school early. He felt it would be in my best interest to be as far away from my hometown as possible, just in case. I packed my things and headed back to school.

"A couple of weeks later, my mother called me and told me that Trey's car had been found abandoned along a lonely country road. His parents had reported him missing. I felt like I got hit by a freight train. My blood ran cold. I felt I was going to throw up. I remember saying nothing to her, just putting the phone down. She called back, and I told her I couldn't speak. I sat by myself in my college apartment, wanting a drink very badly. For a while, I held on to some crazy hope that something might turn up.

"They found Trey's remains two weeks later. There was a memorial service, which I attended, but have no memories of today other than Trey's mother wasn't there. She had a nervous breakdown and was hospitalized at a sanatorium. I said nothing. I was too scared. What good would it do? That's what I told myself. I think I wrote it off to bad luck. My capacity to rationalize and project the evil onto the killers allowed me to go on with my life. I had done the right thing. I had stood up to heroin, and those same heroin dealers had been the ones to murder my best friend. He was the innocent one, and they were the evil ones. I became obsessed with finding who had committed the crime, but other than a brief interview with a homicide detective about Trey's background, I had little to go on. Oh, by the way, I lied to the detective when he asked me if I had any idea who might have reason to hurt Trey. I couldn't even admit that I had inadvertently led him to his death.

"Years went by, but Trey never left my mind. I wondered what his life would have been like had he not gone out drinking with me that night, had I not been busted, had I used any common sense. I wondered about the guys who I helped send to prison. Who were they, and who killed my friend? I think it was almost exactly twenty years later that I thought to call a detective friend of mine with the local sheriff's office about the case. I asked him if he could arrange for the old file to be pulled so I could look at it. I explained that Trey was my best friend. He was happy to help and ordered it from archives.

"I went to his office, and he put me in a conference room with the file, which was very thin. It had a few notes from the homicide detective to whom I had spoken years ago. The police were treating it as a missing person case initially, and only after finding the remains did they classify it as a homicide. They had nothing to go on. This was an outstanding student who was well connected and well liked. After interviews of friends and family failed to produce any leads, the trail went cold. Trey's remains had been sent to the FBI lab in Virginia. The only finding in the report was a fractured clavicle. I was disappointed, but not surprised, by the lack of effort. After I finished with the file, I took it back to my friend's office. He looked up at me and said, 'I don't know if you're interested, but we've still got his remains down in the evidence room.'

"What do you mean? You've got his body here? Why? I was stunned.

"The detective said, 'From what I remember, his mom was hospitalized when they sent the body back from DC. The father said he'd get back with us, but I guess they had their hands full. It's in the evidence room—his skeleton, his clothes, personal effects. You want to view it?'

"We went down to the basement of the old courthouse. The detective pulled down the zipper of an opaque plastic bag, and I saw the bleached bones of my dear friend Trey. His clothes had been torn by animals where he was found. There were obvious gnaw marks on some of his bones. His skull was perfectly preserved. I touched his forehead and made the sign of the cross. I zipped the bag up, and we left the evidence room. I knew at that moment that somehow I had been called to come and retrieve my old friend's body, to give him a proper burial.

"His mother was still alive at that time, so I went immediately to her home and told her what I had found. For some reason, she had supposed that the remains had been disposed of by the FBI. She arranged to have a burial in their family plot. Two weeks later, his brothers and a few close friends joined Mrs. Taylor at a graveside service on a hot summer day. It was just a few days shy of twenty years since his disappearance. Tears flowed down my face in the noonday sun. Everyone thanked me for finding him and giving them closure. I stood mute before them, and just cried for my best friend, and felt nothing but shame. Since I walked away from his grave that day, I've had no further contact with his family.

"I made one final inquiry with my detective friend. I had him check out the boy I had busted—my old teammate who had the heroin dealers over that night. He was murdered by another prisoner at Angola when he was only twenty-two years of age."

I looked at the woman sitting across from me and asked, "So can you absolve me, sister?"

"I just did. I listened to you with my heart," she said. "Your secrets are safe." She walked out of the grotto, and we never spoke again.